She was a puzzle he wanted to solve.

Gray sensed layers and textures in Bree's personality that went far beyond "prissy" or "icy" or "dull"...any of the unflattering names she'd been labelled with. Undercurrents both deep and powerful—and touchingly human.

Well, okay, then, maybe he knew Bree better than he had realized. They belonged to that sorry club— the children who had survived the unsurvivable, and didn't really know why. Or where to go from there.

A large bird, maybe an eagle, landed somewhere high in the pines over their heads, causing the sunlight to shift as the branches swayed. For an instant, the light seemed to catch on two crystal sparkles at the outer edges of Bree's cool blue eyes.

Tears? Gray frowned. Was the ice princess fighting back tears?

She blinked then, and the illusion disappeared. But he was left with a sudden, inexplicable hunger to know her better, to find out more about her.

A lot more.

And...just his luck. He had only thirty days to do it.

Dear Reader,

I'm a homebody. I prove all the clichés. Home really is where my heart lives. I bloom where I'm planted, and I like my roots deep and permanent. However humble my "castle" might be, there's no place like it.

I love reading books that feature fascinating houses—as mysterious as Manderley or as simple as the *Little House on the Prairie*. I also tend to write about characters struggling to find, or to keep, or to reclaim the place in this world that makes them feel whole.

Brianna Wright is, perhaps, the most dislocated heroine I've ever written. When her father killed her mother sixteen years ago, she and her sisters were banished from Bell River, the beautiful family ranch. When we meet her, the patchwork life she's cobbled together in exile has just ripped to pieces. She realizes the one place she wants to go is...

Home. But is there anything left in Silverdell, Colorado, for her?

Surely the answer can't be Grayson Harper III, the charming former heir to Silverdell's marble quarry millions. Disinherited, cynical and determined to avoid commitment, Gray takes a menial job at Bell River. He's made it clear he's staying only a few weeks, just long enough to win his bet and get reinstated in his grandfather's will.

Just long enough to break Bree's already-wounded heart. Or, perhaps, to heal his own.

I hope you'll enjoy sharing their journey back to that powerful, magical, sometimes dangerous place we call home. And I hope that you, too, find the comfort and love that come with home, sweet home.

Warmly,

Kathleen O'Brien

PS—Please visit me on the web at www.KathleenOBrien.com. Come by and say hi on Facebook or Twitter!

Betting on the Cowboy

—

Kathleen O'Brien

HARLEQUIN® SUPER ROMANCE®

Recycling programs
for this product may
not exist in your area.

ISBN-13: 978-0-373-71860-3

BETTING ON THE COWBOY

Copyright © 2013 by Kathleen O'Brien

All rights reserved. Except for use in any review, the reproduction or utilization of this work in whole or in part in any form by any electronic, mechanical or other means, now known or hereafter invented, including xerography, photocopying and recording, or in any information storage or retrieval system, is forbidden without the written permission of the publisher, Harlequin Enterprises Limited, 225 Duncan Mill Road, Don Mills, Ontario, Canada M3B 3K9.

This is a work of fiction. Names, characters, places and incidents are either the product of the author's imagination or are used fictitiously, and any resemblance to actual persons, living or dead, business establishments, events or locales is entirely coincidental.

This edition published by arrangement with Harlequin Books S.A.

For questions and comments about the quality of this book, please contact us at CustomerService@Harlequin.com.

® and TM are trademarks of Harlequin Enterprises Limited or its corporate affiliates. Trademarks indicated with ® are registered in the United States Patent and Trademark Office, the Canadian Trade Marks Office and in other countries.

Printed in U.S.A.

ABOUT THE AUTHOR

Kathleen O'Brien was a feature writer and TV critic before marrying a fellow journalist. Motherhood, which followed soon after, was so marvelous she turned to writing novels, which could be done at home. She doesn't really believe in astrology, but she can't deny that she fits the Cancer profile well—at least in the "home and family first" department. As the poets say, no man is an island—even if we sometimes think it might be easier that way!

Books by Kathleen O'Brien

HARLEQUIN SUPERROMANCE

HARLEQUIN SINGLE TITLE

Other titles by this author available in ebook format.

To my editor, Wanda Ottewell, with thanks.
Your insight and your understanding mean so
much to the stories—and to me.

CHAPTER ONE

BRIANNA WRIGHT PULLED up to the Townsends' elegant Boston Back Bay mansion under a starry black sky, handed her car over to the valet with a forced smile and rushed up the stairs breathlessly. Darn it, she was late. Really late. Ten o'clock. No, almost eleven—thank you *so* much, gridlocked airport traffic!

Now she'd missed three hours of her own party—well, the party her company, Breelie's, had produced, anyhow—and Townsend's fiftieth birthday bash was already in full swing. Music and laughter poured through the open, brilliantly lit windows.

Too much laughter, perhaps, so early? She frowned. The open bar must be getting a workout.

Oh, well. Townsend was a tire magnate, and his millions could cover the liquor tab no matter how high it went. At least it sounded as if the guests were having fun.

She didn't know why that should surprise her—the parties planned by Breelie's rarely flopped. But something about this event had always bugged her a little. Maybe it was just that the "harem" theme had never appealed to her. That didn't matter, of course. Whatever the client wanted, he got. Or, in this case, whatever the client's trophy wife, Iliana Townsend, wanted, she got.

Bree just hoped Charlie hadn't gone overboard. Not that she thought he had. As her fiancée and her business partner, he deserved her complete trust. And he had it…of course he did. It was just that…

She'd been out of town for most of the planning, which obviously accounted for some of her discomfort. She trusted Charlie implicitly, of course, but…

She did wish he had answered his cell phone more often this week. When Charlie went dark, it usually meant he was spending more money than he felt like justifying over the phone. He trusted his ability to persuade anyone of anything, but only as long as they were within the target range of his surface-to-surface ballistic charm.

As she passed under a faux ogee arch and into the unrecognizable entry hall, she suddenly froze in place. She stared, openmouthed, at the glittering, jingling, splashing, sparkling madness before her.

For an instant, she couldn't decide whether to laugh or cry.

This was the high-society party she had hoped would put her event-planning company on the Boston A-list? This… this…*circus?*

What in God's name had Charlie been thinking? The room writhed with half-naked humanity. Belly dancers. Sword swallowers. Eunuchs. Champagne fountains, ruby-grape pyramids, peacock-feather fans and tables groaning with bacchanalian treats. Charlie had created an entire fake Persian seraglio, complete with a hundred over-the-hill sultans flirting with two hundred giggling harem "girls."

Bree's temples throbbed, and her airplane-food dinner suddenly turned poisonously acidic.

Damn it, Charlie! She'd told him a thousand times that, in the upscale Boston society event-planning business, reputation was more important than anything else. *Anything.* Even more important than the bottom line.

And, long before this, she'd had a niggling feeling they were getting a reputation for being…

Well, vulgar.

She set her jaw as a trio of belly dancers wriggled by with

a tinkle of gold coins in the air and a skitter of gold flickers on the walls. A sword swallower followed behind, ogling the dancers' hips. Behind him—a snake charmer with a real live snake slithering around his shoulders.

Oh, dear God. If vulgarity were an Olympic event, this pretentious absurdity would definitely take the gold.

Her hands tightened into fists at her sides. Charlie might be a genius at coaxing money out of rich women, but Bree was going to strangle him for this.

If she could just find him.

Instead, as she scanned the crowd, the only person she recognized was Bill Townsend, the guest of honor himself. But he didn't look honored. He looked furious. His dark eyes and full lips glowered, and he moved like an angry bull, his bulky shoulders plowing a path through the guests as if they were so many inconveniently placed mannequins. His bushy mustache and eyebrows resembled Tom Selleck more than Yul Brynner, but the scimitar at his side suddenly seemed more lethal than any prop ever should.

Though he passed within two feet of Bree, he didn't notice her any more than he noticed any of the others. He kept up his furious stride until he reached the burbling, three-tiered champagne fountain in the center of the ridiculous room.

Iliana, his forty-five-year-old trophy wife who always looked like a beautifully embalmed twenty-year-old, was nowhere in sight. Had the couple been fighting? *Great.* If the host and hostess ended up having a big row tonight, Bree's party would be remembered for that, not the hours and hours of work she and Charlie had put into it.

An elderly, diffident sultan, whose headdress was bigger than his whole body, approached Townsend, hand outstretched, a "happy birthday" smile on his face. Townsend turned his back on the man rudely. He grabbed a silver chalice from a passing waiter, thrust it under the honey-colored stream, letting the bubbles spill all over his fingers, then knocked the champagne back in one harsh toss.

Bree groaned under her breath. This could get ugly. Where the heck was Charlie? He needed to find Iliana, who might be able to handle her drunk husband. The women were always Charlie's responsibility. He was good with bored trophy wives. He could always pump out an extra squirt of charm and coax them into ever-higher displays of extravagance.

Unfortunately, at the moment, he seemed to be just as absent as the hostess. Bree shut her eyes, trying to swallow her fury. But *really.* Maybe strangling was too good for him.

"Ms. Wright?"

She opened her eyes. A tall "eunuch" stood in front of her, holding a tray of wineglasses. She eyed them carefully, wondering how many bottles they'd run through. If Townsend was already in a foul humor, he might balk at an astronomical liquor tab, after all.

"Everything okay, Ms. Wright?" The eunuch hesitated, looking nervous. Poor guy. She had a reputation, she knew, for being a stickler.

"No. I mean yes, everything's fine." It wasn't this poor guy's fault. He appeared as miserable as she felt. So she propped up her artificial smile, hearing her guardian's voice in her head. Kitty Afton, the Boston divorcée who had taken Bree in after her mother's murder, had believed that cheerfulness was next to godliness. Even in the early days, when surely she knew Bree was heartbroken and traumatized, Kitty had scolded her new protégée for letting her lips lose their pleasant feminine curve. "No one likes a sad sack, Brianna. You'll catch more flies with honey."

The waiter-eunuch nodded uneasily, then moved on. Bree checked Townsend again. He hadn't budged from the fountain. He was refilling his chalice, though his eyes glittered, and a sparkling trail of champagne already trickled from his chin like golden spit.

She couldn't wait for Charlie or Iliana. She'd have to try to handle Townsend herself. Reluctantly, Bree merged into the melee of guests, somehow keeping the smile on her lips.

"Mr. Townsend?"

He turned, the chalice halfway to his mouth, and glared at her over the rim. As he took in her simple slate-blue sheath, his eyes narrowed. "What are you supposed to be? Didn't you get the memo? This is a costume party. You've got to look like an idiot or you don't get in."

She deepened her smile, as if he'd meant it as a joke. But the bitterness in his voice was unmistakable. The drinking was a symptom of a deeper problem…not the cause. She really needed to find Iliana and get things patched up.

"I'm not actually a guest," she explained. "I'm Brianna Wright. My company, Breelie's, is the one you hired to—"

"You're…" He lowered the golden vessel, spilling liquid precariously close to her shoes, but ignoring it. "*You* are Brianna Wright?"

"I am," she said. She'd met him twice, during the initial negotiations, but she wasn't surprised that he didn't remember. He'd spent most of both meetings pacing the hall outside her office, barking at someone on his cell phone.

He shook his head for a minute, and then let out a loud, seal-like honk of laughter. Now, that *did* surprise her. She had traveled in a very uncomfortable, very dressy getup, complete with three-inch heels and panty hose, just so that she would look professional when she arrived. She'd even denied herself the luxury of a nap, so that she wouldn't muss the sleek French knot of blond hair at the nape of her neck.

"You seem amused," she observed coolly, irritated in spite of her determination to remain calm.

"Oh, I am definitely amused, sweetheart." He grinned,

showing six very white front teeth surrounded by neighbors far less brilliant. "I really, really am."

She frowned and opened her mouth to respond, but then, without warning, his large hand flicked out and grabbed hers.

"Hey!" She recoiled instinctively from his damp, sticky clutch and the aroma of stale champagne that wafted from his skin. But he had clamped on tightly and didn't let go.

"Come with me, Brianna Wright," he said, turning away from the fountain, tugging her along without so much as glancing back to see if she was willing, or whether she would have to be dragged. "There's something I want to show you."

People were staring at her now, which was saying something, since surely she was the least outlandish spectacle at this particular party. "Mr. Townsend, I really don't think—"

He looked back at her over his shoulder, his eyes suddenly clear and sober. "Your company is in charge of this party, right? Well, there's a problem, and I think you should know about it."

She didn't have much recourse after that, though she did manage eventually to extricate her hand and follow him with a little more dignity and at least the appearance of free will.

The guests seemed to part before them, as if they were just props operated by stagehands pulling levers behind the scenes. Maybe the people smelled danger radiating from their host. Bree certainly did.

When Townsend reached the big central staircase and began to climb, her internal sirens started to go off wildly. Why would he need to show her anything on the second floor? Kitchen, her problem. Buffet table, her problem. Decorations, liquor, security and even valet parking...all Breelie's problems. But her company's responsibilities didn't extend beyond the first floor.

She hesitated, her hand on the polished onyx railing. He

hadn't climbed more than four steps when his sixth sense obviously told him he'd lost her. He turned again, and laughed.

"Really, Ms. Wright," he said, his eyes glittering with some secret, inexplicable mirth. The effect was decidedly unwholesome, and a shiver ran down her spine. "I have a houseful of half-dressed concubines. You think I have designs on *your* icy virtue?"

"No," she said. His tone was so dismissive she found herself flushing, which was ridiculous. She'd worked hard to cultivate "icy" and had always considered it a compliment when people described her that way. Better "icy" than halfmad with uncontrolled passions, as so many in her dysfunctional family tended to be. "Of course not."

"Well, then?" He gestured impatiently.

Still, she hesitated. Something about the moment felt profoundly off. Why was he furious one instant, sardonic the next? And why on earth did he want to take her upstairs? Only the bedrooms were up there....

He laughed again, shook his head as if despairing at her naiveté, then abruptly leaned over the banister.

"Ladies and gentlemen!" His voice rose over the chatter, over the bubbling champagne fountain, even over the string quartet in the corner alcove. "Follow me! I have a surprise for you!"

All the faces tilted up toward him, though half the crowd was clearly too drunk to fully process his words and didn't stir. But at least a dozen laughing sultans and belly dancers churned toward the staircase, ready for anything that sounded different and amusing.

Bree wanted to be relieved. Whatever he had in mind, at least it didn't require privacy. That ruled out the most unpleasant scenarios, surely. So why, as the costumed guests surged up the stairs, creating a tidal wave that swept her along, did she have a sudden instinctive desire to turn around and flee?

She didn't do it, of course. That really would have set the gossips buzzing. Instead, she trailed along as Townsend made his way down the wide hall, turning occasionally to put his forefinger theatrically against his lips to shush his followers.

With every step, though, she felt herself retreating deeper into the numb bubble that had protected her from painful situations in the past. In the sixteen years since her mother's murder, she'd perfected the art of plunging her emotions into a frozen state, much like a medically induced coma, even while, on the outside, she appeared utterly serene and confident.

Icy, as she was always being told.

Finally, in front of the last door on the left, Townsend paused. He made one more "shh" gesture to his guests, then crooked his finger invitingly toward Bree, offering her the place of honor beside him. Unseen hands prodded her from behind, urging her toward her host, and before she could react, she was close enough to see the unholy gleam in his eyes.

"Mr. Townsend," she tried again uneasily. But he put his finger against her lips and grinned down at her, like an evil mime. She felt her heart accelerate. Whatever lay behind this door evoked a strong emotion in him. She wished she knew him well enough to interpret that glitter. Was it anger? Or was it glee?

With an elaborate flourish, he reached out for the doorknob and turned it slowly, so slowly it didn't make a sound. Neither did his guests, who obviously had caught the mystery fever and were craning forward in eager, hypnotized silence.

They pressed so fervently that when Townsend finally pushed the door open, Bree almost stumbled across the threshold.

Before her lay a beautiful room, decorated with a champagne-colored carpet and hunter-green bed linens and drapes. The overhead light was off, but a green-and-gold stained-glass dragonfly table lamp cast an amber circle onto the king-size bed, like a spotlight picking out the important actors on a stage.

In that amber circle, something palely pink and subtly obscene jerked and twisted, making rough, breathless, wordless sounds.

For a shell-shocked moment, Bree's mind wouldn't work. She somehow couldn't identify what she was looking at. It wasn't human, surely…that monstrous shape, with too many limbs, white-soled feet rising out of what looked like a tanned and muscled back…

Only when the people behind her began to gasp, and some to titter, did she finally jerk awake and understand. Two or three in the crowd laughed out loud; those more brazen, who had probably known from the start what the "surprise" would be.

With a cry of alarm, the monster on the bed separated into two parts. Charlie, who had been on top, leaped up, grabbing the green bedspread and awkwardly trying to cover himself with it in a pathetic display of selfishness that left his partner completely exposed.

Furiously, the woman on the bed, who was now recognizable as Iliana Townsend, yanked at the bedspread, too. Charlie, whose face was red and pop-eyed with terror, wouldn't let go, and the momentary tug-of-war was such a farce that everyone in the doorway burst out laughing.

Everyone except Townsend himself, and Bree. She suddenly felt dizzy, almost blind with fury. Oddly, she was angrier with Townsend for setting up this humiliation than she was with Charlie for causing it.

She glanced at the man now, wondering how he'd react to the sight of his wife's expensive breast implants bobbing about for everyone to ogle. Wondering if he would find Charlie's egregious lack of chivalry as disgusting as she did.

To her surprise, Townsend was still grinning.

Catching her horrified gaze, he winked salaciously. "Now look at that. Isn't that sweet? In honor of the occasion, my loving wife apparently decided to wear her birthday suit."

More laughter. Scanning the glassy-eyed, half-clad partiers and their mocking host, Bree realized suddenly that she was way out of her depth here. Back home in Silverdell, Colorado, nobody laughed at adultery. Back home, nobody invited an audience to a cuckolding.

Of course, back home, when her father had discovered her mother's infidelity, he had thrown her down the staircase and broken her neck. So maybe this decadent indifference was more civilized, in the end.

But even so, she couldn't understand it. It shocked her, and made her feel slightly ill. Perhaps that meant that, in spite of all the years living here in Boston, all the college education and the designer clothes and the artificially icy poise, she would always be just a Colorado cowgirl at heart.

What a joke…what a long, ironic laugh fate must be having right now, watching her try to handle these Eastern sophisticates—and fail.

Finally the red-faced, guilty cats seemed to find their tongues.

"Bill," Iliana wheedled. "It's not what it looks like—"

"Bree," Charlie called, trying to move toward her, but pinned in place by his lover's death grip on her end of the bedspread. "Bree, give me a chance to explain. She wouldn't take no for an answer—"

"Why, you lying bastard!" Iliana jerked so hard on the spread that Charlie lost his hold. The sudden full-frontal nudity, which cruelly offered everyone the measure of Charlie's shriveled, terrified penis, sent another wave of laughter through the room.

Bree turned her back on the sight. She eyed the others, drawing on every icy ounce of disdain she could muster, and willed them to move away from the door. Slowly, as if repelled by cold waves emanating from her, they did.

Chin high, she walked out. She didn't look back, though she heard Charlie's plaintive call of "Bree! Bree!" behind her, as if he were some kind of frantic cat stuck in a tree he'd foolishly climbed on a whim and now couldn't figure out how to descend.

She kept walking. Down the stairs, through the other guests, who had gone back to their own drinking and flirting, long ago having forgotten that something was unfolding upstairs. Past the champagne fountain, past the pyramids of grapes and the string quartet, still sawing out Mozart to the tone-deaf crowd.

Out to the valet, to whom she handed her ticket calmly. She tipped him a hundred dollars as she climbed into her car because she was so grateful to him for bringing the means to escape.

Protocol required him to feign indifference. She could have handed him a coupon for a fast-food cheeseburger instead of money, and he was supposed to pocket the paper without looking.

But obviously he knew how to sneak a peek surreptitiously. His eyes widened.

"Thank you," he said, shocked into revealing that he'd checked the denomination. "I mean…thank you, Ms. Wright. I hope you had a nice time at the party."

"Yes," she said automatically. She remembered him now. Tim. Tim Murfin. He owned the valet service, and she'd used his company before. He was honest, and he was smart. "Yes, it was a very interesting party."

In her rearview mirror, she saw Charlie racing toward the portico. He was dressed, mostly, though he was still stuffing his shirt into his waistband with rushed fingers. "Bree, wait!"

"Excuse me," she said politely to Tim, and he stepped away from the door, glancing toward Charlie with a furrowed brow.

As soon as the valet was clear, she pulled the door shut and stepped on the gas. She had no intention of letting Charlie reach the car. She wouldn't put it past him to climb onto the hood and splay himself there until she agreed to listen to his stupid excuses.

Nothing he could say could possibly make any difference at all. He'd be busy trying to convince her that he really loved her, that his dalliance had meant nothing. He might even be craven enough to say he'd done it for them, for Breelie's, to keep a customer satisfied.

He would imagine that he'd broken her heart. He'd think, no doubt, that she was hurt by his betrayal, and mourning their lost relationship.

But he'd be wrong. She didn't give a damn about any of that. The minute she'd seen him jump from that bed, ungallantly covering himself and leaving Iliana helplessly naked before all her friends, she'd understood what the real victim of the humiliating melodrama would be.

Not their relationship. Not her heart.

No. She realized at that moment that she'd probably never loved him, not real love, not with her whole soul.

The damage he'd done was even worse than that.

What Charlie had destroyed, by sleeping with their most prominent client, and making a spectacle before half of Boston society, was Brianna's career.

He had destroyed Breelie's.

And she would never, ever, ever forgive him for that.

THE FRONT DRAWING room of Harper House, where Grayson Harper stood waiting for his grandfather, held at least ten red-silk-upholstered seats. He had his choice of armchairs, straight-backed chairs, two divans and one chaise longue.

All unoccupied. All antiques, all chosen for comfort as well as beauty.

And yet he stood.

Sitting was something you did when you wanted to make yourself at home. Sitting was relaxed. Unguarded. Sitting made you the patiently waiting beta child to the superior alpha adult who would come stalking in, militarily erect, sneering down at his uninvited visitor.

So, no, he'd stand, thanks anyhow. Gray Harper was no one's beta—especially not his grandfather's. After all this time, he intended to meet the old bastard eye to eye.

Two could play the power game, and obviously his grandfather had made the first move already, keeping Gray cooling his heels down here for as long as possible. He glanced at the ormolu clock on the mantel, which ticked in the deep silence like someone tsking sardonically. The housekeeper, a woman Gray had of course never met, since the old man was too irascible to keep employees for long, had led him into the drawing room at least half an hour ago.

"He's dressing," the woman had said when she returned from announcing Gray. "He says to wait here, and he'll be down soon."

Dressing? Gray smiled with tight lips. His grandfather could have had a new suit of clothes bought, tailored and delivered on foot from the haberdashery on Elk Avenue in that much time.

But patience. Patience. After ten years, what was another ten minutes? He had something to say, and he planned to say it, even if he had to wait all night.

He went to the window and, putting his hands in his pockets, gazed out at the beautifully landscaped view of terraced lawn sloping down to the little town of Silverdell below. The sunset gleamed pink against the thin white spire of the Episcopal church and on the blue-gray rim of mountains in the distance.

Instantly, the sight took Gray back to his youth.

His youth. Not a place he wanted to linger. He squinted, imagining he could see rain on the horizon, even absurdly sniffing a hint of wood smoke in the April air, though the fireplace was cold and still.

Maybe that was why his grandfather was keeping him waiting. Letting him simmer in this ghost-filled room long enough to render him weak.

Frowning, he turned around again.

His grandfather stood in the doorway.

Gray inhaled sharply, startled in spite of having known full well the old man would jockey for an advantage somehow.

"Sir," he said, out of habit more than anything else. Certainly not out of respect.

One corner of his grandfather's thin mouth tilted up slightly, as if he understood the distinction. "Gray."

Another family might have made a drama out of the moment. After ten years of complete silence and absolute estrangement, most people probably would have considered a display of feelings relevant. Shock, recriminations, tears, joy…anything. After all, neither grandfather nor grandson had been completely sure, until today, that the other still lived.

But old Grayson Harper the First would have considered any emotional outburst to be a sign of weakness. And young Grayson Harper the Third simply didn't give a damn anymore.

"I'm sorry I kept you waiting," his grandfather lied. He hobbled into the room, using a silver-tipped cane that Gray had never seen before. He had done the calculations before he arrived, so he knew that his grandfather had just celebrated his eighty-fourth birthday. The old man's hair had been thickly silver as long as Gray could remember, and his face lined, so other than the limp, nothing much had changed.

"No problem," Gray said, matching the tone of fake courtesy. "I'm in no hurry."

"Ah. The luxury of time to kill." His grandfather smiled coldly, putting both palms over the head of the cane and leaning subtly forward. "Still not gainfully employed, then? Or… what is the euphemism these days? Between jobs?"

A pulse started to hammer at Gray's temple, and he took a consciously deep breath. That was cheap bait, a quick piece of dirty chum his grandfather probably tossed out by habit. He wasn't eighteen anymore, and he didn't have to rise to it.

"Exactly," he agreed placidly. "Between jobs."

The older man frowned. He shifted his weight, repositioning the cane. Clearly, his injury, arthritis, gout…whatever necessitated the cane…was bothering him. And yet he equally clearly didn't want to be the first to acknowledge the need to sit.

For one ruthless second, Gray told himself he was glad. It served the old man right. Gray would happily stand here all night, if that meant his grandfather might know even a fraction of the pain he'd caused other people. People like Gray's father and mother.

But the thought died instantly. In the end, it was beneath Gray to torture an old man—it was not his way, in spite of what his grandfather had modeled for him through the years.

So he took the nearest chair. Immediately after, his grandfather settled on the edge of the silk divan stiffly, as if his hip didn't bend correctly anymore. He didn't allow himself a sigh of relief, but the lines in his face eased slightly.

"So." He massaged his palm into the head of the cane, eyeing Gray over it. "What brings you back to Silverdell?"

Just like that. No small talk. No "How are you?" or "Did

you marry, have children, stay healthy, make money, buy a house…did you ever forgive me?"

Simply go straight to the point. *Fine*. Again, two could play that game.

"*You* bring me back," Gray answered matter-of-factly.

"Is that so?" His grandfather raised his shaggy white eyebrows. "Not intentionally, I assure you."

Gray shook his head a fraction of an inch. The mean old buzzard hadn't softened a bit, had he? Well, that was probably for the best. His arrogance and unyielding antagonism made Gray's job so much easier. As he'd journeyed back to Colorado from California, he'd wondered what he would do if the old man had grown weak, or senile, or sentimental. He'd wondered what he would say if his grandfather welcomed him home with open arms.

This was much cleaner. Now he could just speak his piece without wasting time trying to be diplomatic. And he could get out of this house before the past swallowed him up and broke his heart all over again.

"Nonetheless, it's true." He gazed at the old man, whose face was tinted a deceptively youthful pink by reflected sunset. "You really are the reason I've returned."

His grandfather frowned, as if he had a sudden gas pain. "Why? Had you heard I was sick or something? Did you hope you could breeze in at the stroke of midnight, butter up a dying man and get yourself written back into my will?"

Gray laughed. "Nope. Hadn't heard a thing. Believe it or not, no one out in California talks about you, your health or your money. Why, *are* you sick?"

"No." More rubbing his palm into the head of the cane, more scowling from under those unruly eyebrows. "I'm old, and my hip isn't what it used to be. But if you're here for a deathbed vigil, you'll have a long time to wait."

"I'm not."

"Well, what, then?" The old man grunted, a deeply skeptical sound. "You don't really expect me to believe the money has nothing to do with it."

Gray leaned back in his chair, smiling. "Oh, the money has *everything* to do with it."

His grandfather's eyes narrowed, but he didn't speak. He simply waited. He obviously refused to give Gray the satisfaction of asking for details.

No problem. Gray had rehearsed this part often enough that he didn't need prompting. He'd been rehearsing it for seventeen years, in fact. Since he was thirteen and filled with impotent fury at being so young, so helpless, so dependent on this tyrant. At being unable to summon the courage to say what ought to be said.

By now, Gray could have delivered this news in his sleep.

"It's one hundred percent about the money," he repeated. "But not your money. Mine."

The expressive eyebrows lifted high. "*Yours?*"

"Yes. You see, I've decided that it's time you returned my inheritance. I've come to tell you that, unless you voluntarily sign over every single penny you took from my father seventeen years ago, I intend to sue you for it."

In the silence that followed, the mantel clock ticked like a time bomb. Gray could hear someone, probably the plump housekeeper, running water in the kitchen, though that part of the house was at least fifty yards away.

Finally his grandfather spoke. "Who told you I took money from him? I'll guarantee your father never said that."

"Not to me. He told other people, who told me. I don't have any proof, of course. But I will get it, if you force me to. And the world will know you stole from your own son."

Finally the old man rose, slowly. Gray watched how he relied on the cane, and wondered whether, without it, his grandfather would be able to stand at all. In spite of everything, pity stirred, and his words suddenly sounded cruel, too harsh for this fragile old man to take.

Gray shut his eyes, annoyed by his own vacillating. This was why he hadn't come back to Silverdell for ten long years. It was just too damn emotionally confusing to feel intense love and intense hatred at the same time, for the same person.

His grandfather didn't seem tormented by any similar ambivalence. He stared at Gray coldly.

"I seem to remember that the last time I saw you I warned you never to mention your father in my presence again."

Gray nodded. "Yes. You did."

"Still you dare to come here and…" The old lips thinned. "You dare to defy me."

Gray shrugged. "Yes." He glanced through the window, where an olive-green gloaming was overtaking the sunset. "I dare. And yet, as you can see, no lightning bolts have struck me down. The earth still turns."

His grandfather's face darkened. "You always were an impertinent boy, Gray. Too clever by half. I blame your mother for that. Hannah foolishly encouraged you to think—"

But Gray, too, was out of his chair now. "Leave my mother out of this." He took one hard step closer. "You don't have the right to speak her name."

"Perhaps not." Undaunted, his grandfather cocked a sardonic glance toward the window. "And yet…the earth still turns."

For a minute, all Gray's hard-won indifference, his emotional independence and rational perspective, melted away, and he was afraid he might hit the old man. Somehow he held himself in check, though the blood throbbed in his head, and his right hand seemed to have frozen in a tightly muscled fist.

God, this had been a mistake. Just being in this house again scrambled his brain. He had overestimated the distance a few years could put between him and the past. Suddenly, the onslaught of memories was just too much… He saw again, as if it were real, that last night…his father standing there, right there by the fireplace, drinking too much, taking offense at everything old Grayson said…

And his mother quietly weeping, her hand on his father's arm, trying to keep him from finishing the last Scotch. The cold rain sheeting across the windows, the shadows of the elms fighting with the shadows of the fire.

Then the slamming doors, the parting threats and the rain-drenched, curving mountain road…

Damn it. Gray's left elbow began to ache, where the bones had knitted but remained sensitive. It might as well have been days since the accident, not years. He couldn't think straight in this room…this house. Maybe not even in this town.

Why on earth had he imagined that he owed his grandfather a warning? Had he really dreamed the old man might have grown a conscience and would meekly agree to admit his error and make restitution?

Fat chance of that. Old Grayson Harper had never been *wrong* in his life.

Besides, what constituted restitution, anyhow? Had Gray really thought that getting back his father's money could *begin* to restore his losses? Grayson had killed Gray's parents, as surely as if he'd put a gun to their heads. He could fill the Harper Marble Quarry with hundred-dollar bills, and it wouldn't begin to make up for what he'd really stolen from that terrified thirteen-year-old boy.

The boy who had awakened in the hospital the next morning, his arms and legs and ribs broken, his head bandaged and his family dead.

With effort, Gray peeled his fingers away from his palm and pumped them to force sensation to return. He had been a fool to come. Warning? *Ha.* He should have just hired a lawyer, filed the suit and let the fur fly.

"Go ahead," his grandfather said quietly, glancing pointedly at Gray's tense hand. "Do it."

Gray shook his head slowly. "I don't hit people."

"No." The scoffing noise his grandfather emitted was eloquent. "And that's the problem in a nutshell, isn't it? You don't *do* anything. You're just like your father. You drift, charming and completely useless in your expensive suits, trying to get by on your clever one-liners and your smarter-than-thou attitude."

He shook his head, as if to shake away the internal image. "You want money? Try *earning* some! If I'd ever seen you do a lick of real work, hard work, I'd leave it *all* to you. Every goddamn penny. Hell, if I could see you hold a real job for even one month, just four lousy weeks, I'd write you a check for the whole kit and caboodle!"

Dismissive old coot! Gray's shoulders twitched, and he felt his legs burn slightly from the urge to stride out the door. The judgmental bastard was so clueless. He hadn't understood his own son, not for a day of his life. Horrified at Gray's father's desire to be a musician, Grayson had forbidden it entirely, and steered him into a dozen "real" careers, each more ill suited than the one before.

And because, in the end, Grayson couldn't make a successful pig farmer out of a poet, he decided the poet was a slacker and a fool.

Gray hesitated, fighting the urge to lash out and give the old man as good as he had dished. But if he let himself stalk off in a huff, what would he have accomplished? He calmed his pulse and considered what his grandfather had said. If Gray could hold a job, he'd return the money. Surely that was almost as good as an admission of guilt.

Could this be the opening he'd hoped for?

For several seconds, fury warred with common sense. Finally, common sense won.

He didn't really want to bring a lawsuit. It would take forever, and it would cost a fortune on its own. He had no interest in humiliating his grandfather publicly. He wanted only the personal, private admission that the old man had wronged Gray's father—and, in doing so, Gray himself.

He eyed his grandfather narrowly. "Will you put that deal in writing? If I do what you ask…if I hold a 'real' job for four weeks straight without bolting, you'll write a check for every penny my father ever gave you to invest for him?"

The old man squinted at him in return as if he suspected a trick. "Not just any job. A hard job. A dirty job. The kind you turned your nose up at all your life."

Gray wanted to ask him, "What do you know of my life?" The last time they'd seen each other, Gray had been nineteen, reckless, defiant and mixed up as hell. Because he'd refused to come back to Silverdell over his college summer breaks and dig marble in the family quarry, the old man had decided Gray was afraid of real work. Just like his father.

How could old Grayson have been so stupid as to miss the truth? Gray wasn't afraid of work. He was afraid of Silverdell and what madness the memories might create in his heart. He was afraid of what living in this house another summer might make him do to his grandfather.

"Of course," Gray said with feigned calm. "I'll accept a job as dirty and demeaning as you want it to be. The only thing I won't do is take a job at the quarry, or anywhere I would report to you."

The old man worked his lips, clearly thinking fast and hard. "It would have to be here. In Silverdell, I mean. So that I could check on you. So that I could be sure it's not a scam."

"Of course." Gray's smile felt twisted. "I wouldn't dream of asking you to trust me."

If old Grayson recognized the sarcasm, he didn't deign

to acknowledge it. He scanned his grandson's face so thoroughly it felt like a scouring.

"Then yes," he said, finally. "If you can hold a real, Joe Lunchbucket job here in Silverdell, one with physical labor and no fancy title, and you can keep it for four weeks straight without bolting, or complaining, or getting yourself fired, I'll write a check for any amount you ask."

CHAPTER TWO

It was two in the morning, and though Bree and Penny had been talking for hours, the conversation showed no signs of sputtering out.

They were ensconced in Penny's suite in Aunt Ruth's beautiful old San Francisco Victorian town house. The sitting area was close enough to Ruth's sickroom to hear her if she called out, but private enough to let them chat in peace. They both still wore their day clothes because getting into pajamas seemed too much of an admission that the night might end.

Bree had been visiting her little sister for three whole days—a true luxury, since ordinarily the entire breadth of the country, and their respective obligations, lay between them.

When the sisters had been split up after their father went to jail, sixty-five-year-old Aunt Ruth had taken Rowena and Penny into her home. But she'd declared herself unequal to mothering all three sisters. After a tense period in which the state seemed likely to get involved, their mother's college roommate had stepped up. Kitty Afton, a Boston divorcée with no children, had always been fond of Bree, and was glad to offer the teenager a home.

Bree had lived in Boston ever since. She told herself she loved it. And yet, three days in a new place, with a fresh perspective and her little sister's calming presence, had done her a world of good. After the mess with Charlie…

She looked at Penny, suddenly wishing she could scoop her up and take her along when she returned to Boston. Without Charlie, without Breelie's, her "perfect" life in the city seemed hollow. Even the trendy Brighton-area condo she'd snagged a year ago—but never had time to decorate—felt lonely and sterile, and she could hardly bring herself to set foot in it again.

But Penny would never agree to leave San Francisco. Ruth, now in her early eighties, had congestive heart failure and needed full-time care. She really ought to be in a nursing facility, Bree thought, but Penny would never abandon the old lady who had put a roof over her head when everything else in their world had exploded.

So Penny couldn't leave, and Bree couldn't stay…not that she'd been invited. Reluctant or not, she had to get back to Boston and see if she could possibly piece her career back together.

Her plane left from San Fran International first thing in the morning.

So they lingered here, not ready to sleep in spite of the late hour. Bree had stretched out on top of Penny's small sofa, her head propped on the heel of her hand, and Penny had curled up in the adjacent armchair, sketching her sister as they talked.

"So what's our plan for Charlie?" Penny's face was still bent over her sketch, but her lips curved upward, and her smile could be heard in her words. "Shall we boil him in oil? Or can you think of something more creative?"

Bree laughed. Only Penny could say things like that and still look and sound positively angelic. She was undoubtedly the sweetest person Bree had ever met, but that didn't mean she was saccharine or dull. In her gentle, Alice in Wonderland face, sugar and spice coexisted in complete harmony.

"Boiling in oil sounds fine to me." But Bree yawned as she said it, which showed that, thank goodness, she'd finally lost her bloodthirsty enthusiasm for revenge.

The first day here, she'd spent hours detailing Charlie's sins—which, it turned out, had only begun with Iliana Townsend, not ended there. He had also been cooking Breelie's books for God knew how long, draining the savings to keep himself in cool suits and hot women. When news got out that he'd been sacked, vendors all over Boston practically set Bree's phone on fire, calling to complain they hadn't been paid in months.

It had taken Bree weeks to straighten it all out—and every penny of her personal savings, too. She'd stayed in Boston long enough to finish the last event already contracted…but, as she'd predicted, no one had called to hire her company for anything new.

She had one appointment still on the books, a golden wedding anniversary consult that had been set long before the Townsend fiasco and, miraculously, hadn't yet been canceled. She tried to be optimistic. Maybe, from that small job, she could begin to rebuild the business.

But she'd had a few days of rare freedom, and, so ravaged by resentment and self pity she couldn't stand her own company a minute longer, she'd impulsively booked a plane ticket to visit Penny.

Her little sister was probably the only person on earth Bree could have been completely honest with about how much Charlie's betrayal had hurt. Though she was four years younger than Bree, and five years younger than Rowena, Penny was without question the kindest of the three Wright girls, and the wisest. She was a good listener, and a true empath, with no trace of the schadenfreude most people—especially Rowena—might feel on hearing of Bree's misfortune.

Bree had always thought Penny possessed a touch of magic, though it sounded primitive and superstitious to say so. Maybe she should just say that, in less mystical terms, Penny was a…a born healer. And sure enough, over the days in Penny's company, most of the poison and pain had been drained out of the topic of Charlie, leaving Bree tranquil for the first time in more than a month.

"Yeah, deep-fried Charlie sounds just fine." She let her eyes drift shut. "You know, Pea, maybe you should have been a psychiatrist."

It was a musing, slightly slurred non sequitur that probably proved she had moved beyond tired all the way to incoherent. A thought struck her. She hadn't meant to discount Penny's art. "And an artist, too. I mean instead of being *just* an artist. Obviously you had to be an artist."

Penny chuckled. "You won't think so when you see this picture."

Bree opened her eyes, though she knew nothing in the sketch could change her mind about her sister's talent. Whatever Penny turned her hand to, whether it was oils, pen-and-ink sketches, photography or interior decorating, she ended up creating beauty.

Take this simple, cream-colored room, for instance. The rest of Ruth's house was crowded, lacy, oppressively Victorian. But up here, Penny had designed a cool, clean haven from all that. Without any cliché Western decor—no antlered light fixtures, no river-rock mantels, no bucking-horse sculptures—she managed to capture the essence of their beautiful childhood Colorado home, Bell River Ranch.

How did she do it? More magic, really. The one gorgeous piece of peach-and-turquoise pottery that always made Bree think of a spring sunset. One painting, a sunlit stand of birch trees that could have been trite, but instead was pure poetry. A love seat upholstered in muted silvers, blues and pinks, like the shimmering pebbles in the shallows of Bell River.

"I love this room," she said, another non sequitur. She laughed at herself, realizing she sounded a little drunk, although they'd been sipping nothing but almond-honey tea all night. She climbed up on her knees and peered over the arm of the sofa. "Okay, let me see the picture. If it's awful, though, it's not your fault. Too bad I don't have Ro's problem and get skinny when I'm upset. I bet from that angle my rear end looks huge."

Penny held out the crisp, thick paper with a smile. "Lucky for you I never got to the rear-end part. I spent the whole time trying to get your face right."

Bree was curious now—and maybe, if she was honest, a little embarrassed. She knew she didn't look her best. She might not have Rowena's problem, but when she wasn't happy her face could look very drawn and hard. She felt hard, since Charlie, and she dreaded seeing that reflected through Penny's eyes.

But when she summoned the courage to look at the paper, the face she saw there didn't look tough at all. In fact, Penny's version of Bree oozed vulnerability. Her blond hair was tousled, and her T-shirt had slid down one shoulder. Her cheekbones were pronounced and graceful, but shadows underscored her abnormally large blue eyes.

She looked wounded, and slightly bewildered, as if she were a child who couldn't understand why anyone would have wanted to hurt her.

She let her hand lower the sketch to her hip. She stared at her sister, frowning. "Is that how I really look?"

Penny raised one shoulder. "Well, you're more beautiful than that," she said. "I'm not good enough to do you justice."

Bree shook her head. "Don't be silly, Pea."

Compliments like that made Bree feel like some kind of criminal fraud. Penny always saw the world through the prism of her own inner sweetness—which was a great beautifier. But right now…

If Bree had really been such a beauty, would her fiancé

have been so eager to sleep with a forty-five-year-old married woman made almost entirely of nips and tucks?

Bree held out the sketch so that Penny could see it again. "I mean, do I look this...weak?"

Penny bent forward and studied her drawing with a small frown of concentration. Bree appreciated that she didn't pretend to misunderstand.

"You look very sad," Penny said finally. She glanced up, her brown eyes warm, and smiled to soften the pronouncement. "Which is why we really must toss the bum in boiling oil, first chance we get."

Bree had a horrifying sensation of stinging heat just under her eyelids, and she knew that, if she weren't very, very careful, she could actually end up crying.

Which was unacceptable. "Smile, Brianna," Kitty's voice in her head repeated, as always. "No one likes a sad sack."

"What if it isn't actually Charlie's fault?" She forced herself to meet Penny's eyes. "He says...he says I drove him to it. He says I'm always so critical, so hard to please. He says if I had ever really been the kind of fiancée who helped and supported his decisions—"

Penny snorted delicately. "Oh, for heaven's sake, Bree. Listen to yourself! You're going to believe that lying scumbag? That's the classic technique for abusive boyfriends, you know. Shifting the blame to you, hoping you'll think it's all somehow your fault."

Penny was right, of course. It was the abuser's easy out... *you made me do it.* But Charlie hadn't just been trying to weasel free of the blame. He didn't say those things until he knew the relationship was truly over and he couldn't ever win her back. Problem was, she could hear in his voice, and see in his face, that he meant it. Really meant it.

It was hard to even think back on the contempt in Charlie's voice as he'd hurled those accusations at her. Harder still, because, deep down inside, she had heard the ring of truth.

"I *am* critical, Pea. You know it's true. I don't know why, but I always seem to be pointing out everyone's mistakes. Especially Charlie's."

Penny was shaking her head. "I don't care if you whipped him with his own belt, mocked his manhood and made him sleep in the root cellar. You still didn't *make* him cheat. You didn't *make* him steal. You didn't *make* him destroy Breelie's. Someone ought to introduce Charlie Newmark to the idea of personal responsibility."

Bree was grateful for the vehemence in Penny's voice, and the loyalty that caused it. But she didn't want to sweep this under the carpet. If she didn't acknowledge her failings, how was she ever going to change anything? If she couldn't get better, she would never be able to put together a relationship that would last.

She didn't want to be alone forever.

"But it's not just Charlie, is it? Every boyfriend I've ever had has said something similar." She flushed as an old, half-forgotten memory came flooding miserably back. The day the sexiest rebel in her ninth-grade class, the boy she'd secretly had a crush on for months, had humiliated her in front of everyone. Wild Gray Harper…he had thought she was cold, prissy and boring…even way back then.

Penny looked at her oddly, and if Bree didn't want to explain that sad old story, she had to recover quickly. "And Rowena," she added. "Charlie might have taken the words right out of her mouth. And Kitty, too—though she sugar-coated it most of the time."

"Kitty was a cross between Pollyanna and a Stepford wife." Penny laughed again, but more softly, as if out of respect for Bree's obvious distress. "She thought it was a sin for a lady to frown, or express a single authentic feeling, or do anything but coddle and flatter the men in her life. I don't know how you stood it all those years."

"She did her best," Bree said loyally. "She wasn't even re-lated to us, you know. She didn't have to take me in."

"I know." Penny's laughter faded away. "That was a dumb thing to say. I'm sorry."

They were silent a moment, remembering, though it was like remembering a nightmare they'd inexplicably all dreamed at exactly the same time. Such horrors couldn't exist in the real world, surely. Their beautiful mother, lying broken and bleeding at the foot of the staircase. Sweet little Penny, so pitiful and bewildered. Penny, who had turned eleven that day, and was unaware that her birthday dress trailed through the blood as she knelt beside the silent body, begging her mother to wake up.

Their father, hauled off to jail for deliberately pushing his unfaithful wife over the railing. A phantasmagoric trial, in which their pathetic, shameful family secrets were trotted out, naked, for all the world to gawk at.

Johnny Wright…rotting in jail for years, so intractably angry. Rejecting the few overtures the sisters could bring themselves to make. Finally dying there of a brain tumor that may well have caused his irrational behavior from the start.

But worst of all was the ripping apart of the sisters, all of them just children, really, as well-meaning social workers, remote family connections and dutiful family friends stepped up, one by one, to offer them a place to live.

Bree shook the memories away. She couldn't let herself drown in them, not after all these years.

She smiled at Penny to show she wasn't angry. They both felt the same grateful loyalty to their respective saviors. Ruth and Kitty weren't perfect, but they'd voluntarily offered the drowning girls harbors in the storm. Ruth had provided stabil-ity and an almost cloistered quiet, which Penny's personality had needed. And Kitty, the compulsively smiling divorcée, had, in her own weird, Stepford way, shown Bree how to snap herself out of the trance of shock and grief.

"The point is that they're all saying the same thing," Bree went on. "It's as if they're reading from the same script. They say I am self-righteous, judgmental. I think I know better than everyone else. I'm never willing to trust other people to do things right on their own."

She tucked her hair behind her ear and looked away, over toward Penny's soothing painting of birch trunks. "They can't all be wrong. There must be some truth in it."

Penny didn't respond right away. She tapped her pencil against the sketch pad and ran her lower lip through her teeth softly.

"Well, even if there is…even if you do find it difficult to trust other people…is that so strange, given what happened to us? Why shouldn't you be afraid that people will let you down? Who, in the end, *didn't* let us down?"

And that, too, had the ring of truth. For a minute, Bree couldn't respond. All she had to do was think back, and she could see that the troubles had begun long before the murder. A mother who had always been emotionally absent…a father who couldn't control his jealous rages. Three little girls who practically raised themselves.

There'd been a whole year—Bree realized now that her mother must have taken a new lover—when a ten-year-old Bree had scavenged in the kitchen almost every night, trying to find something to feed Penny. Rowena, as usual, simply hadn't eaten.

One night Bree turned dinner into a hunt for pirate treasure, filling the bread box with carrot "coins" and radish "rubies." She'd felt such triumph, because Penny, only six at the time, had been enchanted. She had never guessed that she feasted on pirate carrots because there wasn't anything else to eat.

"It did something to all of us," Penny went on softly. "Think about Rowena. She was always so angry. She wouldn't get close to anyone for years. At least you try."

Suddenly, in the midst of her stupid self-absorption, Bree realized that Penny's face had grown sad, too. If she'd had any artistic talent, she could have sketched a portrait of Penny that was every bit as melancholy as the one of herself she held in her hand right now.

"What about you, sweetpea?" She lowered her voice, just in case Ruth was awake. "What did it do to you?"

Penny smiled vaguely. For a minute, Bree thought her sister might not even answer. But after several seconds, Penny held out a hand and swept it from left to right, as if to encompass the whole town house.

"It made me cautious. Too cautious. It made me hide out here," she said. "All these years. Here, where the storm can't touch me."

Oh…. Her heart stabbed, Bree stretched across the footboard and took her little sister's hand. She held it tightly, palm to palm, fingers wrapped around the fragile bones and satiny skin.

They really were like two shipwrecked sailors, holding fast to each other for fear the current would sweep them apart and make them struggle alone.

"We'll be all right, Pea. Somehow, we'll figure it out. We'll find a way to put the past behind us, and we'll be happy again. Who knows? Maybe we'll even find a way to be…normal."

She hoped the joke would lighten the mood, but her voice trembled, and it didn't come out quite as humorously as she'd hoped.

As usual, Penny was the one who knew exactly what to

say. She squeezed Bree's hand, straightened her spine and gave her a mischievous grin.

"Of course we will," she said, "Look at Rowena! After all those years of being the world's prickliest female, she married her true love, became a stepmother—"

Bree laughed. "To a little hellion."

"Maybe, but he worships the ground she walks on. And she's making her dude-ranch dream come true. Frankly, she's so darn normal it's disgusting."

Bree laughed and let go of her sister's hand. "How long before she finds a way to screw all that up, do you think?"

"Brianna." Penny frowned. "That's not fair."

Bree shrugged. She loved Rowena, but she didn't trust her. Ro had pushed everyone away for so long, closing off her heart. It had made her cold and selfish, and it had meant that loving her was dangerous. Marriage seemed to have mellowed her, but Bree was too cynical to believe the change was permanent.

Penny set her sketchbook on the end table and lay her pencil on top of it gently. She stretched, yawned and then rested her head on the arm of the chair, her luminous brown eyes gazing, doelike, at Bree.

"Ro seems absolutely blissful," Penny insisted softly. "Everything's going so well. The ranch has its soft opening in about a week."

"I know." Ten days, in fact. Bree kept tabs on the progress of the ranch more closely than Penny could imagine. It was their inheritance, too, and she didn't intend to let Rowena lose everything.

Ro was passionate, sure, but she wasn't good at the long haul. Every week, Bree half expected to hear that her restless, fiery older sister had grown bored, or fought with Dallas, or come down with her old gypsy fever. "Well, I *guess* they'll have the opening…if she doesn't get claustrophobic and run away again."

The silence that followed Bree's acidic comment made her flush uncomfortably. She heard how bitter and unforgiving she sounded. She wanted to take the words back, but that wouldn't be quite honest.

She had tried to forgive and forget, to believe that change was possible. And yet…she still had a rough, scarred-over spot inside her heart where her trust in Rowena used to be.

"I don't know," she said, trying to explain. "It's just that…" But she couldn't finish the sentence. She'd said it all before, and she knew Penny didn't agree.

"Oh, Bree." Finally, Penny smiled. "You know, if you really think you should try to be less judgmental, Rowena might be a pretty good place to start."

Of his almost thirty-one years of life, Gray had resided in Silverdell full time only about five—from the age of thirteen, when his parents died, until eighteen, when he went off to college. Before the accident, he lived wherever his dad's newest doomed venture took them—a horse ranch in Crawford, a pig farm in Butte. After high school, Gray had never come back to Silverdell, not even when he had flunked out of college and his grandfather cut off all funds.

But those five years had been notable for their intense resentment and rebellion. And for the salt-of-the-earth Dellians, they'd apparently been unforgettable. He must have been even more obnoxious than he remembered, because he couldn't find a soul in town willing to hire him to so much as change a lightbulb.

It was only noon, the Monday after his talk with his grandfather, and he'd already struck out at the hardware store, the brickyard and the ranch over at Windy River. Those businesses were all hiring. They just weren't hiring Grayson

Harper's black-sheep grandson, who had always been a troublemaker and a wiseass and clearly had condescended to return to Silverdell only so that he could sniff around the old man's will.

But Gray wasn't giving up. In fact, the rejection felt like the kind of challenge he loved. There had to be someone in this town who didn't hold his youth against him. Someone, perhaps, who wasn't a fan of Grayson Harper and might be sympathetic to the orphan who had found himself under his dictatorial thumb.

Crusty old coots like his grandfather made enemies, and all Gray had to do was find one.

Meanwhile, the April sun was climbing up a cloudless turquoise sky, and Gray was hot, tired and hungry. Lunch and another study of the classifieds sounded perfect. Luckily, Silverdell had just about the best barbecue in Colorado.

He glanced down Elk Avenue, remembering that someone had said Marianne Donovan was back in town and she'd opened a café that was pretty good.

She might be the perfect place to start. Not that Marianne qualified as old Grayson's enemy—far from it. Her mother had been Gray's grandmother's nurse, years ago, and the families were still close.

But Marianne had always had a soft spot for Gray, too, the way gentle good girls sometimes did when they met a certain kind of bad boy.

He began walking the main street, noting all the new storefronts, checking for her place. She'd been an instinctively domestic female, even as a teenager, so her restaurant was probably great. Besides, seeing her again would be a pleasant fringe benefit of this visit. She'd been such a nice kid—he had actually found himself being careful with her, treating her with a respect he rarely offered anyone during those angry years.

He almost walked right past it. The place was still under construction, and the sign hadn't even been hung yet. It leaned against the front bay window, but at the last minute he registered its kelly-green letters in a Celtic script. *Donovan's Dream.*

He backed up and took a look through the cute bay window, which was framed by white Irish-lace curtains draped over a shining brass rod. He spotted Marianne immediately, and smiled to see how little she'd changed. Still fighting those messy red curls and those extra five pounds. Still unable to fully hide the sprinkle of freckles she'd inherited from her mother. Still a well-bred, classic good girl, even though she was his age—pushing thirty.

She was taking someone's order, listening intently to every word they said. But at the same time, her intelligent green eyes were alert to everything going on around her, as any good restaurant owner would be.

Within a few seconds, she noticed him at the window. He expected her to take a minute to recognize him, and maybe another minute to believe her eyes. But she didn't look the least bit surprised to see him standing there. She simply smiled and extended her free hand, beckoning him in enthusiastically.

So…she had heard. Either she was still in contact with his grandfather, or the Silverdell grapevine was as dependable as ever. He nodded, returning her smile, and moved back toward the front door, which opened with a sweet cascade of bells he recognized as the first few notes of "Danny Boy."

She met him at the threshold, holding out her arms for a hug. "Oh, it's so good to see you, Gray," she said. She didn't stint on the hug, and when she pulled back she gazed at him uninhibitedly. "It's been so long. Too long. But you look every bit as gorgeous, you devil."

He grinned. "So do you."

To his surprise, she flushed and self-consciously put a hand to her hair. "Don't be silly. I—" For a moment, her smile faded. "I don't know if your grandfather told you about...well, it's been a tough year. My husband died just before Christmas. And my mother lost her battle with breast cancer about a month later."

Suddenly Gray felt as if he'd been gone a hundred years. Her mother, dead? He'd liked Eileen Donovan very much— and he'd always understood that his grandfather worshipped the woman from afar, his one grand chivalric gesture in a lifetime of rapacious greed and domineering chauvinism.

But Gray hadn't even realized her mother had been sick. That's what happened when you peeled rubber as you sped out of town, then tore off your rearview mirror and chucked it onto the asphalt at the county line.

He frowned. "No. He didn't tell me. I didn't even know you were married."

"Eight years," she said, lifting her left hand, which still wore a simple gold band. She folded her fingers into her palm, as if to feel the comforting squeeze of the ring. "We met in college."

He touched her shoulder. And then, for the first time, he could see that she had changed after all. Her eyes, once as clear as clover, as simple as grass, held depths and complexities and pain. They looked more like his eyes now—although his had been this way since he was thirteen.

"I'm so sorry, Mari. That's a heavy load, losing them so close together."

"Yes," she said simply. "Of course, you understand better than most."

But then, as if she knew he wouldn't want to open that conversation, she smiled again. She hadn't ever been one to wallow in self-pity, anyhow, he remembered. She had wanted their relationship to go further, but when he told her he just wanted to be friends, she'd accepted it like a trooper.

"But enough about me." She tilted a sideways glance at him. "Let's talk about you. For starters, I know exactly why you're here."

"You do?"

"Absolutely. You're looking for a job." She was teasing. He knew her voice well enough still to recognize its notes.

"I am?"

"Yep. But I'm sorry to say we're not hiring today. I've just found an excellent teenage boy who is happy to wash my dishes for gas money, which is all I can afford to pay him."

Gray tilted his head, smiling down at her. "How did you know that I—"

She laughed and put her hand under his arm, leading him deeper into the café. "Everybody knows, silly. Don't you remember Silverdell? They certainly remember you."

"So I've gathered. Most of them have clearly decided they wouldn't hire me if I were the last day laborer on earth."

"Exactly. No fatted calf for you, my friend. In the eyes of Silverdell, you are *not* forgiven."

He raised one eyebrow. "So...what do you think sealed my fate? Switching tombstones that Halloween? Teaching the naked limbo to Mayor Simpson's cross-eyed niece? Or...I know...maybe it was that thing with the moose head?"

"All of the above." Her green eyes twinkled, and she looked more like herself. "Although that moose head...that was plain nasty."

He chuckled. They'd arrived at the one empty table in the restaurant. She pointed to a chair, wordlessly instructing him to sit. Then she grabbed a bright green laminated menu card from its slot in the nearest wait station and placed it in front of him.

"But don't despair, Gray. I happen to know there's at least

one person in town who will be completely sympathetic to your cause. And, lucky for you, she *is* hiring right now."

Gray looked up. *"She?"*

"Yep. She. Our newest local entrepreneur. The one person in town whose reputation was even half as bad as yours."

He tried to think. Had anyone around here ever been as reckless and rude as he had? Surely no female. Silverdell women tended to be well-behaved and demure. The cadre of bitchy elder ladies, like that skinny harpy Mrs. Fillmore, insisted on it. No one dared to—

And suddenly he knew. His eyes widened.

"Oh, my God," he said. "Crazy Rowena Wright has come home."

CHAPTER THREE

BREE DIDN'T CALL ahead to let Rowena know she was coming.

It wasn't that she thought surprising her sister would be fun. Rowena was as likely to be irked by an unannounced visit as she was to be delighted. Bree didn't call because, right up until the last minute, she couldn't bring herself to commit to really, truly going to Bell River Ranch at all.

Every mile along the way, she kept assuring herself she could always change her mind. Drive away. Get back on an airplane and fly home to Boston.

But somehow merely saying that phrase, "home to Boston," made her realize how little she belonged there, even after sixteen years. And so she didn't turn around. She kept driving, from the Gunnison airport toward Silverdell, every minute bringing her closer to the one place in the world she had ever thought of as home.

And the one place in the world she'd ever thought of as hell.

She skirted Silverdell's downtown area, not ready to be seen by anyone she used to know. Instead, she took the loop-around on what the locals called Mansion Street—though maps and strangers called it Callahan Circle. Bell River was the first ranch you encountered as you exited the city limits, so after she passed the elegant old Harper estate she knew she had only about two more miles to go.

Her heart beat faster, and she tightened her fingers on the wheel. Dread...or excitement? She no longer knew.

Man-made structures thinned out the minute she crossed

the city line, giving way to open spaces, acre after acre of rolling country greening with spring. The occasional cow or horse gazed placidly at her as she coasted by, and a pair of brown falcons watched her sternly from a fence post, but for those two miles she didn't see another human being.

And then, too soon, the acres that spread out beside the road were Bell River acres. She knew every undulation, every tree, as well as she knew the lines and pads of her own palm. The rippling pastures were achingly the same as they'd been twenty years ago when she'd ridden her bike home from elementary school along this same road.

The same—except better. Much, much better.

She hadn't visited since the wedding four months ago. It had been winter, then—and Rowena had still been in the early, messy stages of renovations, the part of the process where you saw only the broken eggs, not the promise of the omelet.

Now it was April, the time when Colorado clouds began to lift, as if the tent of blue sky actually were being winched up higher and higher each day. The air felt fresh, green with sunshine and sweet breezes.

And the creation of the dude ranch was much further along. The first thing Bree noticed as she turned into the long front driveway was how well the grounds had been groomed. The palsied bristlecone pines on either side of the rickety front fence had been pruned up, as if by dancing masters obsessed with posture. The fence itself had had been replaced with a pair of scrolled wrought-iron gates that stood crisply open, smiling a glossy black welcome.

Muddy patches that once had pitted the fields on either side of the driveway had been converted to smooth carpets of emerald grass.

A few more yards and she got her first good look at the house, set like a jewel in its setting of sparkling white paddocks. It had been freshly painted pale green, with a brand-new hunter-green roof and a wide white porch trimmed in lush hanging baskets of ferns, ivy and lipstick-red geraniums.

Her foot almost stalled on the gas, and the rental car slowed to a crawl. "Wow," she said to the empty car. Rowena had worked a miracle, considering how tight their budget was and how short the timetable.

It was gorgeous. No longer a downtrodden, half-neglected white elephant, but a home. Wholesome, peaceful and inviting. All the things the ranch had never been, even before their mother's death.

Bree determined to make a point of telling her sister so. Maybe that would help break the ice…get them off on the right foot. She would show Rowena right away that she wasn't here as judge, or spy, or critic. She was here as a friend.

As a sister.

Sister. As if the word were emotionally electrified, a frisson of fear sizzled through her. It had been a long time since she'd been comfortable with that word, at least in relation to Rowena.

She mustn't let herself get carried away. While the ranch might look inviting, the "invitation" wasn't designed for her. The beautiful scene was, quite literally, a stage set for an ad in a glossy brochure. The goal was to coax paying guests into booking their vacations here.

Her only incontestable credential was her status as co-owner of the soon-to-open enterprise. Her name, Brianna Allison Wright, was listed on those thick loan documents—loans that haunted her every time she thought about how big the numbers were.

She had every right to show up, with or without advance notice, if only to check on the renovations and see how her money was being spent.

Besides, about twenty windows overlooked this front

driveway, so she probably had already been spotted. She hit the gas again, pulled around to the back of the house where a nicely landscaped parking lot had been created and slipped the car into a space.

Then, squaring her shoulders, she got out.

She left her suitcase in the trunk, though. She still felt more comfortable having an escape, just in case. She could pretend she had just stopped by to say hi. She could say she had a reservation in Aspen, or Crested Butte, or anywhere, to…to do…

Something else. Anything else. In case Ro made it clear Bree wasn't welcome to stay here.

She climbed quickly onto the back porch and made her way to the door, which used to open onto a laundry room, but now, she knew, would lead into the expanded kitchen. She smelled coffee, so she knew Rowena was up, even though it was only a little after eight.

All three sisters had always been early risers. Work on a ranch started before the sun came up, and their father wouldn't have tolerated sleeping in.

Eventually, being early birds had been more than a pattern—it had been in their blood. In all the years Bree had lived on the East Coast, she'd never truly adjusted to night-owl hours. Charlie had often laughed at her, saying they should have called the company "Cinderella's" instead of "Breelie's." What a joke, a high-society event coordinator who started yawning at midnight!

"Watch out! Hey, lady! Watch out!"

Startled out of her thoughts, Bree frowned. The child's shrill voice seemed to be trying to pierce through a cacophony of noise—a hectic tizzy of clucking, barking, screeching, fluttering and stomping. Bree grabbed the doorknob instinctively, as if she might have to flee inside the house, and wheeled around to see what on earth…

Good grief! The area behind her whirled with an onslaught of motion. Inexplicably, about a dozen chickens squawked toward her, frantic and brainless, running into each other comically, stumbling over the stairs as they stormed them, feathers flying. Behind the chickens, a glossy brown puppy galloped in ecstatic pursuit. Its long tongue waved like a wet, pink ribbon from its idiotic grin, its soft ears lifted like furry propellers and its gigantic feet churned up contrails of dust in its path.

Behind the puppy, a boy thundered across the grass, trying to catch up, one hand waving to get her attention, the other recklessly swinging a big straw basket.

It was Alec, Rowena's high-strung stepson. Bree didn't have to look twice. She recognized immediately the mop of thick blond hair and the half devil, half angel charm of the skinny, suntanned face.

"Lady, watch out for the chickens!"

Without thinking, Bree twisted the knob and the door swung open in her hand. She wasn't entirely sure why she did that. She didn't exactly need to plunge to safety behind the refrigerator, or beg her big sister for help. She couldn't possibly think a flock of dithering chickens, a slobbering puppy and a nine-year-old imp posed a significant physical threat.

But, jangled, she did it anyhow—and the result of her actions could have been predicted. The chickens streamed through the escape route the open door offered, and the puppy followed joyously, dirt and all.

"Oh, no," she said, thinking they were the most useless words in the English language, and annoyed with herself for being paralyzed by the ridiculous farce.

The imp pounded up the stairs, pausing just long enough to give her a disgusted look. "Great," he said, staring gloomily through the open door. "Brilliant." Then he took a deep breath and continued the chase inside.

After that, what could Bree do but follow? Maybe she could stop being so fuzzy-minded and help....

But it was too late. In his attempt to catch the puppy, Alec had overturned his basket, and the shining new tiles of the kitchen floor suddenly seemed covered in shining yellow glop, disgustingly dotted with islands of white shards.

Oh, no. He had obviously been gathering the chicken eggs. Judging from the wet mess, his basket must have been full of them. As Bree watched in horror, he slipped in the goo and thudded hard on the floor, face down. The puppy ran two demented circles around him, just enough to get its paws thoroughly coated in raw egg, then streaked off to share the excitement with the rest of the house.

Alec lifted his face, his chin seeming to drip lumpy yellow gore. He narrowed his prematurely handsome blue eyes, and opened his mouth as if to say something heartfelt. But then his jaw went slack. "Bree?"

She smiled weakly. "Hi."

"Alec, what the...?" An irritable male voice boomed from around the corner. The sound was followed immediately by its owner, a shirtless, golden-haired god wearing only a pair of half-buttoned, low-riding blue jeans and a few white tufts of shaving cream missed by a recent razor.

Or, as other people knew him, Dallas Garwood. The sheriff of Silverdell County. Rowena's hunky new husband.

"Why the devil are the chickens in the house?" Dallas's attention was at first focused exclusively on his son, who still sprawled on the floor, wearing a goatee of egg yolk. "Oh, hell, Alec. Is that the eggs?"

"It's not my fault, Dad," Alec protested vehemently. He tried to scramble to his feet, but the slippery floor defeated him, and he couldn't get any higher than a kneeling position. "I totally had it under control, no problem. Then *she* went and opened the door."

She would have paid a king's ransom, at that moment, to fall through a trapdoor in the floor.

But in spite of the extensive renovations, apparently no one had thought to add an escape hatch. She could only wait in mute misery as Dallas frowned, turned and finally saw her. She still stood by the front door, her hand on the knob as if magnetized to it.

His blue eyes, so like his son's, widened. *"Bree?"*

"I'm sorry," she said, though she wasn't sure which part she was apologizing for. For opening the door and letting the livestock into the house, for catching him half dressed or for having the dumb idea to come to Bell River in the first place.

"You...you did this?"

"Well. I did open the door," she admitted. Then she shook her head helplessly. "To be honest, I have no idea what just happened. It's all a bit of a blur."

"I can believe that." To her surprise, he grinned, and then he began to laugh. "Welcome to Bell River, Bree. Around here, the forecast is always sunny with a ninety percent chance of Alec."

Without the least sign of self-consciousness, he crossed the rivulets of egg, avoiding them as much as he could, and wrapped her in a warm hug.

"How fantastic that you came. Ro will be thrilled." He turned to his son. "You start cleaning this mess up, Alec. I'll go see if I can corral the circus."

"What circus?" Rowena suddenly appeared on the other side of the large, walk-in freezer. She was smiling, but she looked exhausted, as if the preparation for the soft opening had worn her out. She was also dirty...a real mess, and at first Bree thought she'd somehow become tangled in the chicken-puppy-egg fiasco.

When Ro drew closer, though, Bree could see that she must have been gardening. Her hands were covered in earth, her cheeks smudged and dirty and the knees of her clover-green jeans were black. About half her long dark hair was clipped back with a green barrette, but the rest was in disarray, wisps clinging to the perspiration on her temples, her collarbone and her damp T-shirt.

"Alec!" Smile fading, Rowena scanned the chaos. Then she turned to Dallas, which led her green-eyed gaze to Bree. Her dramatic eyebrows drew together. "*Bree?* What are *you* doing here?"

The minute she said it, she seemed to realize it had come out wrong, because she bit her lower lip and shot a self-conscious glance at her husband.

"I mean…" She tried in vain to swipe some of the dirty, damp hair from her face. "I'm glad you're here, whatever the reason. I am just sorry you've caught us…in such a state."

Bree shook her head. "No, it's my fault. I should have called ahead, or made a reservation or something. I should have given you some warning."

"Warning?" Dallas laughed, and his easy charm smoothed over what was rapidly becoming a very bumpy conversational road. "To stay in your own home? Wouldn't that be kind of silly? Besides, advance notice probably wouldn't have helped. We always seem to be in crisis mode these days. Although—" he transferred his wry smile to his son "—I have to admit the eggs are a special touch. How about you get going cleaning these up, kiddo?"

"Yes, sir," the boy muttered, his tone just the safe side of polite, but his face sour as he surveyed the chore. He rolled his eyes, then bent forward and plucked a large, curved piece of eggshell from the stew and chucked it into the sink just over his head.

In the distance, the puppy began to bark frantically, followed by the crazed clucking of chickens. Dallas groaned. "I think that's my cue."

He put his arm around Bree's shoulder and hugged her lightly. "See you tonight," he said, as if he took it for granted that she would be staying. "Your suitcases are in the car, I guess. Don't bring them in. Barton will be here in an hour or so, and he'll be glad to do it."

Bree nodded. When she'd been in town for the wedding, she'd met their general manager, a courtly older man named Barton James who used to own a successful dude ranch in Crested Butte. It was probably true that he'd be glad to help. He had come out of retirement because he couldn't stand being idle.

Dallas smiled, as if to reassure Bree one more time that she was welcome. Then he stepped to Rowena and kissed her hard on the lips, apparently not in the least deterred by her dirt-smudged face and sweaty hair.

Bree looked away from the intimacy of that simple touch, and her gaze met Alec's. He rolled his eyes again, eloquently, with all the disgust a nine-year-old could express for the mushiness of adults.

"Might as well get used to it," he said morosely, extricating another bit of eggshell. "They're like this all the time."

Then the doorbell rang.

Rowena pulled free of Dallas's embrace, though she kept one hand against his naked chest, as if she couldn't bear to lose the connection entirely. Her head turned sharply toward the front of the house.

"Oh, my God. Has my interview showed up early?" She glanced at the clock on the stove just behind Alec and moaned. "Oh, no. It can't be. It's not really eight-thirty?"

"It's really eight-thirty," Dallas said. "I'm sorry. I should have warned you it was getting late. You always lose track of time out there."

Rowena had begun brushing her palms together, as if she might be able to whisk away the crusting of soil, but her hands remained shadowed with dirt. She touched her chin, checking for dirt there, but she seemed to realize she was only making matters worse.

"I need a shower. I can't interview anyone like this, but especially not—"

"I'll let him in," Dallas offered quickly.

But Rowena shook her head. "You're half-naked, and you know you two have never really gotten along. Besides, you're on chicken duty."

"I'll do it," Alec piped up eagerly, trying to clamber to his feet, but once again finding it difficult. Apparently even playing butler seemed exciting compared to mopping egg gunk off the floor.

"You most certainly will not." Dallas held up his hands emphatically to freeze his son in place. "You're the most disreputable member of the family right now. And that's saying something."

"I can let him in," Bree heard herself saying. She felt a little like Alec, jumping at the chance to leave the room rather than continue an awkward encounter. But her event-planner side had kicked in, and her intervention was the only answer that made sense.

The doubt in Rowena's eyes wasn't exactly flattering. "Bree, I couldn't ask you to—"

"You're not asking. I'm volunteering. I promise I won't blow your chance to hire this guy, whoever he is. This is the kind of work I do all the time. I'll handle the meet and greet, then dance him around a little, maybe tour the property while you guys pull it together in here."

The doorbell rang again.

"That would be terrific. Thanks, Bree." Dallas nodded toward Rowena, who still frowned, obviously uncertain. "You shower, Ro. I'll get the chickens. Alec will fix the kitchen." He impaled the boy with a sharp glance. "Or else."

"Sounds like a plan." Like any good salesman, Bree took the yes as final. She dropped her purse on the counter and picked her way carefully toward the great room on the other side of the kitchen. "Oh…I guess I should know which job this guy's applying for."

Rowena hesitated. "Assistant social director. Part time. Thirty hours. Minimum wage."

Pretty menial job, Bree thought, to be causing such a stir. So what if he didn't like Ro's grubby fingernails or a little chicken poop in the hall? If he got scared off, so what? Surely qualified candidates for that job were easy to find.

"All right," she said neutrally, determined not to show her confusion. She wasn't here to criticize, remember? She had to stop forgetting that, stop lapsing into her old ways. This was Ro's dream, Ro's decision, Ro's hire. "And his name?"

Rowena blinked, her dark lashes shadowing her green eyes. She opened her mouth, closed it, then blinked again. The doorbell sounded its two-note call a third time, which apparently agitated the chickens, who were closer now, close enough that Bree could hear the flutter of wings above their clucking.

"I probably should know his name, Ro."

"Of course." With one deep breath, Rowena seemed to snap out of her weird spell as quickly as she'd fallen into it. "Actually, you know him, or at least you used to. Remember… remember old man Harper's grandson, Gray?"

Bree frowned. Everyone remembered Gray Harper. The bad and beautiful new kid in town. Part jokester, part heart-breaker—all trouble. The heir to the Harper Quarry millions who had become a local legend when he kissed the money goodbye rather than, as he put it, kiss his grandfather's "ar-rogant ass."

"Gray Harper? Applying to be your part-time assistant social director? You're kidding, right?"

Rowena shook her head. "Nope. Sorry. Still want to dance him around?"

"I...well, sure," Bree said with a careful smile. No judging, remember? No criticizing. And definitely no being afraid of a formerly snotty teenager who probably wouldn't even remember what he did to her. "Of course."

She left the room, determined to reach the foyer before he pressed the bell again. She smoothed her skirt and checked her hair in the hall mirror. Everything tidy. She'd do fine.

But honestly...what was Rowena thinking?

Gray Harper?

CHAPTER FOUR

JUST WHEN GRAY thought Rowena must have changed her mind about interviewing him, the front door finally opened.

But the elegant blonde knockout who stood there, smiling coolly, wasn't Rowena. No way Rowena could have changed that much, not even after sixteen years, not even after the mellowing experience of falling in love and getting married. Gray considered himself a connoisseur of beautiful women, and even when he was only thirteen he'd understood that Rowena's fiery good looks weren't a product of cosmetics, clothes or hairstyles. She was all dramatic, gypsy bone structure and primal energy.

And, of course, there was the problem of the coloring. She might have dyed her hair, but no way even contact lenses could transform Rowena's flashing eyes, which had been the color of melted emeralds, into this cool pair of iced-sapphire blue.

Cool. Ice.

The words triggered something. He dug around in his psyche for a couple of seconds, then pulled it out. *Aw, heck.* Wouldn't you know it would be one of the guilty memories, one of those inexcusable episodes from his angry years? He seemed to have an inexhaustible supply. Some more rotten than others.

This one really reeked. God, he'd been such an ass back then.

But at least he recognized her now. This was the middle

Wright sister, Bree. She'd been his age, so they'd been in the same class, but she hadn't been in his group. She had hung with the student council crowd, the prissy, overachiever girls who had annoyed the heck out of him in those days.

He wouldn't ever have guessed that she'd grow up to be so gorgeous. When their mother was killed and the Wright girls left town, the middle sister had still been in that awkward stage, unsure what to do with anything she possessed, from her thick, nearly white hair to her long, gangly legs.

But she knew now. From crown to polished toenail, she was slick and citified and possessed a distinctive eastern seaboard chic. The look might still be a bit icy—alabaster skin, blue suit to match her violet-bluebell eyes, sleek Grace Kelly French twist showing off expensive pearl earrings. But she somehow managed to pack a visceral wallop, even so.

"Hi, Bree," he said, hoping his surprise—and his more pleasantly primitive reactions—weren't too obvious. "I assumed you probably were a partner in the dude ranch, but I didn't realize you had moved back to town, too."

"Hello, Gray." She smiled politely, all professionalism and poise. "I haven't moved back. I'm just here for a visit, and to help out a little with the soft opening, if I can. Most of the time, I'll be a partner in name only."

"That's a shame," he said. And he meant it. He would have enjoyed spending time with a woman this attractive—assuming she wouldn't scuttle his chances of getting the job.

He wondered if it was even remotely possible that she'd forgotten about…the ice.

He had to laugh at his own wishful thinking. No, it was not even remotely possible she'd forgotten. But perhaps she would want to pretend she had. Her whole bearing announced that she had more than her share of pride.

"I'm so sorry we kept you waiting." She took a step forward, putting one foot onto the porch, which surprised him. They were going out, not in?

Suddenly, from somewhere in the house behind her, a strange, high-pitched noise rang out. He glanced over her shoulder, wondering what on earth could have made such a sound. But her face remained utterly impassive, not even a twitch revealing that she'd heard it.

Man, she was good. He wouldn't want to have to play poker with her. Their gazes locked, and he blinked first. After a couple of seconds, he actually began to wonder whether he had imagined the sound.

She stepped across the threshold, pulling the door shut behind her, and gave him another smile. "Rowena is running a bit late for the interview, so she asked me to show you around the ranch. We're all very excited about the plans for Bell River, and we think you will be, too."

She didn't wait for him to agree, but moved on down the stairs without looking back, taking his cooperation for granted—which made sense, of course. After all, she was the boss lady and he was just a hired hand, assuming he got the job.

Mr. Minimum Wage. Still, Gray wasn't complaining. The view he got while she walked ahead of him was pretty spectacular. It made him think like a college kid...it made the phrase "Boss Lady and the Hired Hand" suggest all kinds of interesting, if idiotic, possibilities.

God, what a sleazeball that made him sound like! Good thing she couldn't read his mind. He had to laugh at himself, proving his grandfather right about how unprofessional and self-indulgent he was.

"One day, son, you'll learn that *real* life is not all about games and girls." Gray's grandfather's face, as he stood in Gray's college dorm on Gray's nineteenth birthday, had been rigid with fury. He'd just realized that Gray wasn't going to cave in to his demands to come home for the summer, not even at the risk of losing the Harper Quarry millions.

The old man never had been able to tolerate being thwarted. He'd run his cold eyes over Gray's expensive suit, and then over the equally expensive red dress Gray's girlfriend was almost wearing.

"If you honestly believe you can make your own way, without the safety net of the Harper name, you're going to have to do a hell of a lot of growing up."

Gray had yawned and gone back to knotting his tie. He and Carla had reservations at nine, and she was eyeing him appraisingly, obviously wondering if he had the starch to stand up to the old tyrant.

So Gray had met his grandfather's gaze in the mirror and grinned. "Oh, dear. Will I have to become like you?"

His grandfather's mouth had tightened. "You couldn't be like me if you tried, you insolent whelp. But, like it or not, if you're going to be poor, you will have to get serious. You will have to get focused. And by God, for once in your spoiled life, you will have to get *dirty.*"

Well, the old man hadn't been lying about that, as Gray had soon discovered. But he'd been wrong to assume that getting dirty would bother him. He'd thrived on it, actually, and kept himself so focused that it had been a very, very long time since Gray had found any female special enough to take his mind off "real life."

The subtle stirring of interest Bree Wright had just set in motion…well, frankly, it felt darn nice.

Still, she was talking, and he should be listening. He caught up with her and kept his eyes sensibly on the path as they made their way toward the stables. He tried to pay attention as she detailed the ranch's horsemanship program.

They had built fifty stalls, she explained, because, though they had only twenty horses at the moment, the plan was to

increase to fifty head within a year. They also had three ponies for young riders and a "bring your own mount" option
for guests who preferred a familiar seat.

"Nice," he said appreciatively as they entered the large,
well-designed stables and heard the soft nickering of the animals. He gazed down the wide, clean walk between the stalls.
Half a dozen horses poked their heads out, and his practiced
eye evaluated them quickly. All excellent specimens, as far
as he could see.

Bree didn't seem inclined to take him in any farther,
though he was itching to get a closer look. Apparently this
was only the nickel tour, skimming the high points until she
could turn him over to Rowena.

Or else she simply wasn't a fan of horses. He allowed
himself a quick up and down while she was consulting her
watch. That hairdo wouldn't survive five minutes on horseback, and those high heels had definitely not been bought
with the thought of tramping through sawdust and hay. Maybe
more than a decade on the East Coast had eradicated her inner
cowgirl completely.

After a few seconds, he realized he was still staring at her
impossibly long legs, so he yanked his gaze up where it belonged and said the first thing that came into his mind. "Are
you a good rider?"

She glanced at him, as if surprised by the question, and
lowered her arm, letting her watch fall over the back of her
hand.

"I haven't ridden in years, but I used to be all right," she
said, but she touched her earring when she said it, and he
had already learned that the gesture was her tell. The question had made her uncomfortable. "I was nothing compared
to Ro, of course. She was the horsey one."

He winced, hearing in her voice that she still accepted the
childhood labels without question. Big mistake. Labels, he

knew all too well, had a way of being self-fulfilling. He had been "the spoiled brat."

"Really." He tilted his head. "And which 'one' were you?"

Her eyebrows drew together gently. Then she smiled. "I was the prissy one. The ice queen. I thought you might remember that."

Well, that brought the elephant out and plopped it on the table, didn't it? He admired the cool aplomb that allowed her to mention it first. Maybe the episode really didn't bother her as much as it bothered him. Maybe it was easier to live with the memory of having looked foolish than to live with the memory of having been cruel.

"I do remember," he said flatly, without any attempt to make light of it all. Yes, they'd been kids. But even ninth graders bled when they were cut. "I remember that I was an insensitive jackass. You deserved better, and I knew it, even then. It may be sixteen years too late, but I want you to know I'm sorry."

When he had started his speech, she had already begun to exit the stables. At his final word, *sorry,* she stopped walking and gazed placidly back at him, her elegant, symmetrical features half in shadow, half in sunlight.

"Thanks," she said, but he didn't know her well enough to guess whether the simple word was sardonic or sincere.

Truth was, "jackass" might be an understatement. He and his friends had always made fun of girls like her, the ones who were so bloody virtuous and civic-minded, always on committees to organize this and decorate that. But then, that January, just a month or so before her mother's death, she had ratted on his best friend for smoking behind the bleachers.

Irked, Gray had decided she needed to be taken down a peg.

So, inspired by the instructions on one of his grandfather's housekeeper's frozen foods, he had printed out bold red letters on a piece of plain white paper. Then he'd recruited the girl who sat behind Bree in biology to surreptitiously tape it to the back of her shirt.

Caution: Contents Are Frozen. Thaw Before Eating.

She'd worn it for two whole class periods, in which apparently she had no allies. Finally, after school, one of her buddies saw it and yanked it off. By that time, the joke had made its way around the building like a virus, becoming more vulgar by the minute. Even Gray had felt naive when he realized some of the nasty interpretations that could be applied— though of course he pretended to have meant them all along.

"Don't be too hard on yourself, though," she added with a smile. "You had good reason to be rebellious. What happened to your parents…it was so unfair. I didn't understand anything about it that day, of course, but I found out soon enough. When you're furious with life, with fate, with *everything,* it can make you…" She seemed to search for the right way to express herself. "Less than kind."

He nodded. "True. Although in some ways isn't that just a cop-out? People still have choices about how they'll express their anger." He appreciated her generosity, though. "I have to say," he added, "that tragedy doesn't seem to have had a similar effect on you."

Flushing, she rolled the pearl of her earring between two fingers and laughed softly. "That's nice to hear. But then, you've known me all of…ten minutes? I suspect that the people who know me better would emphatically disagree."

People who knew her better… He wondered whom she meant by that. A husband…an ex-husband? A lover?

Or…he glanced toward the pine-dappled path they'd taken to the stables, and saw Rowena striding briskly toward them, her black hair blowing out behind her in the breeze.

Or a sister?

"Gray!" Rowena met them at the stable door and held out

her hand. "Gosh, it's been a long time, hasn't it? But you haven't changed a bit! I would have known you anywhere."

He accepted her warm, welcoming handshake. He would have recognized her, too, of course. Those eyes. Those cheekbones. But he couldn't say she hadn't changed. Though she had been in the eleventh grade the last time they met, and she was now probably nearly thirty-two, a married stepmother juggling family and business, she didn't look a day older. Instead, she seemed, paradoxically, to have grown younger. Softer.

Was that what marriage to Dallas had done for her? Had love really erased all that dangerous tension that had once tightened the muscles in her face and in her body, until she had seemed a hairsbreadth away from exploding?

"I'm so sorry to keep you waiting," she went on. "You've seen the stables, then? I hope Bree has been persuasive. Her mission was to convince you that Bell River Dude Ranch is the perfect place to work."

Bree frowned, as if this was the first she'd heard of such a mission, but Gray spoke up quickly. "Absolutely. She's made it sound terrific. I'd want to work here even if you weren't the only place in town willing to hire me."

Rowena laughed, but Bree's deepening furrow told Gray that she hadn't been brought in on the joke. When Gray and Rowena had spoken on the phone yesterday, he'd laid everything out frankly, black sheep to black sheep, and asked for her help. In the strictest sense, this meeting wasn't even really an interview, because she'd already offered him the job.

"I was just about to show him where the Phase Two construction will start," Bree said, obviously treading carefully. She pointed west. "We'll be adding a pool and a lodge, just over there. Both of them will allow us to offer many more activities. Your position would be greatly expanded during Phase Two, I'm sure, and—"

Rowena laughed again, reaching out to touch Bree's upper arm gently. "I don't think Gray really cares much about Phase Two," she said. "He'll be long gone by then."

Bree's face went very still, and she twirled her left earring with a studiously careless motion. "Long gone?" she repeated without inflection.

He glanced at Rowena, who nodded subtly, giving him permission to tell Bree the details. "I talked to your sister yesterday, and I explained my situation. I need the dirtiest, most menial job she has, but I need it for only a month. Four weeks, to be exact."

"Only a month?" Bree raised her eyebrows. "And that's because…?"

"Because that's what my grandfather requires, before he'll put me back in his will."

She stared at him a long minute, and the expression in her eyes subtly hardened as she did so, as if she was revising down her estimation of him.

Finally, she turned to Rowena. "You think this is the best decision for the ranch?"

"What do you mean?"

Bree glanced once, quickly, at Gray, then returned her gaze to her sister. "Shouldn't we have employees who really want to work at a dude ranch? At *this* dude ranch? Surely that's in our best interests. And yet, knowing that Gray wants this position for his own personal agenda, and no other reason, you hired him anyway? Sight unseen?"

"Not exactly *unseen,*" Rowena corrected, a slight edge creeping into her voice. "We've known Gray for years, Bree. But otherwise, yes. I knew, and that's exactly what I did."

"Why?" Bree's one-word question dripped disapproval.

As Rowena prepared to respond, Gray thought he detected a spark of the old firebrand. Her green eyes narrowed, and they seemed to blaze hot inside her thick fringe of black lashes.

"Because he is willing to work for practically nothing, which is about what I've got left in the budget. Because a month will get me through the soft opening and give me time to replace him. Because he's handsome and smart and charming, and the guests will be eating out of his hand."

"But, Ro, he—"

"I'm not finished." Rowena's syllables were crisp and staccato, and Bree subsided. "Most important, I'm hiring him because no one else will. Because I know what it's like to try to outrun a reputation that got tied to your tail so long ago it feels grafted to you. In a town like Silverdell, that's pretty darned hard to do."

Gray watched as Bree tried to swallow her opposition— a self-control that seemed to be something of a struggle. As complex emotions swept across her classically beautiful features, rendering them infinitely more interesting than perfection ever could, his curiosity was piqued.

Though of course everyone had gossiped about their mother's murder, Gray hadn't really known the Wright sisters very well. Rowena had been older, too sophisticated to bother with a boy like him, and Bree had always seemed too deadly wholesome to be worth his time. The little one…he couldn't remember her name…hadn't registered at all.

Now, though, he sensed layers and textures in Bree's personality that went far beyond "prissy" or "icy" or "dull." And layers between the two sisters, too. Undercurrents both deep and powerful—and touchingly human.

He suspected that, at its heart, this mini-confrontation had very little to do with Rowena's choice for a job as insignificant as the part-time assistant social director…and much more to do with years of unresolved family baggage.

Well, okay, then, maybe he knew them better than he had

realized. They all belonged to that sorry club—the children who had survived the unsurvivable and didn't really know why. Or where to go from there.

A large bird, maybe an eagle, landed somewhere high in the pines over their heads, causing the sunlight to shift as the branches swayed. For an instant, the light seemed to catch on two crystal sparkles at the outer edges of Bree's cool blue eyes.

Tears? Gray frowned. Was the ice princess fighting back tears?

She blinked, then, and the illusion disappeared. But he was left with a sudden, inexplicable hunger to know her better, to find out more about her.

A lot more.

And…just his luck. He had only four weeks to do it.

CHAPTER FIVE

WHILE ROWENA WENT over the payroll paperwork with Gray, Bree decided to head up to her room and regroup. In the early planning stages, they'd all agreed that one of the upstairs rooms should be set aside for family, always to be left unrented, in case Penny or Bree wanted to visit.

The sister suite, Penny had called it. Because of its size, the space they'd chosen was Rowena's old room. All the upstairs bedrooms had been subdivided to create more guest space. In this one spot, though, they hadn't formed two separate rooms, but one suite with a connected sitting area and a bedroom.

Bree entered slowly. In the old days Rowena had been possessive about her private sanctuary. Her younger sisters had been forbidden to enter without permission, which she rarely granted. Even now, the remnants of inhibition were so strong that Bree felt odd waltzing in as if she belonged there.

Once in, Bree almost imagined she could detect a hint of Balenciaga Paris in the air. Rowena had received a bottle of the expensive perfume from some secret admirer that Christmas—the last they'd ever celebrated in Silverdell.

Ro had pretended to scoff at girly things like perfume, insisting that she preferred natural scents…wildflowers, the wind coming off the river or rain. But Penny, who sometimes crawled into one of her sister's beds after a nightmare, had innocently told Bree that she chose Rowena now, because Ro always smelled of the pretty perfume while she slept. Ro had denied it, but she had clearly felt embarrassed and exposed. She'd been huffy, even with Penny, for days.

Bree knew the smell was only her imagination, of course. Old ghosts were stirring.

She went to the window of the sitting room. It overlooked the back parking lot, but it also had a peaceful view of the misty salmon-and-sapphire-tinted mountain line in the distance, and the view called to her. The physical beauty was shockingly different from anything in Boston, and at the same time it was deeply, hauntingly familiar.

She was still standing there when Gray and Rowena came strolling outside, their paperwork obviously completed. She moved an inch to the right so that the curtain veiled her, embarrassed to be caught watching.

But she needn't have worried. Neither Rowena nor Gray looked up toward the second-floor windows. They seemed completely engrossed in their conversation. Bree couldn't make out words, but occasionally Rowena pointed to various buildings, as if describing the activities planned on the property. Gray occasionally pointed, too, clearly adding suggestions of his own.

Lots of nodding and smiling, interspersed with laughter. They seemed to communicate awfully well for people who hadn't seen each other in more than a decade.

But then, Gray had chatted comfortably with Bree, too, in spite of their touchy history. Obviously the man possessed formidable people skills. He always had, even in high school, which was probably what had allowed him to be so rough and rebellious without ending up expelled or slapped in jail.

Leaning easily against the driver's door of his white truck now, he suddenly tilted his head back and laughed at something Rowena said. Bree smiled wryly, aware of a quick, supremely female reaction deep in her own body.

Okay, so it wasn't just his people skills that gave him

power. He was also dangerously sexy. His body was a six-four, athletic arrangement of rippled muscles and animal grace. She wondered what he did for a living, when he wasn't in Silverdell, trying to vacuum out his grandfather's wallet. Did he do some kind of serious labor? Or did he simply live at the gym?

And his face…she studied it now, trying to pinpoint where exactly its appeal lay. His golden-brown whisker stubble, square jaw and sun-weathered smile lines were all male, hinting at long days on horseback or wielding a jackhammer. But his lush eyelashes, the waves of chestnut hair that tumbled over his broad forehead and those sensually bowed lips belonged in an art gallery, a pirate ship or an eighteenth-century duchess's boudoir.

Above the rest, his intelligent, honey-brown eyes simply said he found the whole question absurd. He was who he was.

Finally, he pulled his keys out of his pocket and beeped open the truck's auto lock. For the first time, Bree actually paid attention to his vehicle. It was nice, a shiny new model, but somehow she'd expected something glitzier. Like maybe a purring silver Jag with a vanity plate that read GRAYT.

He and Rowena hugged goodbye—Bree couldn't help shaking her head at that. When had her prickly older sister developed a warm fuzzy side? Then he climbed into the truck's cab, cranked the engine, executed a deft three-point turn and guided it out of the parking lot and around the house, heading back to the main street.

She wondered where he was staying…and where he would stay, once he reported for work. Phase One of the dude ranch had included creating staff quarters out of the old stable, but she had the impression that, with at least a dozen employees already hired, those bunks were full.

Minutes later, she heard a low rap at her door. She braced herself, assuming that Rowena had come to finish their argument. She moved from the window and shot a glance into the dresser mirror to be sure she didn't look frazzled.

"Come in," she called, trying to sound as benign as possible. She didn't want to fight with Ro. She'd come to Bell River for one reason only…to see if she could start repairing their relationship. The last thing in the world she wanted was to add to the destruction.

But when Rowena entered, her body language was surprisingly relaxed. Bree had always imagined she could see invisible sparks shooting from her sister when she was angry, but she sensed nothing like that now. Nothing but the fatigue she'd noticed earlier.

Apparently Rowena came in peace. Bree hadn't realized she'd been clenching her midsection until the muscles released.

"I showed myself around up here," she said quickly, determined to start right. "Everything looks fabulous, Ro. You've done a masterful job with the guest rooms."

Rowena's smile broadened. "It did turn out well, didn't it? I had a lot of help. Did you know that Cindy Sedgwick got two-thirds of the way through architecture school before she found herself pregnant with twins and had to come home to marry Joey Incanto?"

Bree only vaguely remembered who Cindy Sedgwick was, but she made an impressed face, anyhow. "Cindy designed the rooms for you?"

"Yes, and the new guest cottages, too." Rowena glanced at her watch. "I don't have another interview until eleven-thirty, so I could give you a tour, if you'd like. I figure you might as well see them now, before guests come in and the Trash Clock starts."

Bree chuckled, but to be honest, the joke surprised her. That had been one of their father's favorite lines. He'd always complained that he'd rather postpone buying new equipment as long as he could, because the minute he made the purchase the Trash Clock began ticking, and the new stuff started turning to garbage that would, in its turn, have to be replaced.

Was Rowena really ready to start quoting their father's cranky humor so casually? But then Bree corrected herself. Ro wasn't quoting *their* father—just Bree's. Rowena had found out last year that mad murderer Johnny Wright's DNA didn't match hers in any way.

Zero percent probability that Johnny was Rowena's real dad.

To which Bree and Penny had said…*lucky Ro.* Penny had no hope of a similar reprieve, because she was Johnny Wright's spitting image. But Bree had sent a sample of her DNA off, too, crossing her fingers and saying a prayer.

Her results had been very different. Percent probability of a match? Ninety-nine percent.

Unfortunately, she was the old bastard's daughter through and through, and she'd simply have to live with that. Must be where her grudging, judgmental streak came from, and her difficulty trusting anybody.

But, damn it, DNA wasn't destiny. She was her own person, and if she wanted to be more tolerant and trusting, then she could make it happen. Starting right now.

"I'd love to see the cottages," she said.

For the next hour, her positive attitude was easy to maintain. Four new guest cottages—one that slept six, one that slept four and two smaller units that slept two—had been built as part of Phase One. And each cottage was a perfect jewel.

She loved every detail. She loved their names…River Run, River Song, River Moon and River Rock. She adored their quaint exterior styles, each one unique—some quaint, like fairy-tale storybook cottages, some rustic, like log cabins, and some a hybrid of the two.

And she adored the floor plans, which all included great

rooms with big windows overlooking the stunning views. Even the interior decorating was perfect, cozy without being cliché.

Kudos to Cindy Sedgwick. And, of course, to Rowena.

No wonder Ro looked tired. Having staged so many events, Bree understood that every room in every cottage represented about a hundred decisions to make, a hundred details to oversee. She was deeply impressed and didn't pass up any opportunity to say so.

Even cynical Rowena, whose antennae had always been finely tuned to detect empty flattery, was glowing under the effusive compliments by the time they stopped at the last cottage.

"Enough." She smiled, holding out her hand. "I believe you're sincere right now, but one more and I'll start to think you're blowing smoke."

Bree laughed. "Okay. Nothing but insults from this moment on."

She could hardly keep that promise, though. River Moon, built right at the edge of one of the small creek offshoots of Bell River, was a storybook charmer. This cottage, with its round blue door, steeply pitched, sloping roof and climbing yellow roses, would probably be used as the honeymoon suite. Phase Two included marketing the ranch for destination weddings.

They wandered through the adorable rooms, all the way to the sunny bedroom at the back.

"Oh, this quilt is—" But somehow Bree bit her tongue, holding back the word *fabulous.*

Rowena smiled, shaking her head. "I mean it, Bree. Enough."

But the quilt, which had been draped over a Bentwood rocker, *was* fabulous. Bree ran her hand over the intricate blue-and-yellow pattern of entwined hearts. Each cottage bedroom had its own signature antique quilt, the one theme that ran through all four cottages, but this was the most beautiful of them all.

If Bree had wanted to say something less fawning, she might have voiced the one doubt that had niggled at her throughout the tour. Were the interior decorations maybe almost *too* beautiful?

Too beautiful for their tight budget, anyhow.

But obviously she didn't utter a peep about that. She might have reached her limit of compliments, but she hadn't reached the point at which she could dare to express a criticism.

Besides, Ro wasn't exactly a shopaholic. She wouldn't have spent the money if she hadn't thought it was important. Bree forced the worry from her mind, and instead strolled the perimeter of the airy room, drinking in the romance of every charming detail.

"This may be my favorite of all the cottages. That's not a compliment," she hastened to add. "Just a fact. Just a personal preference. The colors…the creek. I don't know, something just appeals to me."

"I thought it might," Rowena said. She lowered herself onto the rocker and leaned her head back against the quilt with a sigh, as if she didn't get to sit down very often these days. "I used the colors from your old room. Remember?"

Bree scanned the area with new eyes. She hadn't noticed it before, but now… Her childhood bedroom had once been painted this exact shade of powder blue, and her canopy bed had been trimmed in bluebell-daffodil patterned linens that she had loved with an innocent, absolute passion. She'd felt like a fairy princess in that room.

"I'd forgotten," she said softly. "I can't believe it, but I'd actually forgotten."

Once the floodgates were open, she felt the memory rush through her. She suddenly saw Rowena and their mother, arguing quietly at the Mill End store in downtown Gunnison. Ro had tucked a bolt of flower-sprigged fabric under her arm with the grim tenacity of a quarterback protecting a football.

Ro couldn't have been more than nine years old at the time, because Bree had been eight when she got her dream room. But the determination on Rowena's face was intense and unshakable, far beyond her years.

"You helped me pick out that print," Bree said suddenly. "You talked Mom into buying it for me, even though it was much too expensive. And I know you couldn't have liked it, really. It wasn't your style at all."

Rowena had shut her eyes, but she was smiling, as if her mind's eye had summoned the pictures, too. "You should have seen the look on your face. Clearly, you were going to curl up and die if you didn't get it. Whether or not *I* liked it was irrelevant."

Bree remembered that. Somehow, her future had seemed to depend on the sweet, feminine flowers in that bolt of fabric. She had believed with all her heart that if her room looked like that she would always be happy. If her room looked any other way, if her bed was draped in any other material, she would be forever unrealized.

Like a rose that never opens, like a candle that won't light.

Of course, she wouldn't have been able to express it—in those terms or any others—back then. But somehow Rowena had intuited all those incoherent emotions, and had been willing to go toe to toe with the grown-ups on Bree's behalf. She wanted to thank her, belatedly. But it seemed silly, after all these years, to make a big deal out of a bolt of fabric.

Still, she suddenly felt a surge of optimism. Rowena had loved her once, and Bree had loved and trusted Ro, too. Completely, without question. She hadn't been afraid of Ro's ferocity, not back then. She had understood that her big sister was a warrior, but they were on the same side of the combat, and Ro fought for her, not against her.

Bree took heart from the memory. If it had been so once, it could be so again. If Bree could just keep from messing anything up...

"Ro, I...I want to tell you that I—"

Out of nowhere, she heard the sound of the cottage's front door opening, and a woman's voice calling out, "Rowena? Are you here?"

Ro opened her eyes and blinked sleepily. "Georgia? I'm back here. With Bree."

Bree cast a questioning look toward her sister, but there wasn't time for Ro to answer it. Two seconds later, a young redhead in a crisp red suit poked her head through the door.

"You busy? I just picked up the banner and I thought you should see it."

Rowena didn't stand up from the chair, which surprised Bree. She just smiled at the newcomer and waved her in. "Georgia, you haven't met my sister Bree, have you? Bree, this is Georgia Brooke, our social director. Other than Barton and me, Georgia is the most overworked, underappreciated person on the payroll."

The redhead, who was more beautifully groomed than beautiful, and who looked, if anything, even more exhausted than Rowena, smiled wanly at Bree.

"We're all tired," she said, her voice proving the truth of her words. For a social director, she certainly didn't project any energy or enthusiasm. Bree hoped the woman could fake it if she had to, when the guests arrived.

"Speaking of which..." Georgia turned anxious, deep-set brown eyes toward Rowena. "Did Gray take the job?"

"He did."

Georgia let out a deep sigh, as if her life had depended upon getting that answer. Rowena obviously noticed the doleful sound and raised her eyebrows. "Hey, shouldn't you be happy? We just hired you a Cadillac assistant for a go-cart price."

"I am happy," Georgia assured her. But she put her hand to her forehead and shut her eyes briefly, as if she felt dizzy, or sick. "I'm just feeling a little off at the moment. Kind of queasy."

Rowena leaned forward in the rocker and eyed her social director closely. "You're not getting the flu, are you? If you think there's the slightest chance, go home. We can't afford to spread germs around the rest of the crew, not this close to the opening."

"No, no." The smile Georgia dredged up, in an attempt to be reassuring, was worse than her frown. "It's nothing like that. I'm thinking maybe the sausage at breakfast was a mistake."

Rowena didn't look completely convinced, but she leaned back again and didn't press. Bree's estimation of the social director went down another peg. She wondered whether Rowena had hired the woman out of desperation, or whether she was an old friend who had played on sentiment.

Something had to account for this…

"What about the banner?" Rowena glanced at the folded cloth in Georgia's hands. "You're happy with it?"

"Well…" Georgia's frown was back in full force. "It looks fine, but when I picked it up the guy charged us twice what he'd estimated. I argued, but he wouldn't budge."

"That's absurd." Bree was so incredulous she spoke without thinking. "If the correct price is on the estimate, he *has* to honor it."

The other woman glanced up, flushing, as if she resented Bree's intrusion. "It wasn't a written estimate," she said, lifting her chin. "We discussed it over the phone. I didn't have any reason to doubt his word."

Bree glanced at Rowena, and she could tell from the tension around her sister's eyes that she was unhappy with this explanation, as well. But, unlike Bree, Ro seemed to be working hard to cover her displeasure.

"Okay. Well, lesson learned. We'll be getting all estimates signed in blood from now on." Rowena smiled. "Let's see this two-hundred-dollar banner, then. I hope it's pretty darn amazing."

Two hundred dollars? Bree opened her mouth, then shut it over the exclamation of disbelief. She couldn't judge until she saw it. Maybe it was fifty feet tall, or lettered in pure gold.

She watched as Georgia unfolded the white vinyl, which read Welcome to Bell River Dude Ranch. It was an extra large, probably the eight by three, simple grommets, black letters in a standard Booker bold italic.

Nothing misspelled or off center, but nothing impressive, either. Not double-sided or custom shaped. No background, no color, no graphics, no special effects or…anything.

For heaven's sake. Even in Boston, where the cost of living was crazy, Bree could have ordered that banner for a third the price.

Not that she would have—not for an unpublicized soft opening, where all the guests would be friends and family… and staying *free.* The thin vinyl wouldn't hold up well enough to reuse during the more important grand opening in June. Maybe if Georgia had ordered it on canvas, or aluminum…

This time, Bree didn't have to force herself to be silent. Even she knew the comments bouncing around in her head shouldn't be spoken aloud.

But her expression must have said it all without words, because Georgia's flush deepened to a splotchy plum color, and her eyes seemed to be watering. Under her deftly applied makeup and chic dress, she suddenly looked like a little girl who found herself in the deep end of the pool and had forgotten how to swim.

She was younger than Bree had initially realized, as well. Early twenties, tops. Looking at Georgia's miserable face, Bree felt something in her chest soften. She remembered what it felt like to be a newbie and to get everything wrong. Breelie's had almost gone out of business in its first year because Bree, still a college senior and overeager to hit the big time, had made every stupid mistake in the book.

It was only two hundred dollars. The dude ranch wasn't going to sink under the cost of one disappointing banner. She put out a hand, smiling at the other woman, trying to think of something encouraging to say.

"Did you plan to hang it on the front gates? The black lettering will look quite nice there, against the wrought iron of the—"

But then, right in the middle of Bree's awkward attempt to console, Georgia emitted a choking sound, stared around the little room with wide, glistening eyes and finally, with a small groan, vomited helplessly.

All over the banner.

CHAPTER SIX

TWO HOURS LATER, while Rowena interviewed several college kids who wanted jobs on the waitstaff, Bree sat in the beautifully renovated great room with Alec and Barton James.

Though the afternoon had turned chilly, the fireplace in the center of the room was crackling contentedly, and Bree could see what a delightful gathering spot this would be for guests after long days riding or hiking outdoors.

Bree sat on the wide, comfortable sofa, her laptop open, working on her proposal for the golden wedding anniversary party. She'd pitch to the Everlys next week—assuming they didn't call between now and then to cancel. They weren't part of the Townsend set, so she kept her fingers crossed that the gossip hadn't reached their elderly ears.

Over on the wide river-rock-fireplace surround, Barton was trying to teach Alec how to play "Mamas, Don't Let Your Babies Grow Up To Be Cowboys" on the guitar. He'd said it would be fun for them to perform a duet at the opening-night barn dance.

Alec had done pretty well for the first thirty minutes or so. His puppy, a mutt who had turned out to be named Trouble, but who also had turned out to be surprisingly sweet and mellow, slept at his feet.

The boy had a clear, true tenor that sounded charming when mixed with Barton's mellifluous bass. But after about half an hour he'd started to fidget and cast longing glances out the window, and his fingers were too impatient to form the chords correctly.

"Oh, never mind," Barton said finally, propping the guitar on the floor beside him. He ruffled Alec's hair. "I'll handle the music. You just stand there and look adorable. Wear your cowboy hat. And maybe…you got any little rattlesnake boots with spurs?"

Alec glared at the old man as if he were daft. *"No,"* he said, as if that should be obvious. "I have regular boots, like regular people."

Barton didn't seem to hear. He tilted his head and squinted at the boy, apparently imagining the possibilities. "Yes, definitely boots." He nodded, as if satisfied with whatever he had seen in his head. "Silver belt buckle…the works. I tell you, kiddo, all the old cowgirls in the audience are going to eat that stuff up with a spoon."

Alec snorted. *"Gross."*

"Gotta please the ladies, son. That's the first rule of show business. You please the ladies, the menfolk gotta follow. It's kind of interesting, how menfolk don't very often think for themselves. I always say it's because—"

But Alec clearly wasn't in the mood for Barton's cowboy wisdom. "Okay, fine. I'll tell Dad I need rattlesnake boots." He glanced toward the window again. "It's getting dark, and I said I'd help muck the stalls today. I'd better get going."

Barton hesitated. "With spurs?"

Alec groaned. "Yeah. Okay. Spurs."

Over the boy's head, Barton winked at Bree. She lowered her gaze to her laptop, hoping she could hide her smile. Old rascal. He obviously knew Alec would agree to anything right now, if it was the price of busting free. Dallas's son was the outdoorsy type, and his fidgety energy needed an outlet or he'd pop like an overinflated balloon.

Just one of the reasons he and Rowena got along so well,

no doubt. Bree could remember that same twitchy tension tormenting her big sister. Ro used to sneak out of the house sometimes in the middle of the night—not to meet up with boyfriends, or drink, or joyride in stolen cars, as most people might think. She just wanted to be outside, because a whole night lying motionless in a narrow bed was more than she could stand.

"Let's go play, Trouble." Alec grabbed his dog, who woke up instantly and licked Alec's face, his tail thumping. He obviously knew the word *play,* and was delighted to be invited.

Ten seconds of sneakers pounding, puppy toenails clicking, and the two of them were gone.

"So what do you think about Gray Harper and this newfangled glamping thing?" Barton had returned to idly strumming his guitar, and he spoke over the music. His tone was pensive, as if he was continuing a conversation he'd been having with someone—maybe himself.

Bree glanced up, and saw that he was looking at her, obviously awaiting her response.

"What is glamping?" She closed her laptop, curious. The word was odd, but it was the connection to Gray Harper that cinched the deal. She had a feeling Rowena wasn't going to tell her much, not after she'd made her disapproval so clear.

"Glamorous camping," Barton said, plunking the guitar strings to accentuate the two words. "It's all the thing these days. Instead of building permanent structures everywhere, a resort'll put up high-end luxury tents, with beds and fireplaces and bathrooms and all that mollycoddle stuff. Rich people pay a lot of money to spend the night in 'em."

She did have a vague recollection of reading something about the concept. Maybe. "But what does it have to do with Gray Harper? We're not planning to offer that at Bell River." She paused, noticing the smile on the old man's face. "Are we?"

"Well, it's a little idea I've been wanting to try," he said.

He shrugged his shoulders, as if to say it was no big deal. "I talked Rowena into letting me put one out by Cupcake Creek. Just thought we'd see how it played, you know? I'm a sucker for newfangled things. Keeps me young." He grinned. "Well, keeps boredom from killing me even faster than old age will, anyhow."

"I had no idea." She wondered where the money for such an extravagant purchase had been found. She knew their budget pretty well, and "glamping" wasn't listed anywhere. "Rowena didn't mention it."

"Yeah, well, she thinks I'm crazy, no doubt. But so what? If it doesn't pan out, no sweat. I bought it on a lark. I can always sell it to some other old fool who is itching to try something new."

So Barton had bought it. She mentally apologized to Rowena for even considering the possibility that she'd been hiding expenditures. She really, really had to stop judging everyone as if they were as immoral as that hound dog Charlie Newmark. "And you...you're *glamping* out there now?"

"Gawd, no!" Barton laughed and intoned a few notes of a funeral march. "With these old bones? We're putting Gray Harper out there. He needs a place to stay. We need a guinea pig. So there you go. Everyone wins."

Apparently delighted with his turn of phrase, Barton bent over his guitar and began picking out a new song.

"There you go," he sang, starting off on a plaintive note. "Walking away. I know you think..." He smiled, finding his next line easily. "I'll ask you to stay. But when I'm rid of you, that's when the good life begins. So there you go. *Everyone wins*."

He ended with a playful wink and a flourish of finger-picking. Bree applauded softly, laughing as the old man took a small bow. Barton billed himself as the best cowboy poet west of the Mississippi, and she suddenly had a feeling that he might be right.

Alec's littlest-cowboy routine wouldn't be the only thing the old cowgirls would eat up with a spoon.

She started to reopen her laptop and return to her proposal when suddenly, like a grenade tossed into the middle of the easy camaraderie, Rowena appeared, obviously stressed and angry as hell.

Bree frowned, watching Ro's body language, realizing that the sparks she knew so well had finally made an appearance. She wondered what she'd done now.

"Barton, could I talk to Bree privately for a minute, please?" Ro's voice was as tight as the reins on a runaway horse.

"Sure," Barton said easily, slipping his guitar strap over his neck, and sliding the instrument around so that it rode against his shoulder blade. "I can't be sitting here singing all day, anyhow. I've got all kinds of general-managing things to do."

"Thanks," Rowena said, though she didn't seem to notice his little joke. Obviously all her energy was focused on reining in her temper until she and Bree were alone.

Bree waited calmly, refusing to let herself feel anxious or defensive. After that rocky start about the hiring of Gray Harper, she'd bent over backward trying to be supportive. But there was a fine line between bending over backward and allowing yourself to be a doormat. She didn't intend to cross that line, not even for Rowena.

As soon as the front door shut behind Barton, Rowena took a deep breath. "Georgia Brooke just quit."

"What?" That certainly wasn't what Bree had expected her sister to say. "She did? Why?"

"She said it's because of you. She said you made it very clear you think she's not up to the job."

Bree set her laptop aside, stunned. "That's absurd."

"Is it?"

"Of course."

"No, Bree, it isn't." Rowena's eyes flashed. "That is *exactly* what you think. Just because you didn't say so outright doesn't mean your feelings didn't come through, loud and clear. Georgia may be young and inexperienced, but she's not a fool. She sensed your disdain."

Bree knew there was some truth to that, but not enough to account for such a dramatic reaction. If an employee made a mistake, surely they had to expect their employers to be disappointed. Bree hadn't said a single negative word about any of it. If the young woman was so thin-skinned that she couldn't tolerate the idea of a negative thought passing through someone's mind…

Quitting simply wasn't a proportional reaction. If Rowena weren't so tired and stressed herself, she would see that, too.

"I'll talk to Georgia," Bree said. "It probably all seems worse because she's not feeling well. You saw how sick she was. Maybe she's embarrassed about throwing up on the banner. I'll talk to her, and—"

"You can't," Rowena said flatly. "She's already gone. She was in tears. I told her she didn't have to work out her notice if she didn't want to. She didn't want to."

Oh, heavens. "Ro, I really think she's overreacting."

"Maybe she is. I'm not sure what difference that makes. A very nice young woman is still without a job she needed. And I'm without a social director. Good thing Gray Harper isn't as easy to scare off, or I might have lost him, too. I'm sorry my hires don't meet your standards, but do you have any idea how much we have left to do in these next eight days?"

"Not precisely, but I can guess. I do this sort of thing for a living, you know." Bree stood. "So what do you want me to do? If you don't want me to talk to her…"

"I'll tell you exactly what I want." Rowena's shoulders

squared tightly. "I want you to find someone to take her place. As you say, you do this for a living. You must know someone who might be interested. Or you can take the job yourself. I don't really care. All I know is…you broke it, Bree. You should fix it."

BY THE TIME Bree reached Cupcake Creek late that afternoon, her feet were killing her, and she realized she'd made the typical city-slicker mistake. She hadn't changed out of her regular heels and into boots.

She honestly hadn't thought she'd need them. Cupcake Creek was hidden between two thick stands of woodland, giving it an air of isolated wilderness, but it actually was only about a ten-minute walk from the main house.

So when Barton James, whom she'd sought out after her talk with Rowena, told her that Gray Harper should already be out here, setting up camp, she didn't bother going back to her room. She just headed for the creek.

As she moved through the trees, though, she had begun to doubt herself. Was it possible she'd forgotten the route? Cupcake Creek was only one of many tributaries of Bell River that branched off from the main flow, crisscrossing the ranchland like curious children wandering away from the safety of home. Some were just tiny, shallow fingers of water that died out after a few yards, and others were large and deep enough for tubing.

After so many years, wasn't it possible that she might get lost and follow the wrong stream?

She had just decided to turn around—she was only a few yards from forming blisters—when the trees suddenly parted, revealing the creek, twinkling silver and salmon-pink in the late-afternoon sun. She stood still, hardly breathing, and drank in the familiar sight.

Cupcake had always been the prettiest of Bell River's

branches. A placid, curving stream about ten feet wide, nature had decorated the two-foot-deep water with sparkling granite boulders. In summer, riffles of white lace formed where the creek broke around the bottoms of the rocks, and when winter brought the snows, a smooth white frosting collected on the tops.

Bree, who as a small child decided they looked like cupcakes, had given the place its name.

Late afternoon was a magical time out here. Chipmunks chattered, unseen, in the trees, and somewhere she heard the complicated whistling and trilling of a lark bunting. Forgetting her sore feet, she moved closer to the creek, and when she did she finally got a glimpse of the glamping tent.

Wow. Glamorous was the right word. A beige-and-green-striped canvas room erected on a hard floor, the tent looked more like a small house, really. Big enough to stand in, at least twelve by twelve, with several open windows to take advantage of the breeze.

A covered veranda extended the living space, also with a hard floor. It seemed to be set for dinner—Bree saw two chairs and a small table covered with food.

Through the tent doors, which had been snapped into the open position, she spotted a huge bed draped in green linens, rugs on the floor, a potbellied fireplace and a cushioned armchair.

And then she saw Gray, standing beside the bed, smiling as he opened a bottle of wine. She froze in place, shocked by her own body's quick, unmistakable reaction...a very female, very sexual warmth that flooded her before she could even register consciously how gorgeous he really was.

But he was. Those broad shoulders... Her gaze dropped. And those narrow hips. The easy disorder of his wavy hair, as if someone had been running fingers through it. The dimples at the edges of his smile, the sparkling teeth between...

And then she realized he wasn't alone. He was smiling *at* someone.

Bree took another few steps to get a better angle. There were two people in the tent. The other was an auburn-haired woman who seemed vaguely familiar, but Bree couldn't be sure... Someone from Silverdell High School, maybe.

Was that how Gray knew her, too?

Probably. But on the other hand, Bree had learned that Gray had left Silverdell right after high school, and this was his first trip back. So, if he'd known this woman in the past, it must have been thirteen or fourteen *years* ago.

Bree shook her head, marveling, trying to dislodge the melting-female reaction and achieve a little wry perspective on the man. He certainly didn't waste any time, did he? She could imagine him flipping through his little black book and coming across a half-forgotten number. Then the call. "Hey, gorgeous, remember me? I've unexpectedly happened onto a safari tent for the night. Interested in a little glamp from the past?"

Or maybe it hadn't been like that at all. She had to be careful. She couldn't start assuming that all men were as superficial and selfish as Charlie.

The woman was sitting on the edge of the generous bed, gazing around her as she bounced slightly up and down on the mattress. She said something Bree couldn't hear, then let her head fall back and started to laugh, as if the luxurious setup struck her as funny.

Bree wondered very briefly if she ought to just back away, but she decided not to. Though her hope had been to avoid interacting with anyone she used to know, it was time to revise the plan. Having an extra person here was actually a bonus. Bree needed help, and the more people she could ask, the better.

Besides, it was clearly safer not to be out here alone with

this man—not if she was going to go all hot and shivery just at the sight of his sexy hips. The last thing in the world she needed was for Gray Harper to realize she was attracted to him. His ego was already robust enough, thanks. If they had to work together…

"Hello?" She moved forward, calling out loudly enough to be heard, she hoped. "Gray? It's Bree."

Both Gray and the woman came to the tent door, looking curious, but not annoyed. Bree waved, and they both waved back, as if they welcomed the idea of company. Even Gray. She felt a subtle sense of relief.

"Hey, Bree," Gray said as she drew close enough that he didn't have to holler. He had stepped out onto the veranda area. He set the wine bottle on the small table, along with the rest of the food, which looked like gourmet fare…and quite delicious.

But not as delicious as Gray himself, who, as he stepped into the sunlight, almost took her breath away. She felt her neck grow warm, and she was uncomfortably aware that even a witness couldn't completely protect her from this man's incredible sex appeal.

"What brings you all the way out here?" He smiled, then glanced at her feet. "Particularly in those shoes?"

The woman looked down, too, and made a pained sound. "Ooh, ouch," she said sympathetically. Then she smiled. "Don't you remember me, Bree? I'm Marianne Garp. I mean Donovan. I was Marianne Donovan back then. We were in Mrs. Havelock's class together. Ninth grade?"

Bree searched her memory. Now that the woman had emerged from the shadows and the sunlight caught flame-red strands in the auburn curls, her hazy memory began to sharpen.

Oh…yes…Mari Donovan. Of course! Mari had been a quiet, pleasant girl who came from a family so normal they seemed to have stepped out of a Norman Rockwell painting. No one noticed her much, even Bree's student council–honor society types. But then, briefly, around the holidays in ninth grade, she'd become something of a celebrity. Her claim to fame? She had dated wicked Gray Harper for three whole months without, as far as anyone could tell, losing her virginity.

"Of course I remember you." Bree hugged the other woman politely. Of all the Dellians she could have run into, Mari was probably the least difficult. They'd never been close, but Mari had been as quietly kind after the murder—and Rowena's scandal with Dallas Garwood—as she had been before.

Bree remembered Mari and her mother bringing over a casserole, and the two of them standing with Aunt Ruth in the kitchen. Their manner had been respectful, even though the circumstances certainly didn't engender respect for anyone in the Wright family.

While the adults talked, Mari had stood with her gaze cast down, silently compassionate, instead of ogling everything within eyeshot so that she could gossip later about what the murder house looked like.

"Did you come to check out the tent?" Gray waved a hand to indicate she was free to explore the splendor behind him. "Doesn't feel much like roughing it to me. But Barton is certain it's the next big thing, and apparently he likes to stay cutting edge."

Bree nodded, grateful to have something else to think about—something other than the big, comfortable bed she could glimpse through the doorway. "For an eighty-year-old man, he is amazing."

"For a *twenty*-year-old man, he's amazing." Gray laughed. "I have a feeling that, as the Bull Moose at Bell River, he's going to keep us all hopping."

Curious that he should use that expression…Bull Moose.

Top screw, it was sometimes called. The boss man on the ranch. Her father had always called himself that. No one back East would have had a clue what it meant.

It wasn't the kind of terminology she'd have expected Gray Harper to use, either. As the pampered grandson of a marble-quarry millionaire, he had never dressed like a rancher, or talked like one. Not even in high school, where all the boys fancied themselves James Dean in *Giant*. Silly hats that swallowed their heads and belt buckles that could blind you from fifty paces. Boots like trophies, proudly constructed of reptiles they had killed themselves.

Gray had his share of affectations, of course. But his had been edgier. More the James Dean of *Rebel Without a Cause*. Careless hair, slouchy jacket and dangerous, haunted eyes.

He had changed so much—at least on the outside. He seemed generally healthier, calmer, more at home in his own skin. His jeans were old and softly molded to his body, not a statement of anything except his preference for comfort and functionality.

The only remnant of the old Gray was this tawdry charade to get hold of his grandfather's money. And maybe the fact that it hadn't taken him more than four hours to get a married woman out here and onto his luxury safari-tent bed.

She bit her lip. Was that fair? Or was it more bitter echoes of Charlie? Mari might be divorced. That her name was now Garp didn't mean anything. She could have changed her name ten times in all these years, for all Bree knew.

Either way, though, she wondered whether Mari understood that, if she got involved with Gray, the whole thing would be merely a one-month wonder.

"Come see." Gray touched Bree's arm, tilting his head toward the tent. "Even I have to admit, it's impressive. On the other hand, I've been staying at the Big Horn Inn the past few nights, so I'm pretty easy to impress."

Mari shuddered comically, although as Bree remembered it, the Big Horn hadn't been so terrible—just ancient, and rumored to have a naked gold miner ghost who ran up and down the halls all night, laughing because he'd finally struck a vein.

"Actually," she said, edging away from his fingertips, which felt strangely hot against her skin, "I didn't come only to see the tent, although it does look very cool. I came because Rowena and I need some help."

His gaze sharpened subtly. "Everything okay?"

"Yes. It's just that Rowena's social director quit today."

"Georgia?" Mari's eyes widened. "I can't believe it! She was so excited to get that job. When Troy broke the engagement, she was really in pieces, but—"

She broke off, wrinkling her nose sheepishly. "I keep forgetting you guys haven't been living in Silverdell your whole lives. Around here, we all still live in each other's pockets. Nothing's private."

For just a moment, Bree's gaze slid to Gray. He was looking at her, too, and she knew what he was thinking. Marianne Donovan might find it warm and cozy to know your neighbors poked around in your trash cans to see whether you finished your peas, maxed out your MasterCard or discarded a home pregnancy test.

But that was because Mari Donovan's trash cans never contained anything sad or embarrassing. For families like the Harpers and the Wrights, all that unrelenting "interest" could sometimes feel more like having the skin flayed off your body in bloody strips.

"I don't know what else has been going on for Georgia, but for Bell River, this is the worst possible time to lose a critical employee, as you can imagine. I told Rowena I'd help find a replacement, but…"

She thought of the dozens of calls she'd placed in the past couple hours. "So far, I'm coming up empty. I was hoping maybe you knew someone in town who might be a good candidate."

Gray shrugged. "I've only been in town since Friday. I don't know much about anyone local." He turned to Mari. "How is the job market around here? Are there good people hungry for work?"

She shook her head. "Not really. We had a kind of mini-boom a few years ago, when the lumber mill located nearby, and then last year two clean-tech companies came, too. I finally was able to find a full staff for Donovan's, but it was a struggle. Hard to open up a restaurant right when a shiny new dude ranch is hiring."

Bree could imagine. "Sorry." She smiled apologetically. "Bad timing, huh?"

"Oh, that's okay!" Mari waved it off. "We're all thrilled for you guys, and for Silverdell as a whole. I just mean the pool of good hires is pretty shallow right now."

Darn. Bree's hopes sank. No wonder Rowena had been so frustrated when Bree had been picky about her choices. She kept forgetting Silverdell wasn't Boston, which teemed with talented, educated, experienced people, young and old, who were hungry for good jobs.

And even in that environment, she had made the colossal mistake of hiring Charlie. She almost laughed, thinking of the irony. Who was she to criticize Rowena, indeed?

Mari bent down to one of the chairs and picked up a sweater she must have tossed there earlier. As she draped it over her shoulders, she shivered slightly. "Getting chilly, which means I'd better head back to handle the dinner rush."

She put her hands on Gray's chest, and rose on tiptoe to give him a peck on the lips. "Don't let the arugula get cold. It's my best dish, and I only brought it because I want some free publicity. I will expect you to tell everyone in town how fabulous Donovan's is."

"Done," he said, and he chucked her lightly under the chin. "Thanks, kid."

She wrinkled her nose. "Kid? I'm not the one sleeping in a tent." Before he could respond, she turned to Bree. "It was great to see you. Maybe you'll get a chance to stop by the restaurant? How long are you staying?"

"Not long." Bree had intended to stay about six days, until right before her meeting to bid on the Everlys' anniversary party. But now, with Rowena so upset, she wondered whether she might have to cut that short. "A few days, at most."

"Aw, too bad. Still, come by if you can. Lots of people would love to say hi, I know. Everyone always hoped things went well for you and your sisters, after you..."

She didn't finish the sentence. Bree nodded, sensing that Mari, at least, believed what she said. Rowena believed it, too. When Bree had expressed doubts that Silverdell would welcome a return of the Wrights to Bell River, Ro had insisted that Dellians were, on the whole, prepared to start fresh, and didn't hold their father's insanity against them.

If that was true—and, judging by the degree of town support the dude ranch was getting, it must be—then Bree and Penny should sail in on relatively smooth waters. Rowena had been by far the wildest of the three girls—the scandalous one who had led the beloved young town hero astray and caused him to get shot in the face. Comparatively, Bree and Penny had been like fully domesticated house kittens: quite harmless.

Bree wondered whether she should leave with Mari. Her instinct to avoid being alone with Gray in this strangely romantic setting was smart. She was far too aware of him, standing there beside her, watching Mari go. Too aware of the scent of him—minty and sweet and very male. And the way his hands looked, one cocked against his narrow hip, the other raised in a goodbye salute. The long, manly fingers.

The sharp bones of his wrist, followed by the thick taper of muscle in his golden forearm.

She swallowed. Yes, definitely. She should leave.

But surely she wasn't that big a coward? Her mission wasn't complete. She didn't have a replacement yet for Georgia Brooke—and she still had one more idea to explore.

The two of them watched, and waved, until Mari finally disappeared around the first sharp curve in the wood's path.

"Want a sandwich?"

Bree turned, and saw that Gray stood by the loaded table, surveying the pile of lovely sandwiches. "There's more here than I possibly could eat alone, and it'll hurt her feelings if any goes to waste."

Bree glanced toward the nearest bushes, where a couple of squirrels squatted, short front paws pressed together in mesmerized longing, and stared at the bounty. "I bet you could find plenty of takers."

He followed her gaze and grinned. "Can't feed the wildlife. It's not good for them. Don't you remember the field trips, and the warning signs? Don't you remember poor Mr. Driggs?"

She turned up one side of her mouth. "I remember you tormenting him."

"Exactly." Gray bit into one of the sandwiches, chewed appreciatively, then swallowed. "Poor Mr. Driggs."

He would be unrepentant, of course. And, to be honest, Mr. Driggs had been exasperating. Their English teacher, and a grand pooh-bah Nature Boys master on weekends, he'd spent that year trying to get them to revere the Romantic poets, and to believe that wandering "lonely as a cloud" was the primal pathway to spiritual bliss.

As healthy fifteen-year-olds, they'd naturally had other ideas about bliss.

"They're delicious," Gray said, gesturing one more time for her to help herself to the sandwiches. When she shook her head again, he shrugged and picked up another for himself. "So…what's Rowena going to do about the social-director job? Any chance Georgia will rethink and come back?"

"I doubt it." Bree had called the young woman first, of course. And last. And about a dozen times in between calling every other contact she had in the hospitality industry. But Georgia hadn't answered her phone. "But I was thinking…what about you?"

He paused in the middle of chewing. "What about me?"

"I know you weren't planning to take on a full-time job, but would you consider it? Obviously you were always ridiculously overqualified for the assistant spot."

His eyebrows went up, but he swallowed politely before he spoke. "Think so? I got the impression you found me… somewhat lacking."

She felt herself flushing. Her pale complexion never hid much. But the sky had taken on even deeper tinges of pink as the sun slid west, so maybe that helped to cover the problem.

"Lacking in motivation, perhaps," she said. "Not native intelligence or ability."

He smiled. "Maybe. But I'm definitely *under*qualified for the social-director position. The only thing I know about parties is how much to tip the bartender."

Something…some hint of amusement lurking at the back of his eyes…made her think he was making a joke at her expense. Once again, she wondered what he did for a living these days. If he was in dire need of an inheritance, he couldn't have spent the past decade sitting around counting gold coins on Easy Street.

Of course, that didn't mean that he necessarily knew a single thing about taking little kids on trail rides, ordering food for barn parties or organizing a horseshoe tournament at a dude ranch.

"You don't have experience, perhaps. But it's not as if you'd have to do heart transplants, or anything. You're smart, able-bodied and you are…you have excellent social skills." She almost said "capable of charming anyone at will" but that seemed too likely to make him laugh. "Those are the only raw materials needed. After that, it's just a matter of picking up the details."

He didn't answer for a few seconds. Instead, he lifted the open wine bottle and poured an inch or two of deep red liquid into one of the glasses. Raising it, he turned the glass in almost imperceptible circles.

"And where would I pick up the details?"

Hope rose like a living thing in her chest. He was considering it. Oh, how she'd love to walk back into Bell River and tell Rowena she'd found a solution!

"Well, I'll be here a few days," she said. "I've got an event-planning business in Boston, so I'm fairly familiar with the process."

"A few days wouldn't be long enough."

She frowned. That faint spark of amusement still gleamed behind his eyes, and it made her uncomfortable, though she couldn't quite say why. "Why not?"

He held his wine up to the sunlight, as if checking for clarity. It glowed ruby-gold, like some magic potion. He tilted the glass to his lips and let some of the wine slide into his mouth.

She felt her insides warming, as if she were the one who drank. She forced herself to look in another direction. The squirrels were still frozen in prayer, still staring at the food, as if they could will it to float their way.

"Why not?" she asked again. "I'd teach you everything I could before I go, and I could leave information behind. And my phone number, of course, for emergencies."

"I'd never be up to speed by then," he said reasonably. "If I don't know what I'm doing, I'd be more of a liability than a help to the ranch."

She frowned. She couldn't risk rescheduling the Everly meeting. If they'd heard the gossip finally, they might seize on any excuse to go with another company. But perhaps she could fly back for the meeting, then return to Colorado a little longer.

"A week?"

He shook his head sadly. "Probably still not enough."

"Well…you tell me, then. How much training do you think you'd need?" She gave him a straight look that demanded he not play games. "After all, we'll still have to be looking for someone permanent. You'll be here only a month your-self…so…"

"True." He gazed at her thoughtfully. "It's hard to set an exact time frame, given how little I know about the job. But I'd say at least…two weeks?"

Two weeks… She tried to imagine being here, living with Rowena and Dallas and Alec, for two weeks. That would take them through most of the first soft-opening week.

She tried to decide whether they'd even want her….

"Two weeks," she repeated aloud, in a voice even she could hear was heavy with doubt.

He chuckled. "You make it sound like a life sentence." Putting down his wine, he reached out and placed his hands lightly on her shoulders. With a subtle pressure, he angled her so that she looked down the creek instead of at the tent.

"Would it really be such a hardship? Spending a couple weeks in a landscape like this?"

Before her, the river sparkled like a sequined ribbon, curving gracefully between the trees until it narrowed and seemed to disappear. The trees shifted overhead, stirring the pink-honey sunlight and tickling the birds into riffs of merry song.

He was right…it was magnificent.

"No, of course not, but—" And then, abruptly, she glimpsed

motion, and she realized what he had really wanted her to see. She inhaled softly, thrilled.

Two small otters were playing in the creek. Just playing, apparently. Without any sign that they had noticed the nearby humans, they slid down the muddy bank, then paddled aimlessly for a few seconds, doubled back and slid down again. Their deep brown fur was soaked, glistening almost as black as their adorable button noses, and their powerful tails propelled them quickly through the water.

In the old days, Rowena had proclaimed that otter sightings guaranteed good luck, and the two younger girls had believed her, of course, as they almost always did. The sightings were rare, even back then, when the three of them had been free to wander these open acres for hours every day.

Maybe some of Mr. Driggs's nature worship had rubbed off, after all, because Bree suddenly felt an almost mystical peace and beauty floating over this spot, like a blessing. Crisp air, pure water, sunlight and the company of squirrel and bird and otter. How long had it been since she'd noticed how much healing power those simple things really had?

She needed healing. And not just from Charlie's betrayal. She might have run away from everything that happened here at Bell River, and covered over the damage—"No one likes a sad sack, Brianna!"—but the underlying wound had never healed.

She'd waited much too long to admit that, even to herself.

"It's beautiful," she said, quietly enough that she didn't disturb the animals. She looked at him. His hands had remained on her shoulders, though his face, too, was turned toward the creek. With his handsome profile rimmed in the colored sunlight, and the five-o'clock stubble tracing the strong jaw… He was beautiful, too. Dangerously beautiful. But surely not really dangerous to her. She hadn't ever been his type, not even when they were teenagers, and not now, either. Marianne, with her red hair and her easy laughter, was far more likely to please him and earn an invitation to share that big, splashy bed.

Besides, Bree could get control of this…this foolishness, which was probably some weird hangover from her youth, an absurd overreaction to his good looks, just because she used to have a crush on him in the ninth grade.

With a little time, that would fade. She would get tougher. After the lesson Charlie had taught her, that wouldn't be so hard.

"Two weeks, then," she said. "Unless you decide that you're ready sooner."

He turned back to her. He smiled.

"Don't count on that," he said.

AFTER SHE LEFT, and the sun went down, leeching the colors from the creek and sky, Gray felt restless. The tent might be comfortable, but it didn't offer much in the way of distraction from his thoughts.

So he got into his truck and drove into town.

It was only a little after nine when he pulled up in front of his grandfather's house. He killed the engine, but he sat there a while without climbing out, just getting used to seeing the old place again.

French Second Empire, that's what his grandfather always called the architectural style, in his usual self-important way. But Gray's mother had always laughingly referred to it as "the marble wedding cake," and that was the image that had stuck.

It truly was a silly piece of conspicuous consumption. Eight thousand square feet and twenty rooms under a high mansard roof, it would have been little more than a tall, boring white box if it hadn't been for all the frills. Iron cresting on the roof, elaborate cornices and balustrades, window hoods like eyebrows and endless yards of intricately scrolled gingerbread trim. Even the porte cochere dripped curlicues, like something out of a Victorian fairy tale.

Every possible feature was white marble, naturally. It was, Gray had always thought, not so much a home as a three-dimensional billboard advertising Harper Quarry.

The night was turning cold and he hadn't brought a jacket, so finally he got out and headed up the steps to the elevated entry pavilion that projected from the center of the house. Tonight, under the full, silver moon, and wreathed in cold, black sky, the house looked more like a big block of ice than a wedding cake.

He shivered as he touched the frigid metal doorbell.

The same plump, poker-faced housekeeper answered the door. So she was live-in, he deduced. He felt an odd sense of relief. He hadn't enjoyed thinking of the old man rattling around in this marble mausoleum alone, night after night.

Why he should care, he had no idea. Just another of those exhausting ambivalences. One more proof that love and hate remained equipoised just above his heart, like a knife on a fraying string.

"Hi," he said. He smiled, because none of this was her fault. "I'm sorry…I don't think I ever got your name."

She glanced over her shoulder before answering. "Almeda," she said stiffly, minimally, as if she had a limited ration of words. But then to his surprise she smiled. Well, almost smiled. Stopped frowning, anyhow.

"Almeda. I'm Gray. I'm sorry to call so late. Is my grandfather available?"

The woman hesitated, one hand on the doorknob, the other on the edge of the door, that universally recognized position of impending rejection. The one you used when you'd made the mistake of opening to the salvation salesmen.

"I think he's already retired for the night, Mr. Gray. But if you'd like to leave a—"

"That's all right, Almeda." His grandfather's voice floated out of the darkness behind the woman. "I'll see him. Let him in."

She swung the door open, then let go and backed away to give Gray room to enter. "He's in the library," she said. As she shut the door behind him, she seemed to register his lack of a jacket. "You must be cold. May I get you a cup of coffee? Some hot tea?"

He would have loved to show his appreciation for her friendliness, but he had a feeling his grandfather would dislike the liberty. He probably already had that sour look on his face, just because Gray had dared to ask her name.

"I'm fine, thanks," he said. "I probably won't be staying that long."

She nodded wordlessly, immediately reverting to her usual dour demeanor, then quietly melted away down the dark hall. Gray blinked, trying to adjust to the gloom. Would it kill the old miser to run a few kilowatts now and then?

The library was the second room on the left, just beyond the parlor where Gray had waited that first night. The parlor was unlit, as was the dining room on the right. In fact, the only illumination Gray could see on the entire first floor was an eerie orange light emanating through the open library door.

The light was restless, shifting randomly, throwing strange shadows on the opposite wall. As Gray made his way down the hall, he felt surprised. His grandfather had always read before retiring for the night. Were the old man's eyes still good enough to read by firelight alone?

"Damn it, Gray. Have you forgotten where the library is located?"

His grandfather's tone was crabbed and petulant, as if he resented being kept waiting. Gray took a deep breath.

"No," he responded dryly as he reached the doorway. "Just feeling my way in the dark."

His grandfather didn't rise to greet him, of course. Manners didn't require it, and his leg probably didn't allow it. Gray entered the room with an exaggerated air of indifference, though internally he braced himself for the sight of the portrait.

The goddamn, nauseating portrait.

It had always hung where you couldn't miss it, right between the center stacks of floor-to-ceiling books. And there it hung still.

An impressive, ten-foot canvas, made even more imposing by an extravagantly ornate carved and gilded frame, it was a full-length painting of his grandfather as a young man. Dressed in an elegant brown Western show coat, camel breeches and high, glossy oxblood boots, Grayson Harper the First stood with his broad shoulders squared, his chin high and proud. His thick waves of brown hair lifted slightly in the wind. In one hand, he held a riding crop. In the other, he held the reins of an exquisite black stallion with sleek coat and spirited eyes.

Old Grayson had sat for the portrait when he was twenty-five, and had just made his first million. By then, he'd accepted that his childhood dream of becoming a rancher and horse breeder would never come true. There was just too much money to be made carving up the mountains and trundling blocks of marble down to the hungry towns below.

The picture was his official goodbye, the ten-foot tombstone erected to mark the spot where the rancher dream had died.

But that wasn't what made the portrait stressful for Gray. His problem was that, when he hit about fourteen or so, he found that he couldn't look at the damn thing without a dizzying sensation that he was looking into a mirror.

Every year, the resemblance had grown more pronounced. It didn't matter what he did to his hair, long, short, spiked or shaved. It didn't matter what he wore, or what kind of surly, delinquent expression he twisted his features into.

He was his grandfather's spitting image.

What a cruel twist of fate that it should be Gray who inherited the whole, crummy DNA strand, and not his father, old Grayson's son.

God knew, the old man had tried, forcefully, but always in vain, to make his only son over in his image. But ironically, Gray's father hadn't looked a whit like the old man, and hadn't shared a single trait. He'd hated horses almost as much as he'd hated marble. Gray's father, the sensitive musician, wanted only to be left alone to love his wife, love his son, love his art, but he was never given the chance.

Gray, who after his parents' death hated the old man more than anyone on earth, had inherited it all, from his hair to his jaw to his eyes to his temper. There was no escaping it. He wore the loathsome blood tie like a brand.

And when he realized that he, too, secretly dreamed of life as a rancher, a rider, a breeder…when he realized even that dream had skipped a generation and landed on him like a ton of bricks…that's when he refused to set foot in Harper House ever again.

He would not give the old bastard the satisfaction of seeing his grandson fall in line. He would not obediently take his father's place as old Grayson's dream surrogate.

Did his grandfather really believe he was God? Did he think he could just callously eliminate the disappointing son, simply sweep him off a rainy mountainside like a block of flawed marble, so that he could slide Gray into the slot, like interchangeable pieces in some cosmic puzzle?

Gray gave the portrait a long, frank look as he entered the room, just so that his grandfather would see that it didn't have any power to upset him any longer. Strange to think that, at thirty, he was older now than the arrogant, headstrong young man in the painting.

"Hello, Grandfather," he said politely, turning his gaze to the old man. He held no book, Gray saw. Apparently he'd just been sitting here, staring into the fire.

Or at his portrait, perhaps?

His grandfather gave him a steady look. "I assume you have news?"

"I do." Gray rested one foot on the heavy brass fireplace fender and extended his hand toward the flames to thaw out his fingers. "I thought you'd like to know I have a job. I start tomorrow."

He cast a glance over his shoulder at the old man. He wondered whether someone might have already told him. Marianne, perhaps? She said not, but she did still visit. She'd openly admitted that.

But age hadn't diminished old Grayson's ability to keep his secrets to himself. "And what will you be doing?"

"I'll be working over at Bell River. Rowena Wright has come home, and she's turning the place into a dude ranch. I'm ostensibly the social director, but the ranch is obviously on such a tight budget that everyone will have to pitch in with everything."

"Social director." The old man made the words sound more vulgar than *gigolo,* or *male prostitute.* "Meaning you'll be teaching rich old ladies to dance and play canasta while you flirt your way into their wallets?"

Gray chuckled. "Occasionally, I suppose, if I'm lucky. Most of the time I'll be building playhouses and digging vegetable gardens and mucking stalls. Oh, and taking packs of snotty six-year-olds on overnight-camping trips."

He stood and faced his grandfather squarely. "I think, on balance, it qualifies as a dirty job. If you disagree, you'd better tell me now. The four-week clock starts ticking as soon as

I report to work in the morning, and I'll expect your written guarantee of our deal, as promised, by the end of the day."

The old man narrowed his eyes, which caught the reflected firelight, making them difficult to read. For a couple of minutes he seemed lost in thought. He kneaded the studded-leather arm of his chair absently, as if he didn't realize he was doing it.

Finally, he nodded slowly. "I suppose it will do. I suppose they were the only ones who were willing to hire you. With a past like theirs, they probably can't be picky."

Gray thought of the companies who had refused to even grant him an interview. He could hear the truth in the old man's voice. He'd tried to make it impossible for Gray to be taken on anywhere in Silverdell. He wasn't above trying to win this thing unfairly.

"Exactly," Gray agreed pleasantly, refusing to be baited. "Two bad seeds in the same pod. That's Rowena Wright and me."

He put his hands toward the fire one more time, for insurance as he headed back out to sleep in his tent. Then he smiled at his grandfather.

"Good night, then," he said. "I'll look for your document by courier? Oh, and just for the record, tomorrow is Wednesday, April twenty-fifth. Four weeks from that date will be Wednesday, May twenty-third. That will be my last day in Silverdell, so I'll expect to see you then. Or at least your banker."

"You'll see me before that," his grandfather responded testily. "I'll expect weekly check-ins and reports on what you've been doing. I also reserve the right to pay unexpected visits to your place of employment, to verify that you are actually there. And actually digging, mucking, snotting, as advertised."

Gray had to laugh. Micromanaging everyone's life, as always. It reminded him so much of the years his grandfather had demanded weekly reports from his teachers, his coaches, his professors, his dorm leaders and academic advisers, all part of the endless power struggle to force Gray to become the kind of scholar his grandfather wanted him to be.

And how had all that worked out in the end? Gray had damn near flunked out of high school, and he had absolutely, irrevocably, deliberately flunked out of college. He'd lost a small fortune on poker games he didn't give a damn about. He'd bought jewels he couldn't afford for girls he didn't respect.

He'd defied his grandfather at every turn, not caring whether he made a mess of his own life in the process.

But the point was…he'd never once considered giving in. He'd never once considered obeying. How sad that the old man hadn't learned a thing from any of that.

"Yes, you should do all those things," he said, still laughing at the thought of old Grayson trying to make Rowena add this to her jam-packed to-do list.

Dear Ms. Wright, please create a "Little Grayson Has Been a Good Boy" checklist for nosy old Mr. Harper.

Mr. Harper would soon learn the difference between the way teachers at elite, expensive private schools responded to a millionaire's demands, and the way Rowena Wright responded to any bastard dumb enough to try to order her around.

"Yes, indeed," he said again, cheerfully, as he strolled out through the library doors. "You should absolutely do that."

CHAPTER SEVEN

BREE HAD DRIVEN herself half-mad that night. She was unable to sleep, partly because it was so strange being in the family home again. Every groan and creak of old windows, old wood, old tree limbs against the roof…it all sounded slightly haunted. She kept thinking she heard her mother turning her doorknob quietly, as she'd done every night, just to be sure all was well.

But her insomnia also stemmed from constantly second-guessing her decision to stay here a full two weeks. Would she end up regretting it?

As far as the family went, everything appeared okay. Rowena had seemed satisfied, even relieved, when she'd heard what Bree had worked out. Dallas had professed himself delighted. Even Alec had let out a war cry of happiness, and made Bree promise to come see his fort at Little Bell Falls.

Still…she knew that there was one more way this plan could backfire on her.

She couldn't deny it. She was already attracted to Gray Harper. And he wouldn't be averse to accepting any opportunities she offered, however subtle. She'd felt his interest from the start…but it had been fairly open and direct in the gaze he'd turned on her, out by the creek.

Problem was, she knew she was vulnerable right now—or at least her pride was, after Charlie's big public slap in the face. If she and this ridiculously sexy, bored, spoiled, uber-virile male worked closely together, every day…

She could end up making a huge mistake.

Another huge mistake.

Maybe that was something she'd inherited from her mother—a self-destructive preference for bad boys. None of the girls had ever discovered who Moira Wright's final lover had been, though his existence was confirmed by the fact that Moira had been just barely pregnant when she died. The man had never come forward, though, never acknowledged their relationship, never offered to testify against Johnny Wright… so how decent a man could he have been?

And, of course, they all knew how violent and cruel their father had been, though that hadn't stopped him from being shockingly good-looking, openly envied by Moira's acquaintances.

Finally, the mystery man who had fathered Rowena had obviously been someone who couldn't or wouldn't marry Moira, not even when she was carrying his child.

Moira had undoubtedly taken other lovers along the way, but of the three her daughters knew about, all three were cads…or worse. So Bree shouldn't really have needed Charlie to warn her that a weakness for bad boys was in her blood.

She had tossed and turned until she'd finally given up.

Agonizing didn't help. She was here. She was going to stay and help her sister. So she would simply have to keep a padlock on her emotions.

Bree had smiled as she turned over and shut her eyes, finally seeing the humor in her predicament. She'd already taken a vow of temperance and a vow of silence. Should be easy enough to add a vow of chastity to the list.

Three days later, she had come to realize just *how* easy. Both she and Gray were far too busy, often in different parts of the ranch, or even different parts of the town, to waste time in flirtation. By this morning, just four days before the grand opening, she was too exhausted even to put on makeup, or do anything with her hair but pull it back in a hasty ponytail before she tackled her projects for the day.

Yesterday had been devoted to interviewing the many Dellians who had volunteered to lead special-interest classes with the guests.

Bill Friday knew everything about geology. Archie Stout was an amateur archaeologist. Fanny Bronson was an expert on local artists and writers. Joe Gibson had an idea for wildlife watching, and Bill Miller from the hardware store had a treasure trove of local history that made even a town like Silverdell sound exciting.

So much for Bree not having to face the townsfolk. But the meetings had gone surprisingly well. Everyone had been natural and friendly, and eager to share their expertise—free. She'd said yes to all of them. Then she'd stayed up half the night, all over again, putting together a schedule for classes.

Today would be devoted to the kiddie activities. She'd ordered books and games all morning—paying a fortune to get them overnighted, and wondering how long Georgia Brooke had been sick. Surely this should have been done a couple of weeks ago?

She'd picked out a bunch of music for the sing-along nights, and had emailed a file of lyrics to the local printer for binding and laminating in leaflets the children could hold—leaflets they could wash and disinfect and reuse later.

Now, with barely enough time to pull on a sweater from the community coatroom, and no time at all to find one that actually matched, or even fit, she had to jog out to the old barn to choose the perfect spot to hold Saturday-Morning Horse Tales. Once she decided, she could fax the specs and dimensions to Jude Calhoun, the local carpenter who had agreed to design the seats and stage, and fast-track the order at no extra charge.

By the time she reached the barn, she was slightly winded.

She was wearing a pair of Rowena's boots, and her sister's feet were half a size larger, which meant Bree's heel rose up on every step and had to be reseated carefully so that she didn't trip.

As the perspiration met the breeze that blew through the chinks in the barn's sides, she shivered. It was chillier in here than she'd expected. She buttoned the sweater all the way up to her neck, and thanked her lucky stars she'd brought one two sizes too big. It covered all the way down to her knees, and, if she tugged a bit, she could make it drape over her fingers, too.

She gazed a minute, observing the cobwebby corners and wondering if she was brawny enough to shove aside those big pieces of dusty old equipment to see what lay behind. A couple of nooks looked promising, but on the surface nothing was quite perfect.

She unclipped and reattached her barrette, trying to capture as much of the flyaway hair as she could. Maybe better to think it through, before she began muscling things around. She tried to remember what being a kid had felt like. What kind of spot would she have liked at six, or ten, if her mother had wanted to read horse stories aloud?

"Hello, Bree."

She jerked her head up, bumping her crown on a low-hanging beam. A man had just entered the barn, but he stood in the broad, sunlit opening, backlit so dramatically that she had no idea who he was.

"Hello," she said warily. There was something about his voice she didn't like. Some unwarranted familiarity...some undercurrent of sensuality that she registered more with the follicles of her neck hairs than with her conscious mind.

She put her hand in her pocket and touched her cell phone. What was Gray doing right now? How far away was he working? Dallas was downtown, catching bad guys for the rest of the Dellians. And Barton was in the new stables, training the head wrangler.

"It's me, Bree." The man moved forward slowly, hands in front of him, as he might have approached a dangerous horse, or a hissing cat. "It's Charlie."

Her mouth dropped open, and she let go of her phone. Charlie? A sudden anger rose in her, like a nausea. She wasn't afraid of this weasel. If anything, *he* should be afraid of *her*.

"What the *hell* are you doing here?" She took two hard steps in his direction. "And, more important, how fast can you go away?"

For a moment, as the rude words shot out of her mouth, she could almost see Kitty's shocked face. "You catch more flies with honey, Bree." *Yeah?* Well, you also caught rats, and Bree had caught a doozy.

So to heck with always wearing a smile and making nice. Kitty was gone. Breelie's was probably gone, thanks to this jerk. It was time to get real. Way past time.

"Bree." He somehow made her name two wheedling syllables, which infuriated her even more. Did he really think she was just another bimbo who would melt at the sight of his baby-blue sad-puppy eyes? At the moment, she was far more likely to gouge them out with her fingernails.

If she still had any fingernails. She'd broken most of them over the past three days, opening crates and carrying boxes, stringing lanterns and painting walls and saddling horses.

"Bree," he said again. "Be reasonable."

"I *am* being reasonable. I haven't impaled you with a pitchfork." She blew a strand of damp hair away from her face and narrowed her eyes. "You really should go away, Charlie. Right now, before I change my mind."

He didn't move, the darn fool. He just tilted his head and let his lips soften into a pout. "We need to talk. We have to. You can't just avoid me forever."

"Apparently not."

She thought about asking him how he'd found her, but Charlie had ways. She hadn't entered the witness protection program or anything. She'd just bought a plane ticket like a normal person. Right off the top of her head, she could think of three women who could have been sweet-talked into spilling the beans.

"But that doesn't mean I have to talk to you." Irritated, she ad-libbed the next part, piecing together half-remembered TV dialogue. "In fact, my lawyer expressly forbids it. Until the case is closed, I mean."

She almost smiled as she watched the hostility fall over his face like a shadow, banishing the pout, the sad-puppy eyes and anything else he thought was charming. He was angry now. *Good.* She knew he allowed himself to show anger only when he was trying to hide shame or fear.

She didn't really have a lawyer, of course. She hadn't wanted to pay for a civil suit when she needed all her money to make good on the debts Charlie had racked up in Breelie's name. Plus, she hadn't wanted to risk letting some smitten female juror acquit him, and have him go around forever crowing about being innocent.

But he didn't know that, obviously. His mouth was a tight line of fear masquerading as rage. "You're suing me? For what? For having sex with someone else? Is it a crime to want to make love to a woman who actually has a body temperature higher than an ice cube? Is it a crime to want a lover who actually likes sex?"

Where the devil was that pitchfork? "No, but in your case it might be a hopeless fantasy."

To her grim delight, that was a hit. His face flushed red.

"And it is *definitely* a crime to embezzle from your employer," she pointed out. "And since I have the paper trail, and the angry suppliers, to prove it, it just seems simpler, in the end, to go that route."

He was quiet for a moment. He stared at her, a pulse in his jaw working overtime. He blinked steadily, as if it were the rhythm of his brains processing.

And then, slowly, the blood receded from his blotchy face.

"You'll lose," he said in a deadly confident monotone. "I had the authority to make every one of those purchases, and you know it. You gave it to me. You were so busy being the big-shot owner that you couldn't be bothered watching the bottom line."

"I was—" She stopped. "I was—"

But he was right, she recognized suddenly, and the realization stole the angry words right out of her mouth.

He was absolutely right. She'd been a fool, giving him so much rope. She should have known he'd use it to hang them both.

It wasn't as if she was blinded by love. She'd long since realized she didn't feel about him the way she should. She kept postponing the moment when they'd have to set the wedding date—not that he was exactly pushing hard, himself.

But she didn't call it off. It was just so much easier to let the relationship glide on smoothly, even if it was going nowhere, than it would have been to grind their engagement to a halt so that she could jump out and get off.

Besides, she had told herself she was being too hard to please. Who, if not Charlie? He was handsome, articulate and the clients loved him. He was also useful. He handled all the boring stuff, like placing orders and balancing the books.

So what if the sex had become almost nonexistent? They were so often at different events, or even in different cities. Even when they were under the same roof, they were exhausted. If lovemaking was a little disappointing, that wasn't unusual. It wouldn't be any different with a different man. That was just how Bree's body worked.

Probably had something to do with her past, but she didn't have the energy to try to figure it out. She poured all her passion into Breelie's, and life was good enough.

Maybe if Charlie hadn't proposed right after Kitty died...

The death had been entirely unexpected—one minute, Kitty was pouring a glass of wine to celebrate the opening of Breelie's. The next minute, an aneurysm burst, and Kitty lay on the floor in a pool of red wine and shattered glass. She'd never awakened again.

That was four years ago, when Bree was twenty-six. Probably, she would have accepted any man who asked her at that moment. It had been such a relief not to have to be alone. That neurosis she *could* trace back to its roots. Ever since the day Aunt Ruth announced that she couldn't take all three girls, and the social worker had explained to Bree that she might have to become a ward of the state, she'd had a horror of being alone.

But she should have forced herself to master it. She should have been tougher, wiser, harder on herself...

She'd been lazy, and she'd been a coward. And she'd paid dearly for it.

"I hope you *do* take me to court," Charlie said, smiling suddenly, as if he smelled the self-doubt that had crept in, knocking out the underpinnings of her righteous indignation. "There's absolutely no chance a jury would convict me. Everyone knows a woman scorned when they see one."

She raised her chin. God help her—maybe she'd inherited her father's temper, after all. Suddenly she saw red, and she wanted to punch him in the nose.

Instead, she forced herself to settle for hurting him back. "A woman scorned? I wonder if they'll still think that's what I am after they get a look at the new man in my life."

Charlie frowned. He looked at her with cold eyes, his gaze moving from her head to her feet slowly. She flushed, remembering the lack of makeup, the messy hair, the oversize sweater…and probably the stable smell as well, since she'd been feeding horses before dawn.

"You're with someone else? Already?"

Why had she made that up? It was childish, more like a teenager than a grown woman. But it would have been humiliating beyond endurance to admit the truth now.

"Colorado is full of cowboys," she equivocated, hoping she wouldn't have to lie outright again. "Perhaps you don't know me as well as you thought you did."

"Either that…or he doesn't know you at all. I'll lay odds you two haven't had sex yet."

She lowered her eyelids. "You'll lay anything, Charlie. You've already demonstrated that."

"Hey, darlin', you comin' up or not? I can't keep the engine revved forever if there's nowhere to drive the train."

The sexy drawl came from the shadowy hayloft just behind Bree's head. Charlie's gaze shot upward, and Bree turned, equally shocked. It sounded like Gray—if Gray had been a sex-crazed cowboy in a 1950s comic book.

Sure enough, a second later, Gray came sauntering to the edge of the loft, looking like someone she'd never seen before. His hair was disheveled, brown waves tumbling in all directions under an oversize cowboy hat she recognized as having once belonged to her father's foreman.

Other than the hat and a smirk, he wasn't wearing much else. No shirt, no shoes, no belt. His jeans technically were on, but they seemed to cling to the lower edge of his hips reluctantly, as if they'd much prefer to slide on down.

He grinned at Charlie. "Sorry to bust up the little confab, buddy, but this gal has a date up here that she definitely don't want to miss."

"Gray." Bree couldn't decide whether to be mortified that Gray had obviously overheard her conversation, or grateful that he'd decided to step into the role of her imaginary cowboy lover. "This is Charlie Newmark. He was just leaving."

Charlie hadn't fully closed his mouth since Gray first spoke. He glanced from Gray to Bree, then back to Gray again.

"*You're* the new boyfriend?"

Gray let his gaze run over Charlie slowly. The very fact that he was above them and had to look down his nose to see the other man made the inspection seem insolent. He held a piece of hay between his sexy lips, and he munched on it thoughtfully.

"Well, that depends on who's asking," he said finally. He pushed the brim of the hat backward so that Charlie could better read his eyes. "And in what tone."

"I'm the *old* boyfriend," Charlie said, though he did dial his voice a couple of notches toward civility.

"Oh!" Gray stretched out the syllable, and his smile broadened. He bent down, gripped both legs of the ladder that had been propped against the edge of the loft and swung himself down to the barn floor without ever stepping on a single rung.

"Nice to meet you, buddy. Tough luck about losing our gal here, but don't feel too bad. The feisty ones are tricky. Some of them just squirt away, no matter how hard you hang on."

While Charlie frowned, clearly trying to decide how to respond, Gray chuckled. He strode up behind Bree and slid his arm around her waist. Surprised, she stiffened, but she didn't pull away. After a second to let her adjust, he tucked her up against him, confidently possessive.

He was playing this role far, far too well. She ought to call a halt to it before Charlie lost his temper. Gray's chivalry probably wouldn't extend to having his nose broken in this impromptu bit of theater.

But she wasn't exactly sure how to slow things down without spoiling the effect. And, to be honest, she wasn't even sure she wanted to. Though she couldn't see Gray's face, the back-to-front connection was deliciously, almost unbearably, intimate. Her shoulder blades pressed into his bare torso, and she could feel his hard, cool touch of the button at the waistband of his jeans as it pressed into her back.

"You sure do know how to drive a guy crazy, darlin'." Gray's voice was teasing. "Were you going to leave me up there all day, just 'a waitin' and 'a wantin'?"

"I…" Someone had forgotten to give her the script. She wasn't as good at improv as Gray was. "No, I was just finishing up some stuff…"

But then he bent his head and skimmed his warm lips against her collarbone. She broke out in ridiculous shivers and couldn't complete the sentence.

"Oh, yeah. That's right, honey." His throaty voice was equal parts absurd and absurdly sexy. "I've got some stuff you can finish up."

Charlie made a rude sound and rolled his eyes. "Good luck with that, cowboy. All I can say is I think you might end up disappointed. Some things look a lot better than they really are, if you know what I mean."

Gray's arm tightened around her waist. He trailed another slow kiss across her neck, all the way up to her ear. Her heart pounded like a jackhammer, and her eyes drifted shut without her permission.

"Yeah, I reckon I know what you mean," Gray said pleasantly. "And all *I* can say is…there's more to riding a horse than sittin' in the saddle and lettin' your feet hang down."

He nudged Bree's hair aside so that he could reach the tender skin at the back of her neck. She felt his mouth curve in a smile, and she knew he was staring at Charlie without ever raising his lips. "If you know what I mean."

Charlie sputtered, but nothing came out. And then, finally, he turned on his heel and left.

CHAPTER EIGHT

THE MOMENT THEY were alone, Bree made a small twitch forward, and Gray instantly let his arm drop.

He had been walking a fine line, he knew that.

For a while, as he'd listened to their argument, he'd felt his best move was to lie low and never let her guess that she'd been overheard. He'd been up there an hour before she ever arrived because Barton had asked him to clean out the loft.

Bree obviously didn't know that. And, if he was careful, she never needed to know.

As long as she was giving this Charlie jerk as good as she got, Gray was content to remain silent. But then she started letting the bastard get to her. Gray could hear the pain in her voice. The insecurity. The fear that the jackass over there might be right, and the problem might lie in her.

When he heard her tell Charlie she had a new cowboy boyfriend, he had simply succumbed to his impulse. He remembered the moth-eaten old ten-gallon hat he'd set aside in the junk pile earlier. Quietly, he retrieved it, then shucked his shirt and his belt, trading them for the swaggering drawl of the Saturday-morning cartoon cowboys he'd loved as a kid.

After that, he'd simply played it by ear. He hadn't intended to actually touch her, or kiss her neck, but the outrage in Charlie's face was just too gratifying. Still, he wouldn't have gone this far if she'd given him any sign that she wanted him to stop.

Finally, here was the sign. The twitch. So he let go of her.

She took a few steps forward, so that she was just outside the barn, where the sunlight could find her. It was as if she needed fresh air after the contamination of Charlie.

He slowly followed. When they were both just beyond the shadows, she squared her shoulders, then turned to face him.

"How long were you listening?"

He shrugged. "Long enough to be hoping you were going to kick him in the groin. I promise you, if there had been a pitchfork among that junk up there, I'd have tossed it down to you in a heartbeat."

She took a deep breath, her blue eyes cloudy. "You heard it all, then?"

"Yeah. I was there from 'Hello, Bree,' which I'm pretty sure was the opening line. It moved pretty fast after that, and I couldn't find a good moment to announce that you had an audience hiding in the balcony."

"I bet that was…awkward." With three tense fingers, she made small circles on her forehead, nodding miserably. "I'm sorry you heard all those—those ugly things. In fact, I'm sorry I said them. I don't usually allow myself to get openly hostile like that. Nasty fights and name-calling are really Rowena's area of expertise."

He smiled. "Well, you're extremely good at it, if that's any consolation."

"It's not." She tried to smile back, but it didn't work all that well. "I was brought up to value restraint. I've seen what happens if people just say and do whatever they want. It might feel good for a minute or two, but there's always a price to pay later." She sighed. "I don't know why I let him get to me."

"Because that's what *he's* extremely good at," Gray observed. "He's the living illustration of the old adage 'the best defense is a good offense.'"

The sound of running came at them from the eastern side

of the barn. As they glanced over, Alec raced up, Trouble panting merrily at his side.

"Oh, good, there you are!" Clearly oblivious to any undercurrents swirling in the atmosphere, Alec skidded to a halt, looking sweaty and winded. "Bree, Gray, Rowena says she needs you up at the house."

Bree seemed almost glad of the reprieve. She turned her back on Gray and faced the excited boy. "What's wrong?"

Alec shrugged. "Who knows? Dad was fixing the fireplace, but he's got to go back to the station." He turned to Gray. "That's why Rowena wants you, I guess. That's man work."

"Okay, my little chauvinist in training," he said, laughing. He was surprised that Alec apparently hadn't yet noticed Gray was wearing a cowboy hat instead of a shirt. Maybe in nine-year-old land, that was normal. "Rowena would box your ears for that. But not me. Whenever a real manly man is needed, you can count on me."

Alec grinned, then looked back at Bree. Trouble did exactly the same thing, as if he always mirrored his master's movements. His grin included a lolling tongue, and was punctuated by a noisy sneeze.

"And she wants you, I guess, because she's trying to help the housemaids get fresh linens on the beds." Alec smiled. "But one of the maids is nuts and..."

He chewed his lower lip and apparently decided it would be more fun to let them be surprised. "Oh, you'll see. Come on. Let's go!"

"Okay." Casting a brief glance back at Gray, Bree signed a quick pantomime of shrugging on a shirt and yanking off a hat. Then she followed Alec and the puppy out of the barn.

Gray took a minute to climb back up to the loft and redress properly, so the drama was already underway by the time he arrived upstairs in the main house.

Dallas stood by the fireplace of the front guest room, wiping his hands on a rag. Bree and Rowena bookended either side of the king-size bed, each of them deftly tucking a corner of a pale green sheet under the mattress.

In the armchair nearby, one of the white-uniformed maids, a middle-aged woman as fat and pink as a pearl, was fanning herself with a Bell River brochure and talking a mile a minute.

"She was right there, I'm serious, as clear as day, looking just like you or me. Well, looking just like you, of course, Miss Rowena. But it was her. I would know your mother anywhere. I tell you, I nearly fainted."

Gray glanced at Dallas, who widened his eyes with discreet eloquence. He handed Gray a trowel and a bucket of wet mortar.

"Sorry," he said. "We really do have an emergency at the station."

Gray smiled. "Sure you do."

"It's true. It's the answer to a fervent prayer, but it's true." Dallas patted Gray's shoulder sympathetically, ruffled Alec's hair and finally blew a kiss to his wife.

Then, whistling the theme from *The Great Escape,* he disappeared down the stairs.

Gray knelt on the drop cloth by the fireplace, did a quick evaluation of Dallas's progress, then proceeded to apply mortar to one of the remaining cracks. Dallas had been using black mortar, which meant the area would need repainting, too, once the mortar dried.

On the other side of the cheerful, light green room, Rowena and Bree had begun to unfold the bed's top sheet, arranging it carefully on the mattress, perfectly centered and crisp. The maid still jabbered, fanning furiously, as if she was afraid of what would happen if she didn't cool herself down.

"Isamar." Rowena gently broke into the stream of words. "Could you see what she was wearing?"

Rowena's question didn't sound mocking, or even particularly skeptical. Gray flicked another glance at her, wondering whether her staffing crisis was so urgent that she didn't even dare to contradict the superstitious head cases who thought they saw ghosts.

"A dress. Green flowers. Big skirt." The maid groaned and crossed herself with the fan. "Saints preserve me. She smiled right at me. I knew she wanted to tell me something."

Gray groaned inside. But Rowena didn't flinch. She just ran her hand over the top sheet, expertly smoothing out one last wrinkle. Then she picked up a brown blanket and handed one side to Bree.

"It's all right, Isamar. I'm sure it wasn't anything to be afraid of. What else happened? Did she...speak? Did she say anything to you?"

This time, Gray heard a subtle note of melancholy in Rowena's carefully steady voice. He wondered what exactly caused it. It could be any of several emotions—or even all emotions at once.

He tried to imagine how he'd feel if someone told him his mother's ghost walked the corridors of Harper Hall. Mostly, he'd be resentful that such a real and wonderful human being had been reduced to a campfire-ghost-story cliché. But he'd also pity the person who "saw" her, because that person must surely be emotionally or mentally unstable.

At the same time, he knew he'd harbor some tiny, secret, desperate hope that it might, against all reason, be true. Some pathetic desire that the dead weren't really gone forever. That a face so loved, so desperately missed, could really be glimpsed again.

"No." Isamar shook her head so hard her round cheeks ruffled. "She didn't speak. She smiled, and then she was gone."

Gray transferred his gaze to Bree, curious as to how she would react. Just coming back to the house where so much tragedy had occurred must have been difficult enough. Now this…

He assumed that, whether she thought the maid was batty or just silly, she still would find the discussion disturbing.

To his amazement, she looked completely unfazed. Her expression was so serene, in fact, that he wondered for a moment whether she'd even heard what Isamar was reporting. Did she have earphones in her ears, blocking all sound?

But then Rowena asked her a simple, quiet question: "Can you get the spread from the end table?" Bree nodded with a bland smile and picked up the heavy green-and-brown-flowered coverlet, proving that she must have heard every word spoken in this room.

Rowena and Bree unfolded the spread up the length of the bed, like a synchronized team. When it was perfectly smooth, and they had arranged the large, decorative pillows on top, the bed was neat and elegant. Rowena surveyed it from top to bottom, nodded with quiet satisfaction, then went over to the swooning maid.

Squatting in front of the armchair, she took Isamar's hands in hers. "Why don't you take the rest of the day off?"

"Oh, no, Miss Rowena." Isamar sniffed. "I couldn't. There's so much work."

Rowena smiled. "You're tired. You've had a shock. You'll be paid for the day, but I want you to go on home. Bree will help me finish the rest of the rooms."

It took several more minutes of coaxing, but finally Isamar agreed to call her son to come and get her. Rowena and Bree had to watch her down the stairs, and she insisted on waiting out on the front driveway, rather than in the house.

As they returned to the green guest room, Bree was in the middle of a sentence.

"—we have asked her not to say anything about this to

anyone? If people start hearing that we have ghosts, what are the odds the dude ranch will ever be a success?"

Rowena just laughed, as if she quite liked the idea of her mother's ghost floating around, smiling at the maids, and didn't take any threat to the ranch seriously. But Gray wasn't so sure. How many people would risk bringing their families for vacation in a haunted house? Particularly if the gossip ever started focusing on the madness of the father...and whether it might have been passed down to his daughters.

It made Gray angry to think of how fragile the Bell River reputation really was, and how little the Wright women could do to prevent superstitious people from spreading absurd rumors.

But Rowena, at least, seemed quite philosophical, even pragmatic, about the situation.

"I can ask Isamar not to tell anyone, of course. But that's not really going to stop her from telling just one trusted person in deepest, darkest confidence. And that person will tell one person, who will also tell one person. Sooner or later, everyone will know, anyhow. If we've tried to issue a gag order, it's just going to make us seem shady and weird, as if we have something to hide."

Bree lifted one shoulder. "Okay," she said, still projecting an indifference that Gray couldn't quite believe was natural. "Shall we hang pictures in here? Or do you want to do all the beds first, and come back to hang pictures after?"

"Let's do all the beds first," Rowena said. "That way, before it's time to hang pictures, maybe Barton or Gray will be free to help us decide what should go where. They'll hate that, of course, but I'm beyond making good decisions alone anymore."

Pulling his head briefly from the fireplace cave, Gray chuckled. "I can hear you, you know."

"I know." Rowena laughed. "I'm shameless. Desperation

will do that to a person. We've got two days until guests arrive, and we've got at least four days of work."

"We'll make it," he said firmly.

And they would. He knew deadlines. The stroke of midnight had a momentum all its own, like a tidal wave, and the wave would sweep everything along with it as it roared in.

He remembered the night he learned that lesson. He'd been about twenty-two, and anxiously awaiting the birth of a prize foal. He had sunk every penny he owned into the stud fee, the stable, the vet and the trainer. Plus, the mare was his favorite horse—he loved her as much as he'd loved any human since the night his parents died.

So she held not only his financial future, but what was left of his heart, as well. He couldn't afford for a single thing to go wrong.

For days he'd driven himself, and everyone around him, half insane with his compulsive need to prepare for every eventuality, to have every particular nailed down, every condition perfect. But once labor began, and it was too late to do anything but guard and guide the newborn into this life, the truth crystallized before him.

All the unfinished details simply didn't matter. You did what you could, for as long as you could. And then, when the time came, you let the rest go.

"Gray?"

Shaking off the memories, he withdrew from the fireplace again and looked toward the sound of the voice. Rowena had left the room. Only Bree stood there, a few feet from him, her voice as somber as her face. "May I ask you something?"

"Okay." He put the trowel down and gave her his full attention.

"You seem like a relatively sane person," she said.

He smiled. "Guess that depends on relative to what."

He was saner than Charlie Newmark, for instance, who

was lunatic enough to cheat on a woman like her. But he was definitively less sane than, say, Rowena's husband. Dallas was a bona fide saint who had never fallen off the virtuous path and never would, even if it were as high and narrow as a tightrope strung between two skyscrapers.

You wouldn't catch Dallas Garwood gambling away his college-tuition money, just to show his grandfather he couldn't be bought. Or stringing half a dozen girls along at the same time in hopes that more attention, more sex, more admiration might finally fill the bottomless hole where his heart used to be.

Dallas would never have spent years refusing to do the work he was born to do, just to demonstrate his independence. Independence from what? Common sense? Happiness?

Bree shook her head. "Not relative to anyone. Just plain sane. Generally." She smiled. "Anyhow, I wanted to know… what do you think about Isamar's story? Do you think there could possibly be such a thing as ghosts?"

He tried to read her expression. But her face was as impassive as if she'd been carved in marble. He'd like to give her whatever comfort she needed, but he had no idea what she was hoping he'd say.

It had been pretty cut-and-dried for him. In his heart, his mom and dad were both innocent martyrs, loving parents ripped away from the son they would never have abandoned if they'd had a choice.

But for Bree and her sisters, the issue was more complicated. True, if ghosts existed, they might get lucky. They might someday, out of the blue, run into their mother on the stairs.

But they might also run into their father.

Gray decided to be honest. "For a while, when I was a kid, I was pretty desperate to believe there could be. I did just about everything short of joining the spirit world myself, hoping I could find the particular ghosts I was looking for."

There had been a couple of times when he'd considered doing even that. But some remnant of sanity had always held him back. He knew that wasn't what his parents would want. Even if it meant being separated forever, they would have wanted him to live.

"But you never did see them."

"No." He shook his head. "I never did."

He thought he sounded fairly unemotional as he described it—it had been a very long time now, and time did at least give you a layer of numbness.

But her eyes were suddenly shadowed and deep with emotion. "I'm so sorry. When you have to face that someone is really gone forever—there's no hope—" A small, pained line appeared between her eyebrows. "That must have been... nearly impossible to bear."

He dipped his trowel back into the black mortar, surprised and a little unnerved by the intensity of her empathy. It was as if, for a moment, she'd been able to peel back a corner of his heart and look inside.

And what she saw there, she recognized. She knew, really knew, what he had been through.

It was the strangest sensation. It made him feel more exposed—and at the same time less alone—than he had in many, many years.

He didn't like the feeling.

This wasn't the kind of relationship he was looking for. He had no intention of letting anyone get that close. That door was locked—or at least he had believed it was. He certainly hadn't given the key to her. How could he? He no longer had any idea where to find it, even if he'd wanted to.

Yet, somehow, there she was. And that changed everything.

Until this very moment, he'd been indulging in a fun little fantasy about having a no-strings fling with her while they were both at Bell River.

His only hesitation had been the fear that he might hurt her. He sensed the vulnerability beneath that cool, alabaster surface. It was part of her fascination. He craved a chance to learn what lay beneath those carefully guarded depths.

So he'd promised himself that he'd be very clear about what he was offering. If she was interested, on those terms, they might have a lovely few weeks together. If she wasn't, she could say so, and no hard feelings.

For the first time, though, he saw that this fling he longed for could cut both ways. He could hurt her, yes, as his inability to commit had hurt so many women through the years.

But suddenly he realized it was just barely possible that this particular woman…

That she could hurt him, too.

He felt like a chess piece already out too far on a perilous board when, without warning, someone changed the rules of the game. What now? Which moves was he allowed to make? And what about the other pieces? Where did the danger lurk now?

When his phone rang, it felt like a reprieve. He pulled it from his pocket and read the name there. *Agatha*. Hell. She was…what…three girlfriends ago?

He turned the ringer off and slipped the phone back in his pocket. He glanced at Bree. He could make something up, say he was ignoring a wrong number, a telemarketer, a bore.

But why lie? She might as well know the truth about him, before she started imagining he was some kind of tragic hero she could save.

"That's the only kind of ghost that scares men like me," he said with a brittle smile, tilting his head toward the phone. "The ghost of girlfriends past."

THAT NIGHT, WHEN Gray finally got back to the Cupcake Creek tent, he saw a packet waiting for him, propped against the zippered canvas door. It wasn't thick, but it was obviously official. It bore the return address of the same lawyers his grandfather had always used...Pegram and Quick, over in Montrose.

He tore it open, sat in the deck chair and read it by the light of the lantern hanging from the highest pitch of the roof.

It didn't take long. For legalese, it was fairly straightforward.

If Gray retained his job at Bell River Ranch for four straight weeks, and if the job included at least 50 percent legitimate manual labor, as defined below, etc, etc, etc, then a new will would be executed, naming Gray as the sole beneficiary of his grandfather's estate.

The only hitch was that the old man had to live for four weeks. If he died before Gray's month was served, his most recent authenticated will would be placed into probate and considered final.

Nothing else. No mention of Gray's father, of course, or of the money old Grayson had supposedly "invested" for him, then had never been willing to release, supposedly because he didn't trust Gray's father's judgment.

And no mention of any of that crap about weekly reports and spot inspections. Maybe the old man had been ashamed to sound so paranoid and overbearing, even to his lawyers, men who were pretty damn overbearing themselves.

After he'd finished reading, Gray sat there on the deck for a long time, the papers draped across his knee. He stared into the shadowy, moon-eerie trees, and listened to the crying of night birds and the occasional splash of something small trying to make its way across the creek.

He ought to feel victorious.

He hadn't been entirely sure his grandfather would actually keep his end of the bargain. Asking for this document had been like playing one final, giant hand of poker, betting everything on the cards that remained facedown, the do-or-die cards. The cards he couldn't see.

He'd placed the bet, though. And, against all odds, he'd won.

He should feel vindicated. Triumphant.

But all he felt was tired. And alone.

And keenly aware that no piece of paper ever printed, whether it had an autographed admission of guilt on it or a string of zeros lined up after a dollar sign, was ever going to make that loneliness go away.

CHAPTER NINE

SUDDENLY, AS IF THE DAYS disappeared into a maelstrom of frantic activity, it was May first, and the reality of Bell River Dude Ranch was upon them.

Guests began arriving early in the day, several hours earlier than the announced check-in time. Luckily, Barton James had warned Rowena this might happen, and they were ready. They'd set out a brunch in the courtyard between the house and the first cottage. As people trickled in, they dropped their suitcases at the front desk, were handed a map of the Bell River property highlights and then were funneled out to the courtyard, where they ate barbecue sandwiches and hamburgers, and drank milk or lemonade or soda.

Then they had a choice. They could stay put, and bask in the sun, listening to Barton James play cowboy songs. Or they could hike off the calories by following the map to Little Bell Falls, the glamping tent at Cupcake Creek, the rock formations on the eastern perimeter or the Native American message trees on the western slope.

Somehow, the staff made it through the check-in process. By five o'clock, each and every guest had been installed in the correct room, and because by some miracle everyone had the proper number of pillows and towels, and all the hair dryers and telephones and ice machines worked, a brief peace fell over the ranch.

Or so it seemed, unless you were in the barn, helping to get that night's dance ready. The barn doors opened at six-thirty, so for ninety minutes every available staff member scurried about, doing something urgent to the cause.

They hung strands of colored lights, paper lanterns and balloons. They set up tables for the guests and the stage for the musicians, and they lay down the dance floor in lovely parquet squares. They tested the sound system, stocked the bars and checked for spots on the glasses.

The chef, a battle-ax of a woman they called Cookie, who resembled a medieval executioner but created delicacies like a fairy queen, had been snarling through the kitchen all day, and the result was a hundred pastries as light as air, three dozen filets as soft as butter, chafing dish after chafing dish of mouthwatering asparagus and sweet potatoes and endless mounds of salads bursting with color.

At six-thirty, Bree and Rowena stood shoulder to shoulder and, for a moment, held their breath. They gave each other one brief glance, then, while Bree held up a hand signal to the band, Rowena nodded to the waitstaff who stood ready to fling open the barn's huge double doors.

And then the guests began to pour in, and all Bree could do was ride the wave of laughter, eating and dancing that overtook them all.

By ten o'clock, she was exhausted. When she looked up from her last dance to see Gray standing in front of her, holding a glass of iced water, she thought she'd never seen anything so beautiful in her life.

"You are an angel," she said, accepting the tumbler and drinking eagerly. She'd been dancing for two hours without stopping and suddenly realized she must be a little dehydrated.

When she finally got enough, she sighed and pressed the back of her hand to her lips to wipe away the water mustache. "And that is the nectar of the gods."

He smiled. "Time to relax for a few minutes. You've been

working too hard. Rowena's going to have Occupational Safety and Health Administration breathing down her neck if you don't take a break now and then."

She nodded reluctantly. "It's been a great way to get to know people, though. There's just so much to learn about the guests if everything is going to run smoothly." She sighed. "It's so much easier to anticipate the trouble spots and head them off if you can."

"Absolutely." He scanned the crowd with a half smile. "For instance, little Mabel Madison... See her over there, dipping her hamburger into her cola? We're going to need to keep her tuckered out. Otherwise, she'll end up burning the place down, or falling out of a paddleboat, or shooting her dad with a bow and arrow."

She laughed. She'd noticed Mabel, too. "She has ten times more energy than any child should. We will have to be careful to keep her away from Alec. That's a chemical explosion waiting to happen."

Gray nodded, agreeing emphatically. He smiled at Fanny Bronson as she danced by, then leaned toward Bree and lowered his voice. "And we're definitely going to have to find Fanny a man. She's been looking at Dallas the way a starving mutt looks at another dog's dinner."

Bree's eyes widened. She had not noticed that. She'd noticed only that Gray himself seemed to be dancing with Fanny a lot. It shouldn't have bothered her—they all had to sprinkle attention on the guests, especially the wallflowers. He was the social director. He was just doing his job.

But it had bothered her anyhow.

He looked particularly handsome tonight, though he hadn't fancied himself up in buckles, bolo ties, big hats and ornate boots, as some of the guys—especially the teenagers—had done. On his body, though, the soft corduroy pants and crisp broadcloth dress shirt were amazing. Especially now that she knew exactly what kind of washboard torso lay beneath that simple button-down shirt.

She had felt an irrational twist of envy, watching Fanny clutch tightly at his shoulders and letting him rest his hand along her waist. The envy was irrational because just a few days ago, at the moment he'd rejected that phone call from an old girlfriend, Bree had vowed she would not allow herself any more fantasies about Gray Harper, who she strongly suspected had serious issues with commitment.

The past few days had been so busy, and he'd been so completely professional and helpful, that she'd almost been able to make good on that vow.

But tonight felt different, as if the gala atmosphere of the opening made it okay to relax the rules a little. Even Rowena had let her guard down and had been warm and sisterly all night. A logical leap from that to saying it was okay to flirt with Gray, but Bree was too happy to split hairs right now.

"Barton is going to be great with the tween girls," Bree noted, eager to change the subject from Fanny. She pointed toward the elderly man, who was waltzing a ten-year-old girl across the dance floor. The girl, who had been hanging sulkily along the buffet table half an hour ago, giggled irrepressibly, pink cheeked and bright eyed.

"Yep." Gray grinned at the sight of the mismatched pair. "And how about Dallas? His brand of saintliness seems tailor-made for wallflowers of a certain age."

She'd noticed that, too. Her charming brother-in-law had been dividing his time between two elderly spinster sisters with striking, if fading, beauty, and killer line-dancing skills. Right now he stood between them, listening attentively, as if there was nowhere on earth he'd rather be.

"Rowena doesn't dance much?" Gray glanced toward the far corner, where Ro stood with half a dozen guests who were looking at a display of horse portraits.

Bree smiled. "Her mission is like ours. She's doing reconnaissance for tomorrow. By tomorrow, she has to be ready to match each guest with a mount, and apparently that's tricky."

Gray smiled. "Because of the inverse fantasy-reality ratio?"

"Exactly." Bree wondered, not for the first time, whether he might, in "real" life, work at another dude ranch somewhere. He seemed very familiar with the ins and outs of things—in spite of his earlier contention that he needed a lot of training to get up to speed.

She'd realized within the first couple of days that he needed her "training" like he needed more sex appeal. But by then she was too invested in the soft opening to even consider walking away.

On the other hand, he wasn't quite sunburned or callused enough to be a full-time wrangler. So maybe he was just a quick study. But, for whatever reason, he clearly understood that as Ro tried to match a horse to each guest, she'd be working mostly from instinct. Apparently, what people expressed a desire to ride didn't always dovetail with what they had the talent, experience or disposition to handle.

"So everyone seems to have a niche here tonight." Gray's voice had a teasing lilt. "But you, on the other hand…"

Bree raised her eyebrows. "I what?"

"You attract them all. Old or young. Rich or poor. Married or un. There isn't a male in this barn tonight who doesn't want a place on your dance card."

She chuckled. "You should talk."

"I notice you play favorites, though. There's one guy who has been getting more than his share of your attention."

"You mean Alec?" She'd danced with Dallas's son four times—she noticed she was the only one who ever said yes more than once. Sometimes Trouble insisted on trotting right out to the dance floor with Alec and getting in the way. However, even when Trouble stayed on the sidelines, basking in the attention of the dog-loving crowd, Alec had a tendency to stomp on his partner's feet.

"No. I mean Matt Gordon."

"Oh. Yes, that's true."

Gray must have been paying closer attention than she'd guessed. She had given a lot of her time to a guest named Matt Gordon, a sixty-five-ish man, neither handsome nor ugly, neither bold nor shy. Just quiet, self-contained and—though she couldn't pinpoint how she knew this—very, very sad.

She wasn't sure exactly how Matt was connected to the Bell River family-and-friends list. Though everyone invited to the soft opening was handpicked by some member of the staff, she didn't remember the name from the roster she'd seen initially.

But here he was. And she knew a hurting soul when she saw one.

"I like him," she said. "And I get the feeling he needs cheering up. I'm on a mission to make him smile, sometime before this night is through."

"I fear that mission may be doomed to failure. Matt's wife died two months ago."

She frowned. "How do you know that?"

"He told me. We ran into each other at the bar, and we talked for a few minutes."

"That's strange," she said, feeling oddly disappointed that the man hadn't confided in her. They had talked far more than "a few minutes," and she had genuinely liked him. She'd thought the feeling was mutual. "I wonder why he didn't tell me."

He looked at her, his expression matter-of-fact. "Probably because you're trying to make him smile."

"What on earth does that mean? What's wrong with trying to make him smile?"

He hesitated a minute, then shrugged. "I think you may

be missing the more important question. What's wrong with being sad?"

She started to laugh, as if he might be making a joke. *What was wrong with being sad?* What kind of question was that?

But his expression remained completely serious. Her smile faded.

"It seems pretty self-explanatory to me," she said, mildly defensive. "No one *wants* to be sad."

"No," he agreed. "What most people want is to be accepted for exactly who and what they are. What most people want is the freedom to be honest and genuine and not to have to pretend to be anything they're not."

She flushed slightly. Gray was being kind, but he wasn't sugarcoating it, either. Her efforts were wrongheaded. What Matt Gordon really needed, Gray was telling her, was a safe place in which to work through his feelings—not rush blindly to change or deny them.

Intellectually, she could hear the power of that concept. With her conscious brain, she knew Gray had touched on something profound. The freedom to be honest, with yourself, and with others, too. The freedom to stop pretending. That would, absolutely, be the greatest imaginable gift one person could ever give another.

And yet, while her brain understood, her heart and her subconscious reflexes, which obviously drove her behavior, didn't have the slightest idea what that kind of freedom felt like.

"No one likes a sad sack, Bree."

As always, Kitty's words were close at hand. But Bree's need to cover the truth went much further back than that. Other voices, other memories, cautioned her against the danger of honesty, as well.

She could hear her father raging at Rowena. "Say anything like that to me again, you little bitch, and they will be the last words you ever utter under this roof."

She could see her mother at the family dinner table, a smile plastered on her face, but the eyes above the smile as empty as a doll's. Sometimes, while her husband talked, Moira's eyes slid away, focusing on something in the middle distance that only she could see. Her real life, maybe, playing out somewhere else, while her body sat propped up in a chair at home, nicely dressed and smiling.

And then, most painful of all, Bree could see Penny, who had crawled into Bree's bed because their father's angry voice had awakened her. Those liquid eyes staring up at her. "Are you scared, too, Bree?"

And Bree's own voice, answering with a steady certainty she'd never genuinely felt, never once in her life. "Of course not, Pea. There's nothing to be afraid of."

She had no idea how to explain any of this to Gray, who was watching her now with dark eyes. Those memories seemed out of place here, anyhow, under the cheerful colored lights, with the music playing and the guests dancing, and the new dream of a dude ranch being born.

No one wanted a sad sack at a barn dance. Already she felt the urge to simply smile, to make light of it all, to smooth past the moment before she ruined Rowena's party.

"Bree, do you understand what I'm trying to say? You don't have to pretend with me. Whatever you're feeling, it's okay." Gray touched her arm. He started to say something else, and then, abruptly, his touch tightened, and a scowl descended over his features.

"Oh, *hell* no. No way, buster."

She looked to the back of the barn, following Gray's gaze. A spotty teenager was making a beeline for them, his eager eyes locked on Bree. She recognized him as a boy she'd danced with a couple of hours ago.

Gray laughed. "See what I mean? I've been waiting for

hours to get a chance to talk to you, and this kid is not going to spoil it now."

Without warning, he grabbed her hand and tugged her toward the doors, which stood open to provide fresh air and easy movement. Tossing an apologetic smile toward the teen, Bree hurried along after him, dodging balloons and waiters with trays of soda, her full skirt rippling behind her.

He didn't pause to speak to anyone, though several people clearly would have liked to say hello. He kept going until they reached the doors, and then he pulled her another ten feet, until they were all alone in the moonlit darkness.

Just outside the barn, where they still could hear the music, he stopped under the overhanging branches of a live oak strung with colored lights.

He didn't let go of her hand and she didn't ask him to.

Her heart pounded a little faster, as if their exit had been in full flight instead of merely a speedy walk.

He glanced over her shoulder, checking to be sure they hadn't been followed. No one else shot through the doors.

"We've eluded them," he said with a playful smile. "At least for now."

She was still too breathless to speak, so she settled for a nod. She wouldn't have known what to say, anyhow. Out here, being this close to him was ten times as intimate and unsettling as it had been inside the barn. She felt, all of a sudden, as awkward as if they'd just closeted themselves in a bedroom.

Without a trace of any similar self-consciousness, he leaned back against the oak tree trunk and watched her for a long moment in silence. Then, with a light forefinger touch, he slowly traced the ruffle at the scooped neckline of her full-skirted, poet-sleeved peasant dress.

"I can't say I blame them, though," he said softly. "What man doesn't long to dance with the gypsy queen?"

The compliment went through her with a lovely warmth,

like a sweet cocktail. She'd ordered this dress from a catalog last week, expressly for tonight, secretly thinking he might like it. Though she'd paid far too much, when it arrived she'd been thrilled. A soft blue cambric, its smocked waist made her look tiny, and the yellow satin ribbons threaded through the neckline and cuffs turned her hair the color of daffodils.

He brought his hand up and touched the matching yellow ribbon she'd wound through her complicated French braid. It had taken her an hour to create that effect, and suddenly it all seemed worth it.

"You know you're driving every man here crazy tonight. Including me."

Bree laughed, trying to cover the tension his touch always seemed to set off inside her. "Well, I'm one of the few single women in the room over fifteen and under fifty, so it probably doesn't really mean much. Still, it's fun to be popular."

For a minute, she thought she saw disappointment on his face. Would he call her on the glib, artificial response? Would he insist on an answer more "genuine"?

And what would she do if he did?

Before he could say anything, though, the band launched into the first few notes of a slow song. Gray smiled and, tightening his fingers around hers, he tugged her softly toward him.

"I think this one is mine," he said.

Perhaps, she thought as they came together, this was one way of being honest. She wanted to be in his arms, and he wanted her there. The dance was just their excuse.

She felt stilted at first, but after a few seconds she began to relax against him. Once she did, their bodies fit easily, as she had known they would. He put his arms around her waist. She put hers around his neck, turning her face into the warm, pulsing column of his throat.

They didn't talk, and she was glad. All her consciousness

was focused on cataloging the details of him, filing them carefully away in her sensory memory. She might need them... for when one, or both, of them were gone.

His clean, profoundly male scent, with hints of spice and lime and sea breezes. The startling baby softness of his hair tickling her fingers. The strong, steady thump of his heart and the answering nervous skitter of her own.

The graceful power of his thighs as they slowly, almost imperceptibly, moved against hers, creating fire as easily as if her bones were kindling and her skin had been glazed with kerosene.

She began having trouble breathing normally. Everything was tightening inside her, and every new touch brought a shimmer of beautiful pain. She made a soft sound, a sort of choked whimper she was unable to control.

When he heard it, his hands tightened on her hips. And then they pressed slowly, tilting her into him, one excruciating inch at a time. Her muscles coiled in on themselves, and her heart raced helplessly.

"Gray." She lifted her face, fighting to pull air into lungs that seemed to have stopped working altogether. The colored party lights illuminated his dark, liquid eyes, and she clung to them with her gaze.

He bent his head to hers, shutting off the light. He kissed her.

The cold night air, the sad music. The press of light against her closed lids—green, then blue, then green again. The smell of climbing roses and nearby horses. All of it mingled with the magic of Gray's mouth until the kiss was not something they *did,* but rather something they *were.* Their lips moving together, wet and hot and urgent, was as much a part of the night as the rustle of oak leaves, or the smell of Bell River on the breeze.

It went on forever...there was no need to pull back, no

need to part. She breathed him instead of air; she beat with his heart instead of her own.

But at some point the sounds of the night changed, and she sensed that people were coming out of the barn. Gray lifted his head, and as the cool wind touched her lips again she opened her eyes. His gleamed at her, like pools of honeyed moonlight.

"Bree! We've been looking for you!"

It was Alec. Of course it was. Alec, her own personal Jiminy Cricket, the inescapable alarm clock for her sleeping conscience.

Bree took a deep breath, arranged a smile on her swollen lips and turned toward the little boy and his ever-faithful puppy. "Hey, kiddo. What's up?"

"You've gotta come back inside. There's going to be a dance contest, and I need you to dance with me. Will you? You've gotta say yes, Bree, because everyone else said no."

Behind her, Gray smothered a laugh. She glanced at him once, as if to say, *so much for honesty!* He shook his head softly, but he added a wink to show her he understood.

And then his cell phone rang. He glanced at it but didn't answer. He thumbed it off and slipped it back into his pocket. He didn't seem to feel the need to mention who it was.

And just like that, the spell vanished. Whatever magic had held reality at bay was gone, and the regular world came washing over her like cold rain.

Well, of course he understood. He understood that he could have her whenever he wanted her, with just a flick of his fingers. Just as he could have almost any female he wanted.

Maybe that was really what his little speech had been about. *Gray,* not Matt Gordon, was the one who needed the freedom to be exactly what he was. To feel only what he genuinely felt. No pretense, on his part, that this was more than sex. And therefore, no false expectations on her part. She could never say he'd led her on....

Really, she was a walking cliché. Hadn't she predicted, from that very first night, that she'd fall into this trap? She had known from the start that she wasn't up to resisting an expert like Grayson Harper.

She was no gypsy queen. Thirty years old, and she was still just another silly girl who got romanced in the shadows after the dance. And he was merely another bored playboy who knew that a girl with yellow ribbons in her hair was asking to be kissed.

She almost laughed at the soap-operatic predictability. If Gray wanted to know what she was *genuinely, honestly* feeling right now, she just might have been prepared to tell him.

She felt ridiculous. She felt like a fool.

And she felt weak, because despite everything, she still smoldered with a yearning to be back in his arms.

But he didn't ask. So she turned and took Alec's hand. "Come on, Trouble," she said, and they went back into the barn.

SHE SLEPT, BECAUSE she had to. The first full day of activities would be a killer, even at the best of times.

But she woke early, and she sent a dozen emails to people she had overlooked in her first, frantic efforts to find a new social director for the ranch. She sent them to near strangers, and complete strangers, to friends of friends and friends of enemies.

Then she placed a few more calls. She followed up on the people she'd called in the first round, just in case they'd changed their minds, or been laid off, or their companies had been swallowed up by volcanoes.

She grasped at every straw she could find. And came up empty again.

Once, she thought she might be getting a callback from one of the people she'd contacted. But when she answered, it turned out to be the Everlys.

Surprise, surprise. They wanted to cancel their appointment to discuss the anniversary celebration. They'd decided to go with another company.

When she hung up, she was actually too emotionally stunned to think straight. She sat cross-legged on her bed, her laptop open beside her, holding her cell phone in both hands and glaring at it, as if she'd like to strangle it for letting her down.

"Useless piece of—"

Belatedly, as she started to toss the cell toward the foot of the bed, she realized Rowena was standing in the doorway, fully dressed in crisp denim jeans and a white blouse, looking as fresh as a marsh marigold.

Bree stopped the hurl midmotion, the phone awkwardly extended, as if she was handing it to her sister.

Her heart sank as she recognized that look on Ro's face. It was barely repressed anger. She straightened her back instinctively. "Good morning," she said awkwardly.

"If you're that desperate to leave," Rowena responded in a clipped, cool voice, "just go."

Drat. She'd heard enough—maybe all of it. Bree felt very much the guilty little sister suddenly, sitting here in her silk pajamas. She hadn't even combed her hair before starting this scouring of her contact list. She pushed a tangled lock away from her eyes and tried not to get defensive. That always escalated the trouble.

"I'm not desperate to leave, Ro. I just know that the clock is ticking for Gray. You'll need someone to replace him, and I'd like to help with that."

But it wasn't an entirely honest answer, and, in spite of

whatever tensions lay between them, they knew each other too well. Rowena could tell it was, at best, a half truth.

Her face tightened. After last night's camaraderie, this regression to mistrust and misunderstanding was almost physically painful to Bree.

She even considered, briefly, telling Ro what was really behind her desperate dialing.

But what could she say? The truth? The truth went something like this: "I've inherited the worst of both of them, Ro. I'm as weak as Mom, and as crazy as Dad. I'm falling for another guy who is going to break my heart, and, even though I've got nothing to go home to, I need to get the heck out of here before I do something dumb."

She couldn't lay herself bare like that. She wanted to trust Rowena, but she had years of doubt to overcome. It would take more than a week to do that.

Rowena shrugged. "Well, just don't think you have to stay because you think we're desperate. We'd find a way to make do."

"I know you would, Ro."

Bree could hear the injured pride in her sister's voice, and a part of her wanted to just stand up and ask Rowena for a hug. She thought of how freely Ro seemed to dispense physical affection these days. To Dallas, to Alec, to Barton…even to Gray and the rest of the employees at the ranch.

But it had been so many, many years since Bree had felt close enough to ask. So she settled for answering the unspoken question. "I've been staying because I'm enjoying being a part of it all, not because I dream that I'm indispensable. I have seen you in action, and I know you can handle anything."

Rowena frowned, as if to dismiss empty flattery, but Bree wouldn't let herself be dissuaded. This part was the truth, the whole truth, and she needed to get it said.

"I'm serious, Ro. I didn't expect to, but I've learned to love the ranch, and I am very grateful that you've let me be involved. In fact, I'm afraid that when I do have to go back to Boston and resume my old life, it's going to feel…"

What was the right word? Empty? Lonely? False? Meaningless and sterile and forlorn?

All of the above?

Suddenly, her throat grew painfully tight, and she wondered whether she'd be able to finish the sentence at all. Ro was looking at her, head tilted, a strange, searching expression in her fierce green eyes.

Bree coughed self-consciously and forced herself to go on, though she chose her words from a less emotionally loaded vocabulary.

"I'm sorry. I'm just afraid it might be…difficult."

From around the corner, she heard the sound of Dallas's voice calling to Alec. Rowena glanced in that direction, and when she looked back at Bree, her face was composed and neutral once again.

"We can sort all that out later, I guess," she said, her voice neither harsh nor gentle, revealing little. "Right now, you'd better get dressed. We've got about thirty hungry mouths to feed."

CHAPTER TEN

For almost a full week now, though Bree had stopped talking about leaving Bell River any time soon, Gray knew that she'd studiously avoided letting herself get stuck anywhere alone with him.

He found her inaccessibility frustrating. More than frustrating. But his own feelings were a little too murky to sort out, so, even as the days passed, he didn't make any real effort to circumvent her wishes.

He still physically desired her, fiercely. That wasn't the murky part. In fact, ever since the kiss, the *desire* part of the situation had been crystal clear. He thought about her, about the feel of her body against his, the taste of her mouth, the smell of her hair, the heat of her response to his touch…and he thought about those things pretty much every minute he was awake.

And, more and more frequently, she played a starring role in his dreams, too.

So no. He definitely wasn't confused about the physical part. He wasn't even confused about whether she wanted the same thing. He knew the signs, and he saw them everywhere. Fifty-foot billboards. Big, screaming neon blinkers.

The chemistry between them was off the charts. If they ever did make love, it would be amazing.

The emotional part, though—that was where he kept tying himself in knots. Every time she walked by him, all sleek and cool and regal, pretending not to see him, he was like a pile of dry brush in a lightning strike. He'd burst into flames from the inside out, just from wanting to pull that perfect hair from its perfect clip and feel it tumbling messily over his fingers.

It was like torture. So he'd tell himself he was just going to have to go caveman and make it happen.

But then he'd start remembering all the wrong things. The haunted look in her blank face when the maid had reported seeing her mother's ghost. How easy it had been for that asshat Charlie to make her doubt herself. How, when she was with Rowena and Dallas and Alec, she always seemed to be sitting just beyond the lamplight, so isolated by something he couldn't define. So alone it made him ache...

And then he'd remember how startling it had been to catch her looking inside his heart, so easily, almost inadvertently, as if she'd just stumbled onto it lying there at her feet, open and waiting—when he'd been so sure it was locked away and utterly unreachable by mortal man.

Then, before he knew it, he would have changed his mind. No caveman. No hair over his fingers, no kisses in the shadows. He'd carefully count the days until May twenty-third. Another nineteen. Eighteen. Fifteen.

Two weeks now. Just two weeks more, and then he could leave with a clear conscience. After that, if she sat with pain bruising the skin around her eyes, with ghosts at her shoulder and the light always just beyond her reach...well, then at least it wouldn't be Gray's fault. He wouldn't have to carry the guilt around with him like a boulder for the rest of his rotten life.

Their luck ran out that Wednesday, though. It was the night of the Bell River First Annual Costume Party Cookout. The elaborate event had been weeks in the planning, but planning could be coordinated by email and text and telephone. Tonight, for the first time since the barn dance, they'd have to actually work side by side for hours.

This was one of Bell River's rare adults-only events. One

of the college kids on the waitstaff had been temporarily elevated to "children's director" for the night, and she and a few other part-timers would keep the kids entertained with movies and popcorn, with sleeping bags so that the parents could have a little unencumbered fun.

Gray had taken responsibility for the games, decorations and physical setup. Bree was in charge of costumes. They'd never quite found a time to discuss what he would go as, so he'd just told her to pick something, and he'd wear it.

At five o'clock he presented himself at her office to receive his wardrobe.

Foolishly, he had decided that her choice would tell him something about what she was thinking. If she gave him something cheesy, the costume equivalent of the studly cartoon cowboy he'd played for Charlie's benefit, then he'd assume she was trying to make light of the whole thing—to defuse the tension by turning it into a joke.

If she assigned him a character who was foolish, or dull—like a smelly moonshiner, or an aproned greengrocer—then she probably still felt vulnerable. She wanted to be absolutely certain he couldn't tempt her, no matter what he said or did.

If, on the other hand, she gave him a more traditional cowboy-hero look, if she was willing to let him play it straight, then maybe she was still open to the idea that they might...

He shook his head, listening to his convoluted logic. Or maybe he was completely full of bull chips.

Probably she just assigned the costumes first come, first serve, according to size and sex. Undoubtedly she would let the guests have first choice, and the staff would have to settle for the scraps.

"Hey, there," he said as he opened her office door and looked around. "Ready for me?"

"I am," she said. She was kneeling in front of a steamer trunk full of brightly colored items—some clothes, from the looks of them, but also hats and scarves and gloves and jewelry, shoes and umbrellas and bags. "Come on in."

He waited a minute or two while she continued rummaging, and finally she turned, her arms full of red, white and blue things he couldn't quite identify.

"Your costume is going to be really fun," she said with such bright determination that he instantly knew exactly how untrue that statement was.

And he also knew that he'd been right all along. Her choice of costume was definitely going to tell him something about her frame of mind.

Just not necessarily anything good.

He eyed the brightly striped red-and-white shirt she lay on the desk, followed by gigantic blue denim jeans and a tomato-red cowboy hat.

"I'm going as a Western Uncle Sam?"

She laughed. Not a natural sound. "No, not Uncle Sam."

He raised his eyebrows and guessed again. The stripes were enough to blind you. "A cowboy umpire?"

"No," she said, smiling as she continued to lay out pieces. Red elastic suspenders. Some pancake-makeup sticks. Oversize brown hobo shoes. A lasso. An absurd blue flower attached to a pin.

"No, no, not an umpire," she said again, growing more visibly nervous with every item she deposited on the desk. She cut a sidelong glance at him, as if trying to gauge how close he was to figuring it out…and how he'd react when he did.

But of course he already had figured it out. He knew even before she added the clincher: a large, round, honking red rubber nose.

He tried not to, but he couldn't stop himself. He burst out laughing.

She gave him a quizzical look. "You like it?"

He nodded. "I love it," he said emphatically.

She still looked a little anxious, as if his reaction made no sense. She probably had no idea why her choice pleased him so much. She probably never dreamed that she'd just told him everything he needed to know about how she felt.

And it was exactly what he'd been hoping to hear—masochistic fool that he was. She'd just reassured him that he was not alone in his torment. She still wanted to make love to him so badly she could hardly trust herself to be in the same room with him.

Not unless she neutralized his sex appeal in every way she could.

Actually, this *was* going to be fun.

He was going as a rodeo clown.

BREE STOOD AT one end of the great room and surveyed the sea of cowboys, bank robbers, sheriffs, dancing girls, cardsharps, gunslingers, gold miners, Annie Oakleys, John Waynes...and one completely uninhibited rodeo clown.

The party was a smash success, and she was flying high. Rowena had even come over a little while ago and hugged her so hard she practically spun her around.

Twenty guests and ten staff members, and somehow she'd come up with a unique costume for every one of them. A few of the choices had been obvious...no-brainers. Dallas, of course, had to be the Old West sheriff. No one but Rowena could do justice to Annie Oakley. Barton James was a little harder, if only because there were so many options for him. He looked exactly like Gregory Peck, so all those Gunfighter and Big Country movies came to mind. But he was also the perfect cowboy crooner, so she was tempted to go Gene Autry or Tex Ritter.

Finally, she let him choose, and he went with Gene Autry, which was the simplest costume ever—essentially Barton's own clothes, his guitar and a huge white hat.

After that, she made her way down the list, one by one, until she got to the last two—her own costume and Gray's. It had been tempting, so tempting, to cast him as a gunslinger. He would have been mouthwatering in a long brown leather duster and high boots, with that sexy gun belt hanging low on his narrow hips. But even imagining it made her feel a little woozy, which was a very bad sign. If she was already swooning over a mental image, how would she stand a chance of resisting the real thing?

She had a weak moment for herself, too, when she opened the delivery of the saloon-girl costume. The satin gown was a gorgeous peacock-feather blue, with black fringe sleeves that shimmered if you so much as breathed, and a complex bustle that pinned back with a cameo brooch. She would have loved to show up in that, and see how strong Gray's willpower really was.

But they'd both been so careful ever since the night of the dance. Clearly, he was as reluctant to complicate things as she was. The saner, wiser route was to give the costumes to other people....

And so that's exactly what she did. Fanny Bronson got the saloon-girl gown, which Bree thought should earn her some extra brownie points, especially since Fanny had spent the past week flirting shamelessly with Gray every chance she got.

Bree assigned herself the schoolmarm costume. Drab olive green, which made her skin look sallow. Shapeless, buttoned all the way up the throat and down to the wrists. She even added a pair of glassless granny glasses and a severe bun at the nape of her neck for good measure.

She gave the marvelous gunslinger duster to the only other male who had the body to pull it off—little Mabel Madison's dad, Jimmy. He deserved it, Bree thought, for surviving five years as Mabel's father without running away and changing his name.

In the end, she decided to give Gray the rodeo clown. It was almost criminal to hide his good looks in an absurd costume like that, but it was the only way she could feel even remotely safe tonight. Face covered in white pancake makeup, nose bulbous and honking, feet flopping and suspenders snapping…surely even she could drive thoughts of sex from her mind while he was looking like that.

Ha. Wrong.

For starters, he still looked fantastic. The suspenders outlined that washboard chest, and the white makeup just seemed to accentuate his elegant bone structure and sensual mouth. He wasn't the least bit subdued by the foolishness of the costume. Quite the contrary, it seemed to bring out an effervescence, a vitality that was positively magnetic.

He'd been surrounded by women all night. Laughing, fawning women who clearly found his every word hilarious. Women who wanted to "play with" his suspenders. Women who wanted to squeeze his nose or sniff his big blue flower.

Or, after a few glasses of wine, make risqué jokes about the significance of the size of his feet.

But that was okay. If the clown costume couldn't save her, a perimeter of possessive women served the purpose just as well. She settled back, let Dallas bring her a glass of wine and proceeded to simply enjoy the success of the party.

Right now, Barton was singing a set of Gene Autry songs, and had just launched into a particularly plaintive rendition of "Red River Valley," when suddenly the white face of her favorite rodeo clown appeared in front of her.

"May I have this dance, schoolmarm?" He held out his hand and made a deep, courtly bow. "I know I'm just a lowly rodeo clown, but you mustn't blame me for that. Blame the costume gods, who cursed me with this nose, this face…"

She laughed. "Cursed? I've been watching you, clown, and, if anything, you owe the costume gods a prayer of thanks. I'm not sure you've ever been more popular."

"Still." His painted smile didn't obscure the intensity of his gaze. "Dance with me."

She shook her head. "Schoolmarms don't dance. They have their reputations to protect."

"I will protect you," he said quietly. "Dance with me."

"I'll dance with you, Gray!" Fanny Bronson came wriggling over, her fringes shimmying. She gave Bree an arch look. "Saloon girls don't worry about prissy things like reputation. Saloon girls know how to show a man a good time."

For a minute, Bree thought Gray might reject the other woman. He regarded her coldly, though the painted smile hid his sober face—or at least Bree hoped it would hide it sufficiently to fool someone as tipsy as Fanny.

"She's right," Bree said brightly. "Schoolmarms are always on duty. Always working."

She stressed that last word, hoping he would remember that he, too, was supposed to be working, and Fanny was the task at hand. Fanny might have been drinking just enough to cause a scene if he didn't handle this deftly.

"She's right, Mr. Clown." Fanny turned, presenting her backside to Gray, and shook her bustle coquettishly. "Saloon girls just want to have fun."

When he didn't respond, Fanny backed up a few inches and wriggled harder. And then a few more inches. And a few more. As she backed him toward the punch bowl, Gray stepped neatly out of the way and took her arm, trying to guide her to safety, as well. But she was apparently feeling feisty, and insisted on remaining on her original, doomed trajectory.

Consequently, she ended up doing her shimmy right over

the punch, with the lowest layers of the bustle dangling like fat blue spatulas, stirring the chunks of pineapple clumsily.

"Oh," she cried out, realizing her mistake. She tried to correct her course, but she came within an inch of losing her footing and falling, bustle first, into the bowl.

At the very last second, Gray caught her as she tumbled, saving her from the humiliation and discomfort of spending the rest of the evening picking slivers of cut glass out of her rear end.

She collapsed into his arms, laughing. She decided that his chivalry deserved a kiss, and was endeavoring to plant one on him when Rowena suddenly showed up with an elderly man in tow.

"Gray?"

As Gray continued to politely stiff-arm Fanny, the way an experienced parent might keep at bay an infant fascinated by a pair of shiny glasses, he looked over at Rowena. Bree, who had already realized who the old man was, watched Gray's face, and even through the makeup she could tell the instant he recognized his grandfather.

The old man's face was almost as white as his grandson's. He scornfully raked his piercing gaze over Gray's costume, from the red nose to the hobo shoes. And then he did the same to Fanny, who still flirtatiously wrestled with Gray's blocking arms for the right to reach his lips.

"Hello, Grandfather," Gray said casually, as if this was no surprise at all. His tone held no undercurrent of apology, either for his idiotic costume or for the tipsy, lovesick female in his arms. "It's nice of you to visit, but I'm afraid I'm working right now."

"Working? This is what you call a job?" Old Grayson Harper paused, then added a deeply disgusted sound that said more than any real word ever could.

As if he hadn't heard it, Gray simply nodded. "Yes. This

is what I call a job. So perhaps, if you don't mind, we could talk tomorrow instead?"

The old man had already begun to walk away, leaning heavily on his cane. At Gray's words, he paused, his back stiff and unyielding.

"I don't think that'll be necessary," he said over his shoulder, turning his head only a fraction of an inch. "As far as I'm concerned, there's nothing left to say."

Rowena followed Gray's grandfather toward the front hall, tossing Bree a grimace as she passed. Gray seemed to have forgotten the old man as soon as he was out of sight. He had finally pinned Fanny's hands without hurting her, and had forced her to meet his eyes and focus on his voice.

"How about if I get you some coffee, Fanny?" His voice was surprisingly gentle, as if he really were dealing with a child. "Otherwise, you're going to feel like the devil in the morning. You have an early riding lesson, don't you? You wouldn't want to miss that."

Bree watched as Fanny's artificial bravado seeped out of her like helium from a broken balloon. She sagged in his arms and didn't resist when he softly led her to a chair and arranged her on it.

"I already feel like the devil," she said, reaching up to massage her head where the comb of her feather headdress attached to her scalp. She dragged the feather out unceremoniously and sighed with relief. "Ouch."

Bree had expected Gray to chase his grandfather out to the parking lot, hot to defend himself. But instead, when he seemed fairly certain that Fanny wasn't going to topple over in her chair, he headed toward the buffet table, clearly making good on his offer of coffee.

So the old man was just going to swan in here, insult Gray—and insult Bell River, too, really—then swan out again, uncontested? Indignation rose in her, fiery hot. She heard the front door close behind the old man, and she knew she could catch him. His cane made him slow, and her outrage made her fast.

Even so, she almost missed him because he hadn't bothered to park like a normal person. He'd simply had his chauffeur idle his gleaming limo a few feet from the door. By the time Bree made it to the porch, he was about to climb into the limo, while his young, shapely female chauffeur silently held the door for him.

"Mr. Harper," Bree called. "Mr. Harper, wait a minute."

The old man turned, frowning. She tried to run across the porch, but her long schoolmarm dress, with its sprigged green flowers designed to look as if they'd been repurposed from a feed sack, flapped around her ankles, slowing her down. So she gathered the hem up in one hand and jogged down the steps to the waiting limo instead.

"I'm sorry," old Harper said, looking at her down his long, elegant nose that she suddenly realized looked so much like Gray's. "Have we met?"

"We're meeting right now," she said, catching her breath. "My name is Brianna Wright. This is my ranch, and your grandson is my employee."

He raised one silver eyebrow. "My condolences, Ms. Wright."

She narrowed her eyes. "Very funny, Mr. Harper. But I'm not out here to see which of us can be the more bitingly sardonic. I freely concede that, by virtue of having ten times more experience and a hundred times more arrogance than I do, you'd win that contest every time."

Something reluctantly appreciative gleamed behind the old man's eyes as he studied her face. "Perhaps you underestimate yourself, Ms. Wright. Perhaps not *every* time."

She frowned, but he held up a hand. "We'll let that pass.

Your comment does beg the question, though. What *are* you out here for?"

"It's simple. I'm here to tell you that you're wrong. You're one hundred percent wrong about Gray, and you're wrong about this job."

"Really."

"Yes, really." She felt herself flushing. She was already sick of his snarky tone. Why couldn't he just have a normal discussion, instead of using every syllable to convey his superiority to, and authority over, mere mortals like her?

"Does he know you're out here?"

"Of course not. He's already forgotten you were ever here."

"All right." The old man shifted his weight again and grasped the door of his limo for balance. "But please, don't take all night."

Fair enough. She inhaled deeply, registering how cold the night air was, especially for an old man with joint problems, and began.

"The social director job is all about making sure the ranch's guests have a good time. Basically, that means fourteen-hour days, every day. Ten of those hours are spent building, cleaning, planning, painting, hauling, assembling, ordering, accounting and then pitching in for any other area that's short-staffed. Which, around here these days, means every area, from the horse stables to the vegetable garden, from the backed-up plumbing to the busted chain saw."

The old man blinked, cleared his throat and shifted his weight on his cane, all body language designed to encourage her to get to the point.

So she did.

"The other four are spent at the event itself. While you're there, your job is to pretend you're having more fun than a barrel of monkeys, when actually every muscle in your body is screaming and you would gladly trade your left foot for one uninterrupted night's sleep. You have to be interested in, and kind to, all the guests. *All of them*. Even the mean ones, the boring ones."

She narrowed her eyes. "Or, in Gray's case, the drunk ones who just want to have sex with him on the lazy Susan."

The old man laughed. *Good*. That meant he hadn't tuned her out. He was still listening.

"And I promise you, Mr. Harper. Those last four hours are a heck of a lot harder than the ten you spent mucking out stalls and snaking out toilets. But Gray handles them all with an amazing degree of diligence, skill, commitment and compassion."

The chauffeur hadn't moved a muscle during any of this. Bree glanced at her, wondering whether the old man hired only hearing-impaired mutes so that he wouldn't get any annoying backtalk or gossip from his staff.

"That's a very impassioned defense of my grandson," Harper observed placidly. "Do you mind if I ask…are you, perhaps, one of the drunk ones who wants to have sex on the lazy Susan?"

Out of the corner of her eye, Bree thought she might have seen the chauffeur's lips compress, as if smothering a smile.

"Yes," Bree enunciated clearly, smiling when the old man's eyes widened. She finished the sentence slowly so that there was no mistake. "I *do* mind."

"I see," he said dryly. "The question was actually rhetorical, Ms. Wright."

"But my answer wasn't." She made an irritated, tsking sound between her teeth. "What's wrong with you? Why do you find it so hard to believe that Gray is working his behind off at this job? As we all are."

He shrugged. "He has about fifteen million reasons to lie about it."

Well, that just capped it. She was tired of being rational

with this pigheaded old fool. *Sorry, Kitty,* she said mentally. Apparently, ladies do lose their tempers. And it felt just fine, actually. Apparently, it was becoming her favorite new bad habit.

"You know what, Mr. Harper? I suddenly think I can see why your grandson hasn't spoken to you in so many years. You're one nasty piece of work."

He drew his head back, as if offended. "Ms. Wright, let me assure you that—"

"No. You let *me* assure *you.* Two things." She put her forefinger out toward his chest, punching the air for emphasis. "First, your implication that we would conspire with him to defraud you of your millions is damn insulting. And second, your theory that we would hire a useless slacker at a time like this, just to help him steal your money? That you'd even consider it possible shows a profound ignorance, both of the demands of a dude ranch, and of the kind of women my sisters and I are."

She gathered up her ugly dress and prepared to go back upstairs and into the house.

"One last thing. I don't ever want to see you at Bell River again. If you are struck by another urgent need to humiliate and harass your grandson, you'll have to do it somewhere else."

CHAPTER ELEVEN

IT WAS GOING to be a long afternoon, so Gray grabbed a third mouthwatering biscuit from the basket in the kitchen as he headed out to join the Junior Explorers Expedition. As he passed Cookie, who was fiercely dicing onions for dinner, he managed to land a loud, smacking kiss on her cheek.

Her net-covered head reared up, and her thick black eyebrows dived toward each other. "No!" she growled, waving her very sharp knife in the air to express her displeasure. "No kissing!"

He grinned, holding up the biscuit and lowering his eyelids in dreamy ecstasy, a wordless explanation of why he'd been unable to restrain himself.

"You're a goddess," he said as he backed away from her toward the door. He pushed it open and loped down the stairs, glancing at his watch. One-fifteen. They should have left fifteen minutes ago.

He stuffed the rest of the biscuit in his mouth and concentrated on his clothes. He'd just managed to get his shirt buttoned and tucked in when he spotted the collection of children lined up behind the barn.

Most of them had taken off their backpacks, dropping them onto the grass. They all seemed bored and fidgety, and Mabel Madison had already started writing something in the grass with small, carefully arranged pebbles and stones.

As he drew closer, he saw what she'd accomplished so far.

H-E-L. He chuckled, wondering whether she was preparing to curse or send an SOS.

Bree stood in front of the kids, looking adorable in pedal-pusher jeans, white sneakers and a blue-and-white-checked shirt. She'd pulled her hair into a fifties-style ponytail that bounced when she moved and caught the afternoon sunlight as if about half its strands were twenty-four-karat gold.

In one hand she held a clipboard and in the other a pencil, which she aimed toward the children as she counted them off.

"Seven, eight, nine…and ten. Good! Everyone is here." She took a deep breath. "Still."

When she caught sight of Gray, she frowned slightly. "Have you seen Rowena? We're already running behind, and the schedule is pretty tight if we're going to get back before dark."

"Sorry." He held up his hands, pointing his thumbs toward his chest. "Looks as if I'm Rowena today."

A couple of little girls giggled, apparently finding that pretty funny. He joined Bree at the front so that they could talk without every word being overheard. Alec was in the group of ten, and Rowena had been especially adamant that the boy mustn't be allowed to worry.

"She was a little under the weather this morning," he said quietly. "Nothing serious, but Dallas put his foot down, said she can't go anywhere today. I got drafted to take her place."

Her frown deepened, and she tapped the pencil against the clipboard nervously. "What's wrong? God, I hope she hasn't caught whatever Georgia Brooke had."

He lifted one shoulder to say he had no idea. Well, he had ideas, but not the kind you bandied around in public—especially when one of the members of the public was Alec. The kid was already watching them with hyperfocused, squinted eyes, as if he was trying to read their lips.

Just in case the little scamp actually possessed that skill,

Gray angled his torso to thwart him. "A minor stomach bug, I gather. She seems fine, except apparently she puked earlier. She insisted she was good to go, but Dallas…well, he was doing the Dallas thing." Gray smiled. "You know the Dallas thing."

She shook her head, but she was smiling, too. "Definitely."

She bent down and put the clipboard into her backpack, then zipped the pocket shut. Standing straight again, she smiled at the children. "Okay, explorers! Let's get this show on the road."

The cheer that went up from the kids was so heartfelt you'd think they'd just been rescued from man-eating tigers or won a trip to Disney World. Mabel kicked her stones and did a stomping, twirling happy dance.

Apparently, fifteen minutes was a very, very long time to a kid.

As they started hiking, moving fairly quickly across the flat, landscaped ranch land that lay closest to the home and outbuildings, Bree filled him in on the four-hour trip's itinerary. The theme today was tree scarring.

Yesterday, the kids had attended a session led by Barton James, who told them all about the Ute Indians, and the special trees they'd left behind as they traveled through Colorado. They'd seen slides of peeled-bark trees, where the bark had been stripped, probably for medicinal or ritual purposes, and prayer trees, pine saplings that had been roped to the ground so that they grew with a distinct "elbow" bend, and message trees, on which the Ute had carved symbols into aspen trunks, telling stories of their history.

No documented scarred trees had ever been found on Bell River property, though the children were excited at the prospect of discovering the first. Barton had been smart, though, and taught them how to identify other types of scarring, like fire, lightning and animals, so that they wouldn't come home frustrated by failure.

The kids had already eaten lunch. So the plan was to hike, in roughly half-hour-long segments, until three, when they'd stop for a snack and a nap. Then they'd take a slightly different route home, arriving back at Bell River just before six.

"Sorry you got roped into it," Bree said, glancing over her shoulder to be sure the stragglers weren't falling too far behind.

He smiled. "I'm not."

She didn't meet his eyes. "It's a long day, though. The whole idea is to keep the kids occupied while the grown-ups go white-water rafting, and bring them home as tired as their parents will be. But I have a feeling you and I are going to be dead on our feet by the time it's over."

"You can't scare me," he said, still smiling. "The weather's perfect, the scenery's gorgeous and I get to spend an entire afternoon with you. I couldn't have designed a more perfect situation if fate had asked me for a blueprint."

She did look at him then. Her gaze was surprisingly frank. "I got the impression we were trying to avoid spending a whole lot of time together these days."

He had to admire the way she came at the subject head-on. She was getting her confidence back.

"That's part of what's so perfect," he said, smiling. "With ten sets of curious, prying, *tattling* eyes as chaperones, we aren't likely to do anything dumb."

Bree didn't get a chance to respond. Mabel's older brother, Michael, came up at that moment, his normally pleasant face pursed up like a prune.

"Mabel says she has to go to the bathroom." He scowled down at his feet. "I don't know why I have to tell you. She should talk for herself. She's six now, not two."

Bree touched the boy's shoulder sympathetically. "Little

sisters are a lot of trouble, aren't they? I know all about it. I've got one…and I am one." She gestured toward Michael's friends, who were walking together just ahead. "You go have some fun. I'll talk to her."

His face unkinked, and he shot her a grateful smile. "Okay. Thanks. But…just so you know, she doesn't really have to go. Not this soon. Mabel can hold it like forever. She's just trying to get attention. Dad says it's a girl thing."

A girl thing? Surely even geeky Jimmy Madison, who Gray remembered dimly from high school, hadn't said anything as dumb as that. The kid must have misunderstood. But it struck Gray's funny bone anyhow, and he had to exert a conscious effort not to laugh.

He had to hand it to Bree, though. She kept a straight face like a pro.

"Thanks for the heads-up," Bree said evenly, neither buying Michael's evaluation of his sister nor rejecting it. "I'll check it out."

The boy nodded, then sped off to catch up to his friends, as if he'd done the best he could do to prepare her, but now the battle was hers.

Bree turned once, to give Gray a soldier's salute, then she found her way to Mabel, who was sulkily walking just to the right of the path, kicking every stone she encountered.

Gray watched the pantomime that followed with amused appreciation. Bree obviously adopted a neutral position first, just in case the crisis was real. Then she asked Mabel to produce her biodegradable toilet paper from her backpack, and she pointed to the thick stand of trees off to the side.

Mabel's face darkened and tightened, and she folded her bony arms over her chest. Bree didn't look the least fazed. She simply plucked out the simple map Mabel had in her pocket— each child had been given one—unfolded it and then pointed to something not far from where they were.

Gray had spent too many years playing poker in order to infuriate his grandfather, and he understood perfectly what was going on. Bree was calling Mabel's bluff. If the little girl had a problem, step over there and deal with it. If she didn't, then stop fussing and wait until they reached the cabin that was clearly marked, and only about twenty minutes away.

Mabel snatched the map back, refolded it, shoved it in her pocket, then churned her legs faster so that she got ahead of Bree quickly and never looked back.

Slowing down, Bree fell in line with Gray, and when they were at a safe distance, her pent-up mirth came out in smothered chuckles.

"Oh, my dear heaven, she's a pistol. I've never felt sorry for Jimmy Madison in my life, but I do now. Do you remember him?"

Gray nodded. "I think so. Chess club, right? All logic and box thinking. A real rule follower." He watched Mabel storming up the path, kicking at stones, some so big it was a miracle she hadn't broken her toes. "Man. He probably doesn't know what hit him."

Bree's laughter had spent itself, and her face had settled into an oddly pensive expression.

"Still…" She watched the fuming little girl kick her way up the hill. "Maybe it will serve her well later in life."

"What will?"

"All that spunk. All that defiance. Maybe, when she grows up, she'll never be afraid to say what she means, or stand up for what she believes in. Maybe, when she's a grown woman, no one will ever be able to make her doubt herself."

She seemed to realize she'd let the conversation grow too serious, because she shook off the philosophical air and grinned. "But what am I saying? *When* she grows up? I guess it's more like…*if* she grows up."

He laughed. But he suddenly realized he owed Mabel a

thank-you. She'd just provided the opening he'd been waiting for all morning.

"Hey," he began casually. "Speaking of feisty, kick-ass females…"

Bree, who had been silently counting the heads in front of them on the path, making sure all the children were in sight, glanced toward him curiously.

"What about them?"

"My grandfather called me last night."

It might sound like a non sequitur, but she would understand. And, of course, she did. Her pace slowed momentarily, then recovered almost at once.

"Did he? And what did he want?"

"He wanted to tell me about this…this feisty, kick-ass female who got hold of him as he was leaving the costume party Wednesday night. Apparently, she grabbed him by the scruff of the neck and shook him till his teeth rattled."

Bree kept walking, her gaze steady on the path ahead, a half smile playing at her lips. "Ah, the angry-female-as-rabid-dog metaphor. Classic. Did he happen to trot out the phrase 'uppity broad'?"

"No. No, come to think of it, I don't think he did."

She gave him a quick, sidelong glance. "The b word?"

He pretended to search his memory. "Nope."

"Really." She tilted her head quizzically. "I guess he warned you to steer clear of her, though?"

"Actually, he told me I was one lucky fool to have someone like that fighting on my side. He said to be sure to tell her that she'd been very persuasive, in her own eccentric, rabid-dog way, and, because of her, he had no intention of reneging on our deal."

She relaxed then, and let a smile spread across her face, all the way to her beautiful eyes.

"Good, then. Good for him." She caught Gray's gaze. "And

good for you, too, I suppose. Just twelve more days of prison here, and you're a wealthy man."

He nodded. "It would seem so."

They walked in silence for a few minutes after that. She was probably thinking about how much she disapproved of his deal with his grandfather.

But he was thinking something else entirely.

The time had gone by so fast.

When he'd initially shown up at Bell River, asking for a job, a month had seemed an eternity. A luxury of weeks. And he had known, from the very first day, that he wanted to spend that month as Brianna Wright's lover.

He hadn't even felt any particular urgency about seducing her. It had seemed inevitable, like something that would simply happen on its own, the way a piece of perfectly ripe fruit might just drop from a tree and land in your outstretched hand.

When, on that first day, Barton James asked him to test-drive the lavish tent, he'd jumped at the offer. The luxury of true privacy. A romantic setting. It was exactly what he needed. What *they* needed.

That's how sure he'd been. He didn't just assume…he *knew* Bree would come to his bed.

And he knew she'd be happy there. He would make certain of it. He'd belonged to the Bachelor Club long enough to know that was the most important mission—if only because a woman who had been happy in your bed never could bring herself to be quite as bitter when the time came for her to leave it.

Uncomplicated physical pleasure in the moonlit tent, beside the sparkling creek, serenaded by birdsong. What could be more natural?

So he'd launched his plan to make sure she stayed around a couple of weeks, ostensibly to "train" him. From there he'd figured it would be a cinch to make the two weeks turn into four. He had planned to make it a month she'd never forget—and never regret.

But then, like an idiot, he'd gone and let the whole thing get…complicated. And now, more than half the time they could have spent in each other's arms was already gone, never to return. Twelve days. That was all he had left.

If he didn't stop overthinking this act that should be so simple, so ancient, universal and pure, he would wake up one day soon and discover it was too late. He'd shake her hand as he left Colorado. Or maybe he'd kiss her—yes, of course, undoubtedly he would kiss her.

But, either way, they would part as friends.

Just friends.

But no. No, no, no, no.

Something inside him rebelled at the very sound of those words. Already the phrase was a lie. They might not have made love, but they were far, far more than "just friends."

"We're here," Bree's voice suddenly called out merrily. "This is our first stop!"

For a minute, Gray felt disoriented, as if his thoughts had been the true reality and she'd just dragged him into a meaningless, intrusive dream.

In front of them, ten heads turned, ten small faces smiled. "This is it?"

"This is it! Time to get out your journals, everyone."

As the children eagerly complied, digging through their backpacks and pulling out small, spiral-bound books, Bree smiled awkwardly at Gray, her gaze suddenly uncertain.

"Everything okay?"

He wondered whether he looked as crazed as he felt. He couldn't seem to think straight. All he knew was that he couldn't let this happen. Every hour they lost, every minute they continued as "just friends," seemed like a crime.

And yet, what could he do about it? Scoop her up and carry her deep into the trees? Make violent, pagan love to her while ten little nature explorers wandered the forest fearfully, calling, "Ms. Wright? Ms. Wright? Where are you?"

"Gray, are you okay with this?" She knit her eyebrows. "We promised them we'd break into two teams. You'll take five, and I'll take five. They're excited about the prizes. For the team that finds the most trees. Didn't Rowena tell you?"

"Yes," he said. "No. Hell, I don't know. It doesn't matter. I'll take five. I'll take them all. Just promise you'll come to me tonight."

She tilted her head back, her blue eyes wide. *"What?"*

"We need to talk, Bree. We can't go on like this." But then, like a schizophrenic arguing with himself, he shook his head firmly. "No, that's not the truth. We don't need to talk. We need to be lovers. Come tonight. I've been a fool. We've lost too much time already."

"Gray, I—" She twisted her earring nervously and lowered her voice so that the children couldn't hear. "I can't talk about this now. I can't *think* about this now."

"Well, I can't think about anything else."

She shook her head again. "We have to. The children are counting on us."

Damn the children, he wanted to say. But his blood was finally cooling, and sanity was starting to hover at the edges of his brain, the way dawn shows up at the edges of night. He glanced toward the nearest kids, a seven-year-old girl and her six-year-old brother, both of whom wore impossibly tiny pairs of glasses. They bent solemnly over their books, dutifully printing their names in slow, unsteady block letters on the first page.

They really were counting on the grown-ups, though they didn't even realize it. They trusted so completely they had no idea trust was even involved.

"I know," he said. He tried to look normal, tried to *be* normal. "I do know, Bree. I'll behave, I promise. But you should know, it's taking every ounce of willpower I have not to sling you over my shoulder and ravish you in the woods."

In spite of everything, she smiled.

"Ravish me? Remember that feisty, kick-ass lady your grandfather told you about?"

He laughed. "Clearly. That's why I'm in a ravishing mood…."

She shook her head helplessly. "Honestly, Gray, you are im—"

"Ms. Wright? Ms. Wright?" Mabel Madison appeared out of nowhere and began tugging insistently on the tail of Bree's shirt. "Ms. Wright, where's the cabin? You said there would be a cabin, with a bathroom and a door and a roof."

"There is, Mabel," she said, bending down and smiling patiently at the furious little girl. "It's right over there." She pointed west. "See?"

Gray looked, too. And he saw it immediately…a small brown cabin, with a bedroom…no, he meant to say *bathroom*…and a door and a roof.

For one last, irrational moment he pondered whether there was any way, any possible way…

"For heaven's sake! *Forget about it!*" Bree's voice was stern, but when he looked over at her, wiggling his eyebrows, her eyes were alight with mirth.

"I'm serious, you impossible beast. Just put the whole thing out of your mind instantly."

"I can't!" Mabel's eyes widened. Apparently no one had ever talked to her like that before. Her voice rose to a near-hysterical pitch. "I can't forget about it, Ms. Wright! I'm going to pee my pants!"

Bree and Gray looked at her, and then at each other, and then, though they knew Mabel would have no idea what caused them to do so, they both broke down in nearly silent, helpless laughter.

Mabel made a low, growling sound of utter frustration. Gray considered trying to smooth things over, but obviously it was too late. The little girl scowled fiercely at him. And then, as if he'd left her no choice, she kicked him in the shins.

SOMEHOW, GRAY MADE it through the endless afternoon. The countless rest stops, the eternal search for marks on trees, the snacks, the naps, the questions, the noise. And always the tantalizing glimpses of Bree in the distance, her ponytail bobbing and gleaming, her body as lithe and easy in the woods as a forest fairy.

Sometimes, when he didn't see her for long stretches, he could actually stop obsessing about her and start to enjoy the moment. The kids were cute, especially his five. Alec had insisted on working with his aunt, claiming kinship. And after Mabel attacked Gray, she suddenly was terrified to be around him, apparently for fear he'd decide to exact revenge.

So Bree had ended up with both the little devils, and Gray had caught the lucky draw. He felt guilty, especially when it occurred to him that Bree might have engineered the arrangement because she doubted his ability to focus at the moment.

She needn't have worried. He was doing fine.

Sure, every hour or two, he glared up at the sun, which still gleamed high and round in the sky, like a pure gold poker chip, the kind you got when you hit the once-in-a-lifetime jackpot.

Sink, damn you.

He'd bark the command in his head, though he would like some credit, thank you, for being sane enough not to say it aloud.

Just call it a day, for God's sake. SET.

Naturally, the sun didn't respond any better to autocratic

demands than humans did. But gradually, one degree at a time, it lost its hold on the glassy blue dome of the afternoon. It began to slide slowly down the western sky, like an egg yolk on a well-greased pan.

As the air began to cool, the shadows stretched longer and the landmarks grew more familiar, signaling their approach to Bell River's ranch house. Gray felt his temper subside. Festering, stagnant frustration was replaced by a freshly flowing rill of sparkling anticipation.

Not long now.

She hadn't ever promised she would come, of course. He hadn't forgotten that. But she would.

Surely she would.

Belatedly, he threw himself into helping his team accumulate points. Even as twilight approached, and good trees grew more difficult to spot, he found the long, vertical scars of a lightning strike and the curved gouges of animal claws. He even became a momentary hero when he located a heart with the initials MW+BB carved in an aspen, then checked the rules and discovered that nothing said the scarring had to be old.

When they reached the last rest stop, less than half an hour from home, he and his team found a small, charming glen already blooming with early columbine and conveniently furnished with a cluster of fallen logs arranged like a sectional sofa.

They had been sitting down for no more than five minutes, happily tallying up their impressive finds and laughing at Michael Madison's knock-knock jokes, when suddenly Bree appeared at the edge of the glen.

Gray's gaze went straight to her, of course. But for once she didn't send the usual buzz of longing through him. This time the sight of her created a tiny needle of fear. Some unnatural microexpression, or some physical detail that didn't fit… He couldn't pinpoint how, but he knew that something was seriously wrong.

He stood. "Carry on," he told his five, copying his earlier merry tone perfectly, though his mood had already done an about-face, based on nothing more than the fact that Bree stood before him and he didn't feel the instinctive urge to smile.

He made his way to her quickly. "What is it? What's wrong?"

Mutely, she shook her head, but he knew she didn't mean, "No, nothing's wrong." The shake was just an instinctive denial. It was her mind rejecting whatever it was that had happened.

"Bree." He put his hands on her shoulders, shocked by how cold they were. Her eyes were very wide, their blue depths tinged with a peach light from the setting sun. "Tell me. Whatever it is, we will fix it."

"I can't find Alec." She pressed her hands together, as if she needed to hold on to something. "He's gone."

CHAPTER TWELVE

FUNNY, BREE THOUGHT, though she knew that wasn't the right word. Funny how, once something huge happened in a certain spot, you could never go there again without feeling at least an echo, an aftershock, of whatever you'd felt before.

It was like a kind of haunting, when you thought about it.

The spot she had been standing in when she realized Alec was not with the others…now that would always been one of those places for her.

She'd been looking down a pretty, violet-sprinkled ravine when one of the kids had casually said, "Where's Alec?" And even before her conscious mind could react, her subconscious had begun to scream.

Yes, yes, it howled. *That is what I've been trying to tell you. We haven't heard Alec do anything, not talk, or laugh, or make silly monster sounds, for a very long time. Something is terribly wrong.*

So, over the next thirty horrible minutes, whenever anyone—everyone—asked her where was the last place she definitively remembered seeing Alec, she had simply responded, "He was with us when we left rest stop number two, but he was not with us when we got halfway to rest stop number one. That was between 5:30 and 5:45 p.m." Between the moment went everything was all right and the moment when everything turned black.

Thirty minutes, she knew now, could be a lifetime. Thirty minutes to imagine every hideous accident that could have happened. Every rattlesnake, black widow, scorpion or puma he might have encountered unprepared. Every psychopath who might have followed when he wandered off to check out a bird or fossil. Every petit mal, or grand mal, or so-far-unidentified allergy to macaroni and cheese or bee stings that might have stopped his heart, or his lungs, or his brain.

Thirty minutes to imagine facing Dallas and Rowena with the news. Thirty minutes to imagine their pain...

Only two things kept her from falling apart during those harrowing thirty minutes. One was the determination to be a helpful part of the search, not another hysterical female to comfort. The other was Gray, whose calm competence was immensely reassuring. As far as she could tell, Gray never for a single second considered the possibility that Alec would not return, safe and sound.

And at the end of those thirty minutes, just as Rowena and Dallas arrived at rest stop number one, the staging area, Alec came sauntering into view.

For a split second, when she saw his thatch of blond hair coming toward them in the gloaming, Bree thought her knees might simply give out on her. She put one hand out blindly and somehow Gray was there. He took her reaching fingers and chafed them softly so that the blood moved through them again. Then he rested her hand on his arm and looked at her with a one-sided smile.

"Told you," he said. "I'd go throttle the kid myself, but I'm pretty sure Rowena will do a more thorough job of it."

Bree watched numbly as Rowena first nearly smothered Alec in a hug that went on for what seemed like hours. Then she pulled back and took the boy's bony shoulders in her hands.

"What on earth were you thinking, Alec Garwood? Of all the dumb, thoughtless, immature things you could have done! Do you have any idea what you just put your aunt Bree through?"

Alec cast a glance toward Bree, looking absolutely miserable. "I'm sorry, Rowena," he said. "It was an accident, I swear. We got so close to my fort, and I wanted to check on it. But turned out some animal must have gotten into my stash of candy, tried to eat the whole thing. What a mess." He glanced up at his dad. "I'm sorry, Dad, really. But it's actually pretty disgusting what a half-digested Tootsie Roll looks like. I *had* to clean up, didn't I? And then before I knew it, it was getting dark."

Dallas shook his head. "Don't you be telling *me* you're sorry, son. I wasn't scared, because I know you. But Aunt Bree hasn't seen what a little escape artist you are, and she was really, really worried."

Alec might be an escape artist, but he wasn't a coward. Bree had to admire the pluck that made him come over to where she stood, with his shoulders back and his chin up like a man, even though his face was slack with embarrassment and guilt.

"I'm sorry that I frightened you, Bree," he said with a simple humility and a lack of aggressive defense that was very appealing. "I didn't mean to. I honestly *never* mean to upset or scare people or mess things up. The problem is, I never start out feeling like I'm doing anything bad or dangerous. If I did, I wouldn't do it, you know?"

It was a bit convoluted, linguistically, but emotionally and logically, he was on solid ground. Basically, yes, she did know. She bent down and gave him a kiss. "I think I understand," she said. "Mostly I'm just glad you're not inside a puma's belly right now, being digested for his Friday dinner."

Alec's blue eyes lit up. "Gross. Is that what you thought happened to me?"

"That was just one of the things I considered," she said. "It wasn't even the worst."

"No?" He wrinkled his nose, fascinated. "What *was* the worst?"

"Alec," Rowena interrupted firmly. "Enough."

"Oh, well." He sighed. "Anyway, I'm pretty sure pumas would rather eat deer and elk and stuff. Maybe raccoon."

Dallas laughed. "And I'm pretty sure you taste like raccoon. God knows you smell like one. Come on. I'll take you home and hose you off with some Purple People Eater."

Alec smiled up at Bree. "That's what we call the purple gunk Dad cleans machinery with. He's just kidding, though. You can't use it on people or it rots their skin off."

"Lovely," Gray said.

"Yeah, it's really strong. But you never know…he hasn't seen the stuff that got on my shoes. It used to be Tootsie Rolls, I guess, but it's something else now, that's for sure." He shuddered, screwing up his mouth, as if just imagining it made his face pucker. "It might be a while before I buy those again."

Dallas came over and, laying his palm flat on the crown of his son's head, steered him toward the clearing, where he had parked his truck. "It'll be a while before you buy anything again," he observed. "It's hard to go shopping when you're grounded."

"Aww, man…"

Alec's voice dwindled as the pair moved out of sight. Bree looked over at Rowena, wondering what she could possibly say. Rowena had been wonderful, defending her in front of Alec, but she could only imagine how little faith she could have in Bree now.

Gray's hand was still warm and bracing against her arm. She smiled at him, then extricated herself softly and walked to where Rowena stood. If a nine-year-old boy could make an honest apology without any attempt at a cover-up, then surely she could, too.

"Ro, there's nothing I can say that makes this any better, but I want you to know how sorry I am. I wouldn't have put Alec in danger for anything in the world—nor would I have risked giving the dude ranch a bad name. I let you down, and it's just by the grace of God that everything turned out all right. I don't have an excuse. I just lost track, pure and simple."

Rowena was staring at her, almost as if she didn't recognize the language Bree was speaking.

She tried again. "I know the ranch will recover from this more easily if I'm not around, so I'll leave as soon as possible. I don't guess there's any way to keep the story from getting out, but—"

Rowena extended her hands and took Bree's shoulders, much as she had taken Alec's when she really needed him to focus and pay heed to what she said.

"Bree. Listen to me, honey. This wasn't your fault. Alec is…Alec is special. He's a free spirit. When he needs to get loose, not even one of Dallas's jail cells could hold him. If this is anyone's fault, it's ours, because we should have warned you."

"But, Ro, I—"

Rowena shook her head, sighing. "I can't even tell you how many times *we've* lost track of him. That's not hyperbole. I mean literally, I don't want to tell anyone how many times because one of these days someone will call social services and tell them what bad parents we are."

Bree laughed, and Rowena did, too, but darkly. "Dallas says he decided long ago that all he can do is teach Alec as much as he can about how to handle himself in a crisis, then hope for the best. And pray. Or drink. Or both."

"What about those chips they put in dogs these days?" Bree

grinned at her sister. "At least that way when he gets out, you could track him down."

Rowena shook her head. "You think you're making a joke, but Dallas approached the vet about getting the chip. A year or so ago."

"And?"

"Well, he was an officious little guy. Stuffy, can't really think outside the box, Dallas said. Apparently, he got a touch self-righteous." She winked at Bree. "We use a different vet now."

For a minute Bree's vision fractured into a hundred tiny white, iridescent stars. That wink, that slow, sassy, green-eyed cat wink, came straight from the old days.

The *old* old days, before tragedy struck the Wright family, before the daughters were split up and deposited in different parts of the country. It even came from a time when they had seemed almost like twins. Before Rowena's one year of age difference magically seemed to turn into three or four, or ten. It came from back when all three sisters were allies, fighting shoulder to shoulder against a world that didn't seem to care.

It was a good thing Kitty had taught Bree never to cry— *no one likes a sad sack, Brianna*—because she was suddenly so flooded with gratitude and relief that she could feel it racing through her like a cresting river, searching for an outlet.

Most of all, of course, she felt profound relief that Alec was safe. But she also was deeply relieved that Rowena didn't judge her harshly for what had happened. And grateful that Rowena still cared enough to give her that old wink, here in the new life. Grateful that Rowena had been strong enough to stop Bree from killing the dude ranch idea before it was born, just because she was skeptical, or fearful, or jealous... or whatever the heck was really wrong with her.

And Gray...

She was grateful for Gray, too. For his strength and his support, for his patience and his sense of humor, and his...

"Do you want a ride home?" Rowena was yawning, and Bree suddenly remembered that her sister had been sick this morning.

"No, thanks, I'm happy to walk. It'll work off some of the tension I built up while I was worrying. And speaking of worrying, are you okay? When you couldn't come on the tree hunt today, I wasn't sure what to think."

Rowena ran her fingers through her hair and yawned again. "You should think your sister is married to an overly protective Old West lawman who is going to have to learn a few things about women. If he wanted a wife who would retire to her bed all day every time she feels a little woozy, he made a wrong turn somewhere along the way. He ended up in the twenty-first century instead of the 1850s."

Gray laughed, holding up his hand. "I think this is where I come in, ladies," he said. "I remember something about a spunky, feisty, kick-ass..."

Bree's chest tightened, either with excitement or with anxiety. Something about living in Silverdell made it difficult for her to tell the two apart, she'd discovered.

"Are you leaving?" She tried to keep her voice neutral, but her tight throat still drove the tones up two or three notes. "I know it's been a long day. I guess you're pretty tired."

"Not terribly," he said with a smile that made her toes tingle. "How about you?"

"Not terribly..." Her voice was markedly less confident than his. "I mean, if you were in the mood, I might be up to..."

When her sentence died out uncomfortably, Rowena rolled her eyes, chuckling. "Well, over here in my part of the forest, I definitely *am* terribly tired. So, since I'm the one with the car, I'll just say good night and leave you to figure out who is up to what."

Bree smiled. Impulsively, she went over and held out her arms for a hug. This wasn't something Rowena used to do, so it wasn't a familiar motion. After only a fraction of a second's hesitation, Rowena accepted. She moved into Bree's embrace and hugged her without holding back.

One more time, the crystalline stars formed in front of Bree's eyes.

"Have fun," Rowena whispered as their cheeks met. She pulled her head back and touched Bree's flyaway, sun-streaked hair with gentle, almost maternal fingers. "And don't forget what the wise women say."

Bree smiled. "What do they say?"

Rowena cast a quick, meaningful glance in Gray's direction. "That a lady rarely gets a second chance to make a magnificent mistake."

"ARE YOU HUNGRY?" Gray wasn't sure what the maids had left in his tent's minifridge today, but they always brought something simple and delicious. A loaf of Cookie's homemade bread, perhaps, along with some fresh fruit, maybe a couple of tarts or custards from the dessert tray. They restocked his water bottles, and presumably they also checked the liquor cabinet, although he hadn't had any reason to tap that yet.

They did everything but leave mints on his pillow—and they probably would have added that touch, too, if it hadn't been for the problem of attracting too much attention from the local wildlife. Apparently, this culinary pampering came standard with a glamping package, and Barton had wanted to be sure Gray got the full experience before he rendered his verdict.

For the first time since he got here, Gray was glad he had something to offer. Bree's face was dangerously pale under the blue moonlight. Her eyes were glazed, as if she was on the verge of either waking up or passing out. She looked half done in.

She shook her head politely, though. "I don't think I'm very hungry," she said. "But thanks."

Wrong answer. Of course she was hungry. They hadn't eaten since the child-size snack of Bing cherries and cheese crackers at three o'clock. It was almost nine now.

She probably had no idea what she felt, physically or psychologically. The afternoon's drama overload obviously had temporarily cauterized her nervous system.

She'd been the one to suggest coming to the tent— he wouldn't have mentioned it again for a million dollars, given how the day had ended. But now that she was here, she seemed slightly bewildered, as if she couldn't imagine why she'd thought it was a good idea.

With her arms crossed, her hands gripping her elbows, she hovered just outside the tent, watching him. She leaned against the buttoned-back door's aluminum brace, but she kept her toes behind some invisible line, as if crossing the threshold could have profound, near-mystical consequences.

"I'm just not very hungry," she explained, as if she wasn't sure whether she'd already said that.

"Well, I am," he lied.

She was getting fuzzier by the minute. She needed to eat, and she needed plenty of water. She needed to sit down, and she needed to clear her mind.

If she didn't, he was going to end up slinging her over his shoulder today, after all. Only, unlike in his fantasies, he'd be hauling her like a sack of dehydrated potatoes right back up to the main house, where Rowena could boss her into accepting some familial TLC.

No way in hell Gray was going to seduce a woman in Bree's state.

First rule of Bachelor Club: you do not touch females who

are weepy, crazy, high or drunk. Second rule of Bachelor Club: you *do not* touch females who are weepy, crazy, high or drunk.

Right now, Bree's decision-making skills were as impaired as those of anyone in those categories. Essentially, she *was* drunk—in her case, drunk with fatigue and the aftereffects of adrenaline shock.

He unlocked the door to the small refrigerator and checked its contents. A round of crusty Armenian bread and a chocolate mousse topped with fresh strawberries. He pulled them out, balancing the bread on his forearm, and grabbed a couple water bottles with the other hand. "Maybe we could share something small. Just sit for a while and shake off the day."

She didn't say yes, but she didn't say no, either. She was staring at the king-size bed that suddenly seemed to obscenely dominate the interior space. She had a small line between her eyebrows, as if something about it bothered her, but she was having trouble processing exactly what.

Shaking his head, he returned to the door and smiled down at her reassuringly before nudging her out of the way with his elbow.

"Let's sit outside," he said. "It's a nice night."

She nodded vigorously, as though she wanted to stress what an excellent idea that was. She took one of the deck chairs under the awning and lowered herself into it with a long, groaning sigh that undoubtedly sounded a lot more sexual than she realized.

"Do you mind if I take off my shoes?" She extended her feet and stared down at her sneakers disapprovingly. "They're so dirty and so uncomfortable."

She smiled over at him, lifting her eyebrows playfully. "But at least they don't have puma puke on them, right?"

He chuckled, wondering whether she was already feeling

better, just from sitting down in the fresh air, or whether approaching delirium made her witty.

"Of course not," he said. He twisted the cap off a water bottle and handed it across the small table that divided their two chairs. "Make yourself comfortable."

She groaned again as she freed her slim, pale feet, first from the shoes, then from the white ankle socks beneath. She reached down and massaged her arches, closing her eyes and dropping her head back in an ecstasy of relief.

The tightening in his groin was instant and painful. His college fraternity had owned porn videos that were a hell of a lot less erotic than the uninhibited self-pleasuring she was administering to her feet.

Bolting back his water, he forced himself to look somewhere else. Apparently Bachelor Club needed a few more rules.

When she finished, she sighed. "Oh, that's better," she said. She glanced at his shoes. "Don't you want to take yours off, too?"

He smiled through his tightly clenched jaw. "Later, maybe."

She'd finished almost half her water now. Maybe time to add some food. He broke off a piece of bread and extended it.

"Try this," he suggested casually. "It's Cookie's Armenian bread. Pretty fantastic."

She seemed to have forgotten she wasn't hungry, because she accepted the chunk of bread with a simple thank-you and began munching on it instantly. She ate slowly, savoring every crumb.

"It's heavenly," she said, almost as if she was talking to herself. With a deep sigh, she turned her gaze into the middle distance. She did not seem to be looking at anything in particular. It was more as if…as if she rested her tired eyes on the night's peaceful beauty, like a pillow.

And it was beautiful. The purple-blue sky was star-studded

and clear, the air clean and cool. The creek glittered silver in the moonlight, curling through the darkened landscape like a spangled ribbon that had slipped from some celestial gown.

He broke off another hunk of bread and shared it. And then another, until most of the loaf was gone. She shifted, pulling her feet up and cupping her toes in her palms, as if the night air had begun to sting their nakedness.

The movement was completely different from anything she'd done since she got here. Though she still didn't speak, and she still gazed into the darkness, Bree's silence, and her stillness, had taken on a new quality.

A quality of...

Awareness, that was the only word he could think of. Where twenty minutes ago she had been vague, as insubstantial as a ghost, drifting just beyond her physical body, now she had returned to this moment and this place.

She once again inhabited her own skin. She knew where she was. And she knew why she was here.

An owl called somewhere beyond the distant ponderosa pines, a cold and haunting sound. The temperature was dropping fast, and the paper-thin aspen leaves, always the first to notice, had begun to whisper about the rising wind.

"Are you cold?" he asked.

She nodded. "A little."

"Do you want to go home?"

For a minute she didn't answer. Then she shook her head. "No."

"You can do whatever you want to do," he said. "I hope you know that. If you've changed your mind, or if you didn't even realize what you were saying in the first place, it doesn't matter. If you want to leave, I'll take you home immediately."

He sat very still as he waited for her answer. He told himself that he was ready for whatever she decided. He told himself that if she wasn't able to come to him tonight without doubt, and leave him tomorrow without regret, he would rather she never came to him at all.

But he was lying. He was saying what civilization required him to say—but it simply wasn't true. He had been driven half-mad with this unquenched thirst, and, on some deep, terrible level, he'd become more beast than man.

He wanted her on *any* terms. No matter what she said, what she felt or even what she did, he couldn't stop wanting her, any more than he could stop wanting air to breathe just because it was too cold, or too hot, or too filled with smoke or fire.

Every muscle in his body had been stretched unbearably taut from day after day of that helpless desire. If she walked away now and left him here with no relief, he thought the agony might finally break him in two.

Still…she hadn't given him an answer.

And then she stood, slowly, putting her bare feet onto the cold deck carefully. She turned toward him, and with two deliberate steps she closed the distance between them. For however long that took, he didn't breathe.

When she stood before him, she smiled softly. "I want to stay," she said.

He'd expected relief, expected his muscles to unclench and the pain between his legs to subside, just a little, just until he could sweep her into his arms and carry her into the tent.

But instead he felt a cruel twisting of the rack, a new and terrible cascade of fire that pinned him where he was. She had placed her palms on his knees and begun to push softly. He had no power to resist her, and his legs parted. She sank gracefully to her knees, her dark blue eyes locked on his as she descended.

"Bree." His voice was the only part of him he owned, the only part he could control. He felt as if unseen cords bound him to the chair, his hands, his shoulders, his ankles, his straining, burning thighs…

And all his helpless struggle to stand, to protect, to resist, only drove the fire higher. She touched the button of his jeans, working it open, and he felt an arcing pressure on his spine, as if the bones would crack.

"Bree. No." And still he couldn't stop her.

She dragged his zipper down, then peeled back the cloth that had been confining him. He pulsed helplessly, desire coursing through every nerve ending like an unblocked river, swelling him, inflaming him, until, when she closed her lips over the tip of him, he had to bite back a cry.

He was lost....

But somehow, at the final instant—with some instinct that must have been more powerful than life itself—he found the strength to hold back.

He breathed rhythmically, with intention, with a terrible, unnatural control. With his will alone, he created a microscopic invisible sheen of numbness between his skin and his nerve endings, and it helped him to endure the hot, sweet fire of her slow mouth....

For a while. For a very little while. Within minutes—seconds—the magic numbness began to wear off, and he felt himself falling.

He touched her silken, golden hair.

"No," he said softly, though even his vocal cords were on fire. "Not yet. I want more than this."

When she released him, he had to bite back a groan of relief. He stood quickly, pulled her to her feet, then lifted her into his arms and carried her, as he'd dreamed of doing so many times, into the waiting shadows of the tent.

CHAPTER THIRTEEN

HE WAS DISAPPOINTED, as she had known he would be.

When their lovemaking was over, she lay on her side in his big, luxurious bed and wondered what she could have done differently.

Should she have faked it, the way she used to do with Charlie?

It had seemed wrong, somehow, to erect that wordless lie and place it forever between them. Every time she'd faked a climax with Charlie, she had loved him a little less. Not because she thought it was his fault—she knew it wasn't—but because every lie was one more wall erected between them.

Perhaps he couldn't see the walls—from his side they probably were invisible, made of transparent glass. But on her side, they were solid, and growing thicker every day. Eventually, the distance they created between them muffled all honest communication and cut off any hope of true intimacy.

Eventually, it was as if Charlie maintained a relationship only with the pretend Bree, the fake Bree—and the real, frustrated woman who feared she was somehow inadequate... that woman was walled up in the soundproof glass prison she had built for herself.

Ironic, that she had been willing to live like that with Charlie, a man she had assumed she would marry—and yet had refused to risk the same with Gray, a man who, in twelve short days, would exit her life forever and never look back.

She turned her face to the pillow. She couldn't try to sort

all that out now. She was so tired. And she was so sorry that, no matter what else she had done to delight him, his pleasure had been canceled out by that last, disappointing thirty seconds, when he finally realized that she would not, or could not, let go.

That, in spite of his perfect body, his experienced technique and his endless patience and generosity, they still would not end it together.

They would not share the moment of final surrender—the one everyone read about in books, the one that proved two people belonged together because their bodies spoke the same mysterious language, and their souls flew like birds, like angels and heroes and gods, on simultaneous currents of bliss.

It had been too late for him to hold back, but she had seen the dark surprise that altered his face when he realized he flew alone.

And she'd felt the kindness, the apparently inexhaustible generosity that made him reach out for her again, as soon as he could find the strength. She'd stayed his hand, nudged his lips back up to her own lips, asking him to settle for a kiss instead.

"I'm fine," she had said. "It was beautiful, and I'm fine. Really."

He had raised himself on one elbow and looked down at her for a long time with an inscrutable gaze. His hand had slowly stroked her damp skin, from waist to hip, across her rib cage and up again. He had traced his fingers lightly over the soft pink tip of her breast, as if the truth lay there.

"I don't think you are," he had said finally. Then he had smiled, that sweet, sexy smile that made her heart flop helplessly in her chest, and lowered his lips to her neck. "But we can fix that, sweetheart, I promise."

"No, really." She had smiled, too, though her effort felt strained. She couldn't put him through that all over again.

She couldn't put herself through it. It wouldn't work. And besides, it wasn't necessary.

"I'm really fine. Just…a little tired, I think."

And now she lay in the dark, wondering whether it would have been easier, in the end, just to go on pretending. Why didn't he believe that she had loved every minute of it? Why couldn't he accept that a woman like her, a woman whose body just wouldn't cooperate with that kind of ultimate surrender, could still be moved to feel pleasure, even joy, when she touched a man who excited her, who made her breath come faster just to look at him?

She was still a woman. She felt passion. She longed for the hot pressure of him inside her, filling her almost to the edge of glorious pain. What woman would not thrill to a lover as masterful as Gray Harper? The magic, knowing fingers on her skin, the clever lips brushing fire into every secret nerve ending and creating shimmers that crossed her body in waves of light.

Tonight, for a moment, she'd almost thought she could give in, surrender and let her body do what ought to come naturally. For a minute, she'd been filled with light, and she'd thought, *yes, this is why a woman should never pretend.* Because allowing yourself to wait, no matter how exposed and awkward you feel, is the only chance you'll ever have to make things better.

How could any lover ever help her find her way to the real thing if she kept pretending it had already happened?

In the end, she'd pulled back, the same as always. The miracle hadn't come through, but even that moment of hope had been exciting….

And if there could be another moment, and another after that…maybe someday…

But even if it never happened, she could still experience a deep and transporting satisfaction in lovemaking. Just a different kind. Her kind. Her ultimate pleasure would come from seeing his, if only he could accept that it was no failure for him to reach that pinnacle alone.

She would thrill to his thrill. Could she ever convince him that was enough?

And would she even get another chance?

Though she lay there for hours, listening to the melodic murmur of Cupcake Creek as it surged across long, thick downed logs and frothed softly at the undersides of its mounded rocks, she never did find an answer to any of those questions.

After all these years, she hadn't really expected to.

Eventually, Gray's hand softened on her thigh. His breathing changed, and she knew he had finally surrendered to sleep. She eased free of his hand and climbed quietly out of the bed. She dressed in the dark and, looking back at the tent only once, she carefully made her way back to Bell River by moonlight.

WHEN GRAY'S CELL rang before dawn the next morning, he didn't even check the caller ID. He was 100 percent certain it had to be Bree.

"Hey," he said thickly, smiling half into the pillow and half into the phone. "Why did you sneak away like that? I wasn't finished with you."

The awkward silence on the other end was his first clue. *Hell.* He pulled himself to a sitting position, covers bunching everywhere, and brought the phone down where he could belatedly check the number.

Harper Hall.

He chuckled wryly, scraping his hair out of his forehead with his fingers. *Wonderful.* Always helpful to play to your stereotype.

He put the phone back to his ear. "Sorry. Got you confused with a really nice dream I had last night." Another silence. "Grandfather? What, have you fainted from the shock of hearing that I have a love life?"

"Mr. Gray?" A woman's voice spoke haltingly into the phone, sounding bewildered. "I don't know what you mean when you say all that. I am calling you, not Mr. Harper. I am Almeda."

"Almeda!" Feeling absurd, he put his hand on his face and scrubbed hard. He needed to get some blood flowing to his brain, damn it. He wasn't thinking very fast this morning. "I'm sorry. I was—I thought you were my grandfather, and I thought I was playing a joke on him."

"Oh, I see." She didn't seem to think it was very funny, though. And all of a sudden his brain woke up, and he felt a chill pass through him that had nothing to do with the cold, misty Bell River morning he could see through the windows of the tent.

Why was his grandfather's housekeeper calling him at dawn?

Or ever?

It had to mean only one thing. Something was wrong with his grandfather.

"Almeda, has something happened?"

"Yes." She sounded immensely relieved that he finally understood. "Yes, that is why I am calling. Mr. Harper..." She tried again. "Mr. Harper, he..." She choked on something that sounded like tears...but how could it be? Could she actually care about the old coot? Old Grayson always used to say, with a perverse pride, that everyone he'd ever employed had probably wanted to stab him in his bed.

No "probably" about it. Even as a teenager, Gray had known it to be true.

"Almeda, has he been hurt? Do I need to call an ambulance?"

"No," she said. "It came already. It took him to the hospital. They say they think he is having a heart attack. They say—"

She broke off again. Gray kept the phone to his ear, but he'd left the bed and was yanking clothes out of the wicker chests and setting them on the dresser. Jeans, sweatshirt, underwear, socks…where the hell had he put his socks?

"They say it could be bad."

She had finally swallowed her tears and found her voice—and then it was as if she couldn't seem to stop the words from pouring out.

"Oh, Mr. Gray, you should go. The things he says to you… They are not his real feelings. You should go now."

Oh, who the hell cared about socks? Gray jammed his feet into his tennis shoes and grabbed his keys from the dresser.

"I'm on my way," he said.

GRAY HAD ABOUT a million reasons why he would never, ever consider living in Silverdell again, but Silverdell Memorial Hospital had to be right up there at the top of the list.

That's where they'd brought him after the accident. He'd spent two months inside its white-walled prison, locked in a vicious, unresolvable battle with the doctors and staff.

In his eyes, they had seemed like monstrous machine people, devoid of logical thought, guided only by their knee-jerk, one-size-fits-all, dogmatic conviction that every human being should live. Including Gray.

He had violently disagreed. And, when he discovered the extent of his injuries, he figured God did, too.

But the doctors toiled on, clearly believing they knew better than God. And, in the end, they'd held all the cards—all the IVs and resuscitators, all the burn salves and body casts and traction apparatus. All the skin grafts and miracle drugs and needles and antidepressants and shrinks.

He'd had no choice. And so he had lived.

His chest turned to iron for a minute when he first walked through the double doors and approached the information desk. Then he took a deep breath, told both the panic and the memory to go to hell, and his chest opened again.

He'd learned, long ago, that you had to nip that crap in the bud, or you'd end up in a straitjacket, eating your food through a straw.

"I'm looking for Grayson Harper. He was brought in by ambulance an hour ago, maybe? Possible heart attack?"

The reception clerk had that constipated look that told him she was going to require all kinds of paperwork proof, including social security numbers, patient IDs and maybe a secret decoder ring, before she coughed up any information about his grandfather.

"Look, I'm his grandson. I'm his only living relative. If you'll just tell me what floor he's on, or whether he's still in the E.R.—"

"Gray!" Out of the corner of his eye, he spotted Marianne Donovan, who had been sitting by the far door. "Gray, I was waiting for you! Almeda said she'd already called you and you were on your way."

She rushed up, her cherry-red coat folded over her arm, and smiled at the battle-ax behind the desk. "It's okay, June. I'll tell Gray what he needs to know."

As she drew him off to the side, he realized he felt a little less tense already. Marianne wouldn't be smiling like that if the old man were dead. And if his grandfather had made it this far, he was unlikely to kick the bucket now. Gray happened to know for a fact that the doctors here never let anyone die on their watch.

"Was it a heart attack? Do they know yet?"

She shook her head. "From what I can tell, they think this one was a false alarm. Maybe really bad indigestion, or maybe stress related. But apparently when they ran the tests they saw some things that raised some red flags. Bottom line, they think he may have had other heart attacks, and—"

Gray frowned. "Attacks? As in more than one?"

"Yes. They say there may have been quite a few over the past few months. Or years. Who knows? He's not admitting anything, and obviously he never got help. So they're going to keep him awhile and do a whole barrage of tests."

Gray laughed. "I bet he's loving that."

"He's giving them fits." She sighed. "They wouldn't have told me, either, you know, if I'd just shown up and asked. I only know any of this because I rode over in the ambulance with him. Almeda called me right away, and I live so close, so—"

"Hey." He shook his head and smiled. "It's fine. I'm glad you were there for him. It's not as though I'm going to waltz in after all these years and be jealous because he's got a new best friend."

She nodded a bit ruefully. "Anyhow, he's in fine fettle, denouncing everything and everyone, and generally making himself odious all around. That seems to be what he does when he's frightened or hurt."

Gray laughed, and then regretted it when he realized how bitter he sounded. "Excellent strategy. Can't imagine why it never works."

She reproved him with her eyes, but that was all.

"Anyhow, he said he wanted to talk to you, if you showed up." She sighed again, even more heavily, as if the two of them exhausted her. "Heaven only knows what kind of nasty thing he wants to get off his chest. Are you willing to risk it?"

Gray considered. "Sure," he said finally. "I'm already here. What do I have to lose?"

She raised her eyebrows, as if to say he shouldn't underestimate his grandfather in a rage, but she need not have worried. Gray had never underestimated exactly how toxic his grandfather could be, and he wasn't likely to start now.

Mostly, he just wanted to get it over with…so that he could return to Bell River, and Bree. On the way to the hospital, when he'd had no idea whether his grandfather was going to live or die, he'd put all personal issues out of his mind with little effort.

But now, as the slow elevator crawled to the third floor, the doors repeatedly trying to close, then opening again as people wrestled their way on and off with gurneys, wheelchairs, crutches, flowers, medicine carts and IVs, Gray found his mind straying back to last night.

He'd really taken a hit to the old ego, that was for sure. There he was, in the middle of one of the most amazing sexual experiences of his life…

No, not *one* of the most. *The* most. Brianna Wright turned him on, moved him, body and soul…like no one he'd ever known. Ever.

Her beauty was only part of it, although when he finally took her clothes off he almost couldn't breathe. Beauty was the nursery-school word for what she had. She was magnificent, like some timeless work of art, all alabaster symmetry and transcendent grace. Her proportions, from simple things, like the ratio of her breast to her waist, or her waist to her hips, to more profound things, like the relationship of all that to the ratio of everything on him, were impossibly perfect.

If he'd been a poetic man, he might have said that she seemed to have been designed to resonate with the secret spiritual harmonics that regulated everything in the whole damn universe.

So there he was, resonating all over the place, ready to erupt into a brave new world where he finally understood the meaning of life and love and birth and death, and why the rainbow is made of colors and the flowers bloom in the spring…

And in the middle of all that he'd suddenly realized that Bree had, in return, received…absolutely nothing.

Nothing. Except maybe a level of sexual frustration that must have been the equivalent of an undetonated atom bomb.

He leaned back against the elevator wall and shut his eyes. *Well done, Harper.*

She'd led him to Olympus and turned him into a god.

He hadn't even been able to lead her to one average, garden-variety orgasm.

"Gray? Hey. Are you okay?"

He opened his eyes and saw Marianne's mildly irritated face staring at him.

She scowled. "That was a strange look. What on earth were you thinking about?"

He smiled.

"Just something I've got to take care of later," he said.

And he would. That was a disaster he never intended to repeat.

It wouldn't be difficult. Even last night, she'd been so close. He might have been half-crazed with his own desire, but he always registered things like that. She'd been all the way up at the top of the wheel, strung tight and only half conscious. And the wheel was still spinning and sending off sparks.

He knew that spot. It was the sweet spot, the place where it suddenly all got so easy. Where, if she wanted to, his lover could just stay forever, right on the edge, like a bird on a wire, letting the electricity move through her in shivering waves that never quite set her free.

Or…

He could let her fall. He could adjust the angle, or the pressure, or the pace, by even one degree… He could lean down and take her nipple in his mouth, completing the circuit. He could let his thumb graze the tiny, throbbing nub just above where he filled her. Sometimes all he had to do was say her name and she would suddenly lose all control, cry out and shatter in helpless pieces around him.

Bree had been there, he was sure of it. She had been in that sweet spot, over and over. By all the rules that governed the human body, she should have shattered...

And yet she hadn't. And he suddenly resented all the hours that stood between him and the moment, tonight, when he would be able to set that right.

"Don't put your fierce face on already, Gray." Mari was frowning at him again, looking troubled. "Don't go in spoiling for a fight."

He laughed. Was that what he looked like? Like he was spoiling for a fight? He'd have to work on that before tonight.

"I'll be good," he said meekly.

She stopped before a closed door. "He's got a private room, of course."

Of course. Who would put up with him?

She knocked politely, and in response a gruff voice barked, "What *now,* for God's sake?"

She backed away, putting her hands up as if to say she'd had enough for today. "He's all yours," she said. Then she squeezed Gray's hand. "Seriously. Good luck. I hope it goes all right."

"It'll be fine," Gray said. "And even if he tries to beat me senseless, I'm in a hospital, right? They'll save me. They'll probably put me in the adjoining room."

She laughed and turned to leave. At the last minute, as she turned the corner that would take her out of sight, she waved a hand over her shoulder in a playful goodbye.

Okay. His turn now. Time to get this done.

Squaring his shoulders, Gray opened the door.

CHAPTER FOURTEEN

HIS GRANDFATHER WAS sitting up in the room's one chair, undoubtedly violating doctor's orders. He was hooked up awkwardly to a couple of machines that clearly were intended to service a patient who was expected to be lying in the bed.

His face was thin, his nose hawkish, as he glanced up from the brochure he had been perusing. Gray read a few words upside down. Some patronizing little lecture about the benefits of exercise for heart conditions.

Well, stop the presses.

Apparently his grandfather had the same reaction. He tossed the pamphlet onto the bed tray. "Talk about belaboring the obvious," he said acidly. He folded his bony hands in his lap. "So. You did come. Who called you? Marianne?"

"Does it matter?" Gray sat on the edge of the unused bed, if only to show himself that he could. He didn't have any lingering horror of these nasty slabs of plastic torture. "I came."

"Of course you did. You don't want me to die before your month is up, and I have a chance to write a new will. You were probably afraid that I'd keel over prematurely, leaving everything disposed of as it was before."

Gray smiled coldly. "Terrified."

His grandfather didn't seem to have a response, which surprised Gray. Already, after just a couple of weeks in Silverdell again, he'd fallen back into old patterns, and had expected the rhythm of insult-deflect-insult-deflect to continue ad nauseam.

Silence, unless it was a pointed silence created to be its own form of insult or deflect, didn't really fit the pattern. This silence felt more…impotent.

And yet, it stretched on. Old Grayson fiddled with the belt tied at the waist of his robe, then with the piece of tape that held his IV needle in place on the back of his hand.

Gray noted the purple bruising around the ropy blue vein and wondered if they'd had trouble inserting the needle. Then he wondered why he cared. If there had been trouble, it was probably caused by his grandfather's refusal to cooperate.

But as the seconds ticked on, and the old man didn't seem to be able to focus well enough to hold a conversation, Gray felt a small current of sympathy drift into the ocean of cold antagonism that was his normal emotional state around his grandfather.

Grayson's age was finally catching up with him. Though he had always seemed omniscient, omnipotent and immortal, he was, in the end, merely a human being. He couldn't fight nature forever. Being too stubborn to admit you'd had heart attacks wasn't really the same thing as not having them. Just as being too stubborn to *die* from a heart attack wouldn't really be the same thing as continuing to live.

But if he admitted to physical weakness—or even, God forbid, to cognitive decline—then who *was* old Grayson Harper the First? If he wasn't a force to be reckoned with, a powerhouse to be placated, a lacerating wit to be feared… then what role was left for him to play?

Guess that was the final downside of living your life as an unmitigated bastard. When you stumbled, who had any incentive to help you to your feet? If you'd populated your world with people who wanted to stab you in your bed, when the day came that you were too weak to defend yourself, one of them would do it.

"Marianne said you wanted to talk to me." Gray kept his

voice neutral. He'd promised Mari that he'd be good. On the off chance that his grandfather didn't actually have plans to be vicious, Gray would be smarter not to goad him into it. "What did you want to say?"

Slowly, his grandfather raised his hand to scratch the side of his neck. Gray was shocked to see a tremor in the fingers, a tremor so strong the old man had to start twice before he could manage to lift high enough to reach the spot.

"Would you like some water?" Gray wasn't sure what water would do to help, but some atavistic instinct took over, and water was all he could think of to offer.

His grandfather shook his head, waving away the pitcher with that same trembling hand. It was almost as if he didn't notice the tremor. As if it had been with him a long time, and had become a part of his life.

How long? How long did it take to accept something like that?

Gray knew it would be almost impossible for him to *ever* adjust his mental image of this man. In his head, his grandfather would always be about sixty-five, as vigorous as he was ruthless, as sharp intellectually as he was unforgiving and unkind.

"I wanted to tell you something," his grandfather said suddenly, as if he'd just heard the question. "Something about your father."

Gray shot a glance at the old man, who was staring down at his bedroom slippers. His scalp was as pink as a baby's butt beneath his thinning silver hair.

"Well, I'm not sure I want to hear it."

The old man lifted his head and fixed a glittering eye on Gray. "I'm sure you don't. But that doesn't mean I shouldn't say it. Perhaps I should have told you years ago. Maybe you wouldn't have turned him into such a saint. Saints are…tricky.

They loom so large. Makes it difficult to put them in perspective."

Gray felt suddenly very tired. "Is this a joke? You think I canonized my father because of anything *you* said? I can't remember you praising a single thing about him, ever in your life."

His grandfather nodded. "I'm sure that's true. I was very disappointed in my only son, and I may have been too harsh."

Gray laughed. "*May* have…"

His grandfather pretended not to hear that.

"However," he went on, "you are bright enough to see that there are two routes to sainthood, only one of which is to be beloved and praised for great works."

Gray took the bait. "And the other is…?"

His grandfather shrugged. "The other is to be a martyr."

Gray didn't respond. He saw, of course, what his grandfather was getting at. But so what? What did this have to do with anything?

"Your father drank. Not like a normal person drinks. He drank too much. You know that, even if you don't admit to yourself how big a problem it had actually become."

"Of course I know. I also know *why* he drank."

His grandfather made a dismissive snort. "He drank because he was an alcoholic. People don't become alcoholics because they hate their fathers, Gray. Otherwise, half the world would be drunk all the time."

The old man smiled without mirth. "They become alcoholics because they have something on their DNA strand that makes them susceptible to addiction. Your father had that something."

Gray felt the familiar defensive anger rising in his chest, but he didn't let it come out in words. Instead, he tried just to sit with it, and let it be, for now. Perhaps that was because some sliver of honesty told him the old man wasn't lying about this.

Take Gray himself. He hated his grandfather. For a few years there, he'd hated the whole bloody world. And yet, he'd never turned to booze or drugs. He would have, if they had seemed appealing. But they didn't, so he didn't.

Because he clearly did not have that *something*...

He thought of the portrait hanging in the library, and how it had always felt like a prophecy of doom. He had been created in the mold of his despised grandfather—and shared almost nothing with his beloved father.

How ironic. The twist of fate he'd hated the most might, perversely, have been what saved his life.

"All right," he said. "He was an alcoholic. What is the significance of that? Are you trying to say that makes it okay for you to have let him get behind a wheel? You knew he was drunk. You knew he was upset, unstable, incapable of good judgment. And any fool could see the weather was dangerous."

His grandfather didn't deny it. In fact, he nodded, his eyes shut.

"So why the hell didn't you lock the door and throw away the keys? I'll tell you why. Because you *wanted* him to die."

When he started that short speech, Gray had been talking to the wall, but when he got to the last line he turned, wanting to hurl the final words right into the old man's face and watch the blood drain out of it.

To his shock, his grandfather's face was already bloodless, and twisted in a rictus of pain so hideous that it was almost impossible to witness the change without a rush of instinctive pity...without a reflexive urge to do whatever it took to make agony like that subside.

"Don't," the old man whispered through those painfully twisted lips. "You can say I killed him because I didn't stop

him. You can say it was my fault because I didn't prevent him from leaving."

A small, beaded strand of what looked like spittle clung to the edge of the old man's lips, and Gray realized suddenly that his grandfather's face had contorted so hideously, not in pain, but because he was trying not to weep.

"I know you think that, so say it." His grandfather raised his voice harshly. "*Say it, damn you.* I say it, too, every day of my life. But you *will not say* I…"

Suddenly, the tears spilled, slowly tracking the gaunt furrows of the old man's sunken cheeks. The spit he couldn't swallow dribbled piteously down his chin. Even so, he balled his palsied hand into a fierce fist and raised it menacingly toward Gray, as if to say he'd kill him if he had to.

"You will *not,* you bastard. Do you hear me? You will not say I *wanted* him to die!"

"So…" BREE PAUSED dramatically, aware of the five young bodies leaning forward intently, wondering what the angry matador would do to the bull who refused to fight. Then she smiled. "They had to take Ferdinand home."

"Home?" One of the little girls who had come to today's Saturday-Morning Horse Tales gasped with joy, followed by a spontaneous burst of applause from her four friends, all arranged on the colorful padded benches in front of Bree.

Bree let the celebration continue a minute or two, getting a kick out of the beaming faces. Then, as the girls subsided, she read the last line or two of the book about the bull who loved to smell the flowers just quietly.

When she closed the final page, the youngest member of the audience, five-year-old Teegan Ross, stood up impulsively and began to dance.

"I love Ferdinand the Bull!" She spun herself in circles until she got dizzy and had to plop back down on her violet-polka-dotted cushion. Even then, she folded her hands, prayerlike, under her chin and shivered fervently. "I love him *so much*."

What a cutie! This was only the second Horse Tales session, but Bree could already tell it would be one of her favorite rituals. She was already making plans for next week. She and Rowena had agreed that each story time should have at least one horse story, so...maybe "Misty of Chincoteague" next time?

She'd have to double-check the ages of the children expected—they'd have a whole new group by next week.

Right on the hour, one of the part-time kids' counselors, a pink-cheeked sweetie named Rose, appeared at the barn door, ready to collect her charges. As they bustled out, kids began telling Rose all about Ferdinand, and asking if they could have some time today to sit and smell flowers just quietly.

Bree tidied her books away, then pulled out the supplies to sanitize the cushions. Ideas to improve the event tumbled around in her mind.

Maybe they should build up a lending library of children's books, so that the ones who were inspired by Horse Tales time could let it carry over...

Or maybe in winter, when the barn was cold, they could— *Winter?*

What was she thinking? She wouldn't even be here for the *summer* season. Much less the fall. The winter was just a dream, still rough sketches on a drawing board. Rowena was still crunching numbers nightly, trying to decide if they could afford to offer skiing lessons, and what effect sleigh rides and sledding and fires in every hearth would have on the insurance.

One more story time. That was the extent of her hands-on involvement. Then she'd go back to Boston. Gray would go, too—home to wherever that meant for him, doing whatever he really loved. Eleven days now. A week from this coming Wednesday, he'd win his bet and be on his way.

She took out her phone to see if he had tried to call.

He hadn't.

But surely he would soon? Maybe she was simply feeling mellow from breathing kiddie-joy fumes for the past hour, but she couldn't quite believe he would tire of her after only one time.

The fretting she'd done last night seemed kind of silly now. She hadn't broken down all her lifelong barriers. That would have been asking too much. But he had brought her so much further than she'd ever gone before.

She'd been so *close*.

It might not seem like much to anyone else, but she knew it was practically a miracle. She had been so close that for the first time she believed it might be possible, someday, to just let go and let it happen.

She didn't know if it would take two seconds, or two years. She didn't even know whether Gray would be willing to be patient long enough.... But she knew that, for the first time, she didn't just want to give up and run away. She knew she couldn't pretend it didn't matter to her.

It did matter. Deeply. She wanted things to change. She wanted that icy place inside her to melt and disappear. And for the first time she believed it actually might. And, even though the whole concept still embarrassed her—even frightened her, in a way—she desperately wanted to try.

She glanced at her phone again and decided that if he hadn't called by the time she got off duty, she was going to call him. Or maybe she'd just hike down to the tent. Skip the phoning step, save time...

She laughed, listening to herself. Who was this edgy, buzzing, shameless hussy—and what had she done with the ice maiden?

She'd never felt this way about sex with Charlie. Not even close, not even in the earliest days. At the time, she'd assumed it was because she was in mourning for Kitty. When that never wore off, she reluctantly had to accept that she'd probably gotten her "Contents Are Frozen" label the old-fashioned way—she'd earned it.

Not anymore, though.

The Bree who lived in Boston and the Bree of Bell River Ranch were like two different women. The question was... which one was the real one?

Oh, please... The prayer came without conscious thought. *Let it be this one.*

Through the open barn door, a picture postcard advertising the beauty of Colorado spread out before her. Green pastureland, where glossy, healthy horses cantered lazily under a warm sun. Tidy white paddock fences with clusters of blue flax growing at the base of the posts, as if they'd been decorated for a garden party. In the misty distance, silver mountains stuck up like stony knuckles, giving the impression that the whole happy valley was cupped in the protective palm of some silent giant.

Like a huge, natural rush of wind or wave, love for this exquisite land swept into Bree—almost too much emotion to contain in one body. Impulsively, she twirled herself in happy circles, understanding now why Teegan Ross had needed to dance off her joy.

Suddenly, she felt the vibration of her cell phone, and she froze in place, eagerly digging it out of her back pocket. *Gray,* her mind whispered, even her thoughts sounding breathless.

But it wasn't Gray. It was Dallas.

"Hey, Bree," His voice was warm, as always. He had never hinted that Rowena's ambivalence about Bree had created any in him. He always treated her like family.

"Sorry to have to ask, but is there any chance you can handle the pony rides this afternoon? Ro's not feeling great. I suggested Gray first, but she says he got held up in town. And I can't come in till about four because I'm stuck at the office."

"Of course," she said immediately, but it worried her that Rowena was still feeling bad. She'd looked healthy enough last night, although naturally they were all living in a constant state of fatigue. "Is everything okay?"

"Everything's fine." Dallas would say that anyhow, of course, but he had a very comforting way of making it sound sincere. "She's worn herself out over the past few months, that's all. You know how Rowena is when she's determined— she only has the one speed."

So true. Rowena's passions had "all out" and "off." Nothing in between, like "sensible" or "lukewarm." She'd been in all-out mode for about a year now.

"So maybe this is just her body telling her brain who's ultimately the boss here. If she won't voluntarily slow down, it'll make her do it." He sighed. "She's way too bullheaded for her own good."

Also true. But he didn't sound truly critical. Bree could hear that, even though he worried about his wife, he admired her independence and drive.

Oh, lucky Ro—to have a man who understood her so well and yet seemed to love her flaws as much as he loved her virtues.

"I'll be happy to take the lessons. As long as you're sure there's nothing seriously wrong."

He laughed. "Nothing seriously wrong."

Out of nowhere, a thought occurred to her. Once it did, she was shocked that it hadn't occurred before.

"Dallas." She tried to think how to say it. "Is it possible that…well, that maybe there's actually something seriously *right,* instead?"

He didn't skip a beat. Even if she was a bit dense, obviously the idea wasn't coming out of nowhere for him.

"I just don't know yet, Bree," he said with disarming honesty. "But I sure do hope so. If it turns out to be…" He trailed off for a minute, as though lost in the implications of the whole amazing possibility.

Finally, he laughed. "Well, I'll keep you posted. I can't promise you'll be the *first* to know, because once we tell Alec, he'll be shouting it from the rooftops, and all western Colorado will find out at approximately the same time."

When they hung up, Bree felt even more restless and unfocused than ever, and yet oddly buoyant, like a helium balloon tugging free of its string. She needed to do something, anything, to work off all this emotion. And—no offense, Teegan—she'd like it to be more useful than simply twirling in place.

What she really wanted was to do something for Rowena. For years now, Bree had been so pinch hearted, so grudging as a sister. Even as her heart began to unfurl, she still didn't quite know how to express her feelings freely.

She wanted to do something to show Rowena how much she cared. And now, if there was a baby on the way…

She gathered her things and headed out of the barn. She should get some lunch before the pony lessons. But she couldn't really think about food, or ponies, or anything but how happy she would be for Rowena if it turned out to be true….

A child would be such a gift—a child who was Rowena's own in every way. It would ground her, give her roots. She would have an unquestioned, unconditional bond with another human being, something she had never really known.

It had been so hard for her, growing up under the cloud of Johnny Wright's inexplicable rejection. Bree knew that Ro had always felt as if she didn't quite belong, but she'd never known why. Not until she found the picture that made it fall into place—the picture of her mother's long-ago lover.

Rowena had found the picture quite by accident—actually, Dallas's son, Alec, reportedly was the one who had unearthed it from the secret spot where Moira Wright had hidden it. The photo showed Moira with a mystery man. Rowan…his first name, that's all they knew about him. His first name, his tall, lanky body covered in bulky ski clothes and a smile on Moira's face that spoke volumes.

That smile, and the date written on the back of the picture, about eight months before Rowena's birth, had been enough to open a floodgate, and a million questions had poured through. Before long, Rowena's need to know had been greater than her fear of finding out.

She had sent off samples of her DNA and Johnny Wright's—and the verdict had been unequivocal. There was a zero percent chance that Rowena was Johnny Wright's biological daughter.

Rowan, the man at whom her mother turned that dazzling, unfamiliar smile, had undoubtedly been Rowena's real father.

And that meant he would be Rowena's child's real grandfather.

He might still be alive, and if he was, he would be the child's only surviving grandparent, on either side. He would hold the answers to some of the most important questions of the child's life. Not just what name to write on the "Grandfather" leaf of the baby book's family tree, but more profound questions, too.

He held answers that would speak to who the new baby really was, what kind of people he came from and who else in this world shared his blood and had his back.

All the answers that, if they had come sooner, might have filled the angry, confused and empty spot inside Rowena's heart.

And suddenly Bree knew what she could do for her sister. Well, she couldn't do it herself, but she could hire someone who could.

She could track down and identify the handsome, smiling, athletic man in the photo. She could find the mysterious Rowan.

CHAPTER FIFTEEN

AFTER CLEARING HIS absence with Rowena, Gray had spent the day in town. Most of the time, he camped out at Donovan's, where Mari had unofficially dedicated a small back booth for his use the past couple of weeks. The space was a real help. He made a lot of calls and processed a lot of paperwork there, taking care of things back home.

Thank heaven for laptops, smartphones and digital signatures. And for Mari's unquestioning acceptance of his right to privacy.

It wasn't as easy having two full-time jobs as one might think, especially when they had to be kept entirely separate—even entirely secret, if he wanted to get dramatic about it. He had a whole new understanding of how slick those bigamists you read about had to be, keeping two sets of unsuspecting families in different towns.

And how tired. Frankly, he couldn't imagine why they thought it was worth it.

But today he wasn't tending his secret double life. He was trying to figure out what to do about his grandfather. He'd finally cleared the privacy hurdles by hanging around in the hall after the old man kicked him out of the room and refusing to go away until the doctor showed up for rounds.

Then he put his grandfather more or less on the spot. In the doctor's presence, he got the old man to agree, although not without a lot of snide asides about "deathbed vultures," to add Gray's name to the list of people who could be consulted.

A short list indeed. Disturbingly short. Before Gray was added, Marianne and Almeda had been the only names on it. Gray was shocked. Back when he was a kid, his grandfather had been a big mover and shaker. Where were all the hangers-on that sick old rich people were supposed to be surrounded by? His grandfather's isolation was apparently almost absolute.

Not that Gray had any intention of getting sucked into the situation. Wasn't much he could do from a five-hundred-mile distance, and living any closer than five hundred miles from Silverdell was unthinkable.

But neither could he walk away without making sure old Grayson had a network in place to provide basic care.

Which meant he had approximately eleven days to find some nurses, home-health aides and the like. Maybe a part-time maid to help Almeda keep up with that drafty old marble mausoleum.

He was exhausted by the time he trudged back to the tent. The toughest work he'd ever done, either at this ranch or any other, was ten times easier than a day spent wrangling with doctors and hospitals.

It wasn't fully dark yet as he arrived, but the moon had risen in a blue twilight. Maid service had, as always, left the bedside lamp on, which made the tent glow like a big block of amber against the silver sparkle of the creek.

Something out here was oddly healing. The tumble of water over rocks was a soothing sound, and the minute he heard it, that strung-tight feeling between his shoulders disappeared.

Rowena had asked everyone their thoughts on maybe putting in a spa so that the ranch could offer massages and facials and all those other TLC services people splurged on while vacationing. He hadn't weighed in, not being the herbal-wrap type, but suddenly he thought this might be a good spot for it.

"Gray? Is that you?"

A dark shadow unwound itself from the other shadows under the awning. Little by little, it turned into a slender female body, which stretched like a sleepy kitten, arched and yawned softly.

Bree. Instantly, the strung-tight feeling reappeared, but slightly farther south. He reached the deck just as she made it to her feet. Without saying a word, and certainly without asking himself whether it was the smartest move, he dropped his laptop onto the other chair and then scooped her into his arms.

Their kiss went on…and on. Her mouth tasted like violets in the rain. And her skin felt like satin…if satin had been struck by lightning and glowed hotly gold, the sizzle of electricity trapped in its threads.

It was intoxicating, and every stroke of his lips over hers led to another, until, where she pressed herself against his chest, he could feel her heart skittering wildly. He knew then, that he had to pull back. He'd thought about her on and off all day, of course—and by lunchtime he'd decided that they must talk things over before they mindlessly tumbled into bed again.

But with her heartbeat already racing like that, and his own body fired up and straining, he didn't have a chance of staying sane enough for talking. Not if he didn't slow down now.

He lifted his head sluggishly, with tremendous effort, as if breaking a magnetic pull. He couldn't get more than a few inches, but it was a start.

"Hi, there," he said belatedly. His lips felt thick, as if words didn't come as naturally as kissing. "I missed you today."

She smiled, and he saw that her mouth, too, had been slightly inflamed, distended by the intensity of the kiss. Her pale pink lipstick smeared just beyond the beautiful bow of her upper lip. He had to fight the urge to plant one more kiss there, to cool and soothe its sensitive flesh.

But there wasn't anything cool about him right now. Every inch of him, lips included, was on fire, and all another kiss could do was burn them both.

"Are you hungry?"

She smiled. "No. I ate with the guests, and then I came out here to bring you some of the apple cobbler. It was amazing. I hated for you to miss it."

He glanced toward the small table, where a pretty white pleated bowl sat, filled with something rich with red and gold and cinnamon.

"You came all the way out here to bring me apple cobbler?"

"Of course." She tilted her head, biting her lower lip even as she smiled. "What other reason could I possibly have?"

The gleam of her perfect white teeth against that swollen red lip almost undid him. He had to look away, just to be able to keep from scooping her up all over again.

But she clearly had expected him to. And when he didn't, she tensed slightly. "Gray?" She put her hand on his arm. "Was I wrong to come?"

He shook his head. "No. Of course not. It's just—you know what I *want* to do. I want to take you to bed right now and make love all night, until neither of us can remember our own names."

"Um." Her fingers were hot, twitching slightly against his skin where she held his arm. "I think that's a brilliant idea. Why aren't we doing that?"

He wasn't sure he remembered anymore. The plan that had seemed rational, even imperative, while he sat in Donovan's this afternoon now seemed as silly and useless as planning to follow a child's scribbled map to find imaginary buried treasure.

Still…he retained just enough clarity to understand that his brain might possibly be more trustworthy sitting alone at

Donovan's than it was out here, with Bree's slim, pink-tipped fingers shooting electricity through his system.

They *did* have to talk. His conscience required it.

He'd thought back on last night's sex and realized that there'd been something slightly off from the start, when she'd immediately assumed they should begin, not with mutual foreplay, but with her pleasuring him alone. And then, throughout the night, her body had yo-yoed cruelly between acute responsiveness, almost to the point of surrender, followed by a sudden withdrawal that short-circuited the sexual current and sent her back to square one.

And then, even when he'd been ready to tend exclusively to her, to focus solely on bringing her the release she needed, with no distractions, no fears that she was neglecting to take care of him, she had rejected the suggestion outright. She seemed not to fully register how much she needed to finish what they'd started. When he touched her, she hummed like a live wire, but she pretended that was no big deal…that it was simply, somehow, her normal.

He wasn't a psychologist. But he had a very strong suspicion this was more than just exhaustion or an off night. He wanted to probe a little, maybe try to understand what fears were in her way and how he might be able to help her overcome them.

If he could possibly make sense of this without embarrassing or frightening her, he wanted to try. If he couldn't…

He didn't want to think about what he'd do if he couldn't.

"I just think we should talk a little first. There are so many things we don't know about each other."

"Like what?"

"Like…almost everything." He smiled. "And at the same time, nothing in particular. It's only that we skipped some of the steps involved in most relationships."

"Even relationships like ours?" Her eyes were shadowed,

but quite steady as she met his gaze. "Twelve-day relationships?"

He reached out and touched the swollen bud of her lower lip with his forefinger. "Do you really think relationships are measured only in days?"

She hesitated. And then she shook her head, her lips sliding slowly an inch left, then an inch right, grazing his fingertip with a velvet warmth.

"Then let's go sit by the creek and talk," he said. He let his hand fall, tracing the curve of her neck, the sweet line of her collarbone. "No agenda. We'll just talk about whatever comes to mind. It's still early. We have plenty of time."

She smiled ruefully, and he knew what she was thinking. Eleven days was all they had—and by no measure could that be considered *plenty*. But unless he wanted a repeat of last night's inexplicable, unresolved finale, he had to get answers to some very delicate questions.

He ducked into the tent for a minute and grabbed a blanket and a couple of sweatshirts, in case it turned even colder.

"Let's go," he said as he came out. He extended his hand. She was ready. She took it without hesitation and let him lead her down the short, rocky path overgrown with grasses until they reached the edge of the creek.

They found a smooth spot where the grass was low, the ground fairly level. He spread the blanket, and then he stretched himself out on one side, leaving plenty of room for her to take the other. She waited a couple of minutes before joining him, standing instead at the water's edge, watching its gently sweeping current move silver ripples like cargoes of sequins toward the purple horizon.

Finally, she came to the blanket and sat, then lay on her side next to him. She pulled her knees up a little and tucked her hands under her cheek. Their faces were only a few inches apart.

"What kept you in town today?"

He felt his shoulders stiffen instinctively. He stretched them, consciously working out the tension. Funny, he hadn't considered that she might ask him tough questions, too. But if he wanted honesty from her, he was going to have to offer some in return.

"My grandfather was taken to the hospital this morning," he said as matter-of-factly as he could. "They thought he might be having a heart attack."

"Oh." Her eyes were liquid, blue-black in the darkness. "I'm so sorry. How is he? Is he going to be all right?"

"I think so, for now, anyhow. As it turns out, it was a false alarm today, but they think his heart has been damaged by other, earlier attacks that he never sought treatment for."

"Oh, dear." She blinked thoughtfully. "He's stubborn?"

"Very."

"Is that part of the problem between the two of you? That you're both stubborn? Are you too much alike, do you think?"

He smiled. "Me, stubborn?" But she didn't rush to assure him it wasn't true, so he just shrugged lightly. "Maybe. I contend that he's the real problem, of course, and that I'm simply being firm and fair in the face of his pigheaded arrogance. But no doubt he thinks the same thing about me."

She nodded. "No doubt." She shut her eyes for a moment, as if she was focusing on something she saw in her mind's eye. "Family relationships are so fraught with dangers, aren't they? And I don't mean just things like what my father did. He was insane—they say the brain tumor that killed him might have been affecting him a lot longer than we knew. I mean even in normal families. It's always the people we love who hurt us the most."

"Well, who else has the power?" He thought of how, ultimately, it had been easy to develop a genuine indifference to the morons who had spread some of the worst rumors about the accident that had killed Gray's parents. Creeps like that idiot Farley Miller, the ferret-faced little kid who thought he was a big deal just because his father owned the hardware store. Indifference was easy because Gray didn't actually give a rat's ass what Farley said or thought about anything.

But ever reaching the point that his grandfather's insults would bounce harmlessly off his skin like rubber bullets? Wasn't ever going to happen.

"And besides," he added, "I think the whole notion of 'normal' may be an illusion. Have you ever known anybody who was really normal, once you scratched the surface? I haven't."

"I guess not." She shook her head slowly. Then a small smile lit her face. "But I've definitely known some people who were a whole heck of a lot more 'not-normal' than others, if you know what I mean."

He rolled over on his back and stared up at the stars so that he could begin to get to the point without making her feel cornered. "What about Charlie? How normal was he?"

She didn't answer at first. Then she sighed. "It's hard to be sure. If a person does rotten things while they're involved with me, isn't there a possibility it's my fault, not theirs?"

He turned his head briefly, gave her a very direct look, then returned to perusing the stars. "No."

She chuckled softly, clearly appreciating the absolute certainty of the word. "Well, in that case, Charlie is a rotting fish corpse with legs, and if he's normal I think I'd rather move to Mars."

He liked that, and he smiled, though he remained on his back. She was still on her side, watching him. He could feel her gaze touching him softly—on the jaw, down his arm, across his chest. He tingled everywhere he imagined her eyes, and when she reached the spot between his legs, he turned his head.

She was staring exactly there, her lips parted slightly, her eyes sparkling slivers under her lowered lids. He felt himself stiffening, as if her gaze had actual pressure.

"How long were you with him? Was he the love of your life?"

A beat of silence.

Then she reached out and put her hand on his hip. "Gray, what is it you really want to know? Are you asking me if sex with Charlie was better than the sex I had with you? Because if that's what's bothering you, you should stop worrying. I came closer to…to letting go when I was with you than I had ever imagined possible."

He turned back on his side so that he faced her again. He'd been wrong. Artificial physical distance didn't help, not when the conversation was getting so emotionally naked.

To make this work, he needed to be closer, not farther apart. He needed to touch her while they talked. He reached out, put his arms around her waist and gathered her in. It wasn't sexual—her knees still were tucked against her stomach and grazed him just above the belt.

But it was intimate. It was united, and that was what they needed right now.

"Close doesn't count, Bree," he said softly. "Not in sex. If anything, close is worse. Close hurts."

"I know." She was so near now that when she tilted her head in slightly, their foreheads touched. She rested there, as if the connection soothed. "I learned that last night. But…you have to understand. Close is a big step for me."

Overhead, the shadow of a long-legged bird passed, stirring the air rhythmically with a soft whuffle of beating wings. As if in response to the sensual sound, Bree's fingers kneaded his shoulder softly, and then she restlessly shifted her knees.

"Close is progress," she said. "Close could be…hope."

He could feel the tension building in her even now, and every instinct told him to start over, try again and just keep

loving her, learning her body, teaching her to trust him—
and herself—until whatever stood between them collapsed
and floated away.

But he wasn't quite arrogant enough to be so sure he could
overcome absolutely every bad possibility in the world. And
if he pushed, and pressed, and insisted, and exhausted her,
and still failed…wasn't it possible that he'd do far, far more
damage than she'd already endured?

"Bree, what happens? Do you know? When you realize
that you're not going to be able to…let go…what does it feel
like? Is there something I do—or say? Do you remember
something else? Some*one* else?"

She shut her eyes, but she shook her head. "I don't know.
Everyone tells me it has to be connected to my mother's death,
but I have no idea how. There was no sexual abuse in the family. My father didn't—hurt her that way. They were arguing,
and he pushed her. She fell down the stairs and broke her
neck. He may not even have intended to do it."

"What were they arguing about?"

"She…" Bree's voice suddenly grew thready, and he tightened his hands on her back, as if he could silently remind her
that he was holding on. "She had a lover, and he found out.
He was furious. I think her infidelity was a problem…a problem they'd had before."

She was trembling suddenly, not on the surface, but somewhere deep inside, below the fragile bones and satin skin.
He knew, instinctively, that this must be the dark place….

Of course it was. Could it be any more obvious, when you
thought about it? Her mother had surrendered to passion, to
lovers, to the comfort and thrill of illicit affairs. And she had
been punished for it.

She had, essentially, been executed for the crime of sex.

Maybe that was an absurd layman's oversimplification. He
was no psychiatrist. But how could such a situation not have

created a twisted logic in her daughter's mind? Sex equaled danger. At least the kind of sex that was purely for pleasure. Duty sex, cold, obligatory marital-responsibility sex…that might be safe. But passion? Desire? Abandon?

Too dangerous to consider.

"Did you ever talk to a therapist?" He'd take her to one this minute if he thought it could set her free. Not so that he could have the pleasure of using her body—that was out of the question, no matter what else happened tonight.

But he'd do that, or *anything,* if he thought it would make her happy.

"Every week for more than four years," she said in a dry tone. "Kitty was a wonderful woman, and she did her best to make sure I wasn't scarred by what happened. And the therapists were good. They helped me come to terms with a lot of things."

"But four years…that means you stopped when you were only eighteen or so? Did you even have a clue, that early, that you would find it difficult to—"

"No. But I sought my own doctors when I got engaged to Charlie. They gave me anti-anxiety pills. They tried lots of things, actually, and so did I, for a while. But eventually I just decided it wasn't worth all the fuss. Charlie and I hardly ever—" She smiled. "Well, I figured I just wasn't all that attracted to him. He is a rotting fish corpse with legs, after all."

He reached up and traced her smile with his fingers. He loved her smile. Out here, it caught the moonlight, and it lit her entire face.

When his fingers reached the bow of her upper lip, she kissed them softly. "You, on the other hand…"

He felt his breath come faster. "Yes?"

"You are…" She gave him a look through her lashes. "*Not* a rotting fish corpse."

He shook his head, smiling. Then he put his hands around

her waist again and tucked her as close as their knees would allow him to bring her.

"I want you to spend the night with me, Bree. The whole night. No slipping away in the darkness. Will you do that?"

"That's why I'm here," she said simply.

He knew, though, that she still didn't understand. He hoped he could find the right words. Ducking his head, he sought her gaze and held it.

"But I'm not going to make love to you. Not tonight."

"You're not?" Her voice was small, like a child's, and her eyes were dark.

"No. We both need peace tonight, far more than we need sex. I don't want to bring those old shadows into the tent with us. No talk of letting go, or surrender, or 'coming close,' or any words that are really synonyms for failure and fear. No memories of other struggles or other people. Just the two of us, easy together. And sleep."

She touched her hand to his hair. He took a deep breath. "Can you do that, Bree?"

"I can try," she said.

CHAPTER SIXTEEN

IN THE END it was easy, so much easier than she could have imagined.

He gave her a heavy sweater to wear, and she slipped it on before sliding her jeans off. Without awkwardness, he donned sweatpants and a T-shirt. After she climbed into bed, he fed the wood fire in the small black stove that vented through the roof of the tent, until gradually its crackling warmth overcame the chilly night air.

Then, for a long time, they simply lay in the luxurious king-size bed, with soft, downy quilts and blankets and pillows to keep their body heat close. They talked about the silliest, most irrelevant things. Movies, books, trips they'd taken that went nightmarishly, comically wrong, sights that had been magical and unforgettable. They talked about Bell River, and she told him about having hired a private investigator to identify Rowena's biological father.

She even told him about Charlie. They were tired by then, a little punch-drunk, and had reached the point at which everything seemed hilarious. When she described Charlie jerking the sheet off the bed, desperately and futilely trying to cover himself at the expense of his ladylove, Gray had laughed out loud.

"Well, at least now I know where the rotting-fish-corpse image came from," he said. And realizing he'd hit on a truth even she hadn't consciously seen, Bree began to giggle so goofily she actually couldn't breathe, and he had to reach out and grab her hand to make sure she didn't slide off the side of the bed.

It was nonsense, more like being best friends who felt free to be ridiculous together. With sex off the agenda, there was no need to be self-conscious, to worry about how you looked, or whether you said or did the "right" things.

You could simply say the things that were true.

And then, deep into the night, he offered her answers to questions she hadn't ever felt free to ask, like where he lived—northern California—and what he did for a living—he worked on a ranch that bred horses.

He even told her about how he'd avoided the whole ranch-cowboy life for years just because he knew his grandfather longed for him to take that route. He said it had taken him far too long to wise up to how incredibly self-destructive that had been.

"I was late catching on because I was blinded by my anger. But I finally understood that if I made my life choices merely to annoy my grandfather, I was still letting him control me. I wouldn't have real independence until I stopped caring what he thought—good or bad. So I decided to follow my gut, which led me straight to the ranch."

Bree mulled that over, nestled in her warm cocoon of downy blankets and soft sheets. So that explained why he was such a natural at Bell River. He really was a cowboy, not just the playboy heir to a marble-quarry fortune.

But it just made the mystery of the money even more inexplicable. She blinked heavily, feeling her tiredness overtake her. She wondered whether he'd waited this late to share anything meaningful because he'd *wanted* her to be too drowsy to be terribly analytical or ask persistent follow-up questions.

But if he had, he'd chosen the wrong tactic. Actually, she would have been much more diffident if she'd been fully awake. Exhaustion always hit her a little like liquor. She didn't think all that clearly, but she had very few inhibitions about sharing her muddled thoughts. It had driven Charlie crazy.

"Can that really be true, though?" She yawned. "That you entirely stopped caring what your grandfather thinks, I mean. If you had, I don't believe you'd be here."

"Here? You mean in Silverdell?"

"At Bell River." She shut her eyes, letting the words free-associate, since she was far too tired to be entirely logical. "The thing is, I don't believe you're really after the money. I've spent a lot of time around people who are money crazy, and they're obnoxious. Really. Just awful. They're nothing like you."

He chuckled. "It's a lot of money, Bree."

"I know." She forced her eyes open. "But still…" She yawned again, and her eyes insisted on shutting. "I just can't believe that's what brought you here. Not entirely, anyhow. You're here because some tiny part of you wants to fix things between the two of you."

"Nope."

"Yep." She snuggled deeper under the covers, reaching out her hand to touch his shoulder, enjoying the hot-velvet feel of his skin over the rounded muscle. She just let her palm curve around it, fitting as if it belonged there. "You know how I know?"

Almost absently, as if he, too, did it without thinking, he put his hand over hers. It felt so warm. Strong. And safe. Her body was relaxing, her mind drifting even further away on this unmoored, king-size dream craft with downy, billowing sails.

"How do you know?"

"I know," she said thickly, "because I've done the same thing. Last year I came to Bell River, and I said it was about money. About Rowena spending too much or something. But really, way down deep inside, I just wanted to be around her, because maybe then we would work it out."

"And did you?"

She laughed, realizing her example was dumb. But it was the best she could think of when she was drifting so far above the conversation, above the tent and the creek and the whole of reality, really.

"Nope. I made a giant mess of it. But that's not the point. The point is, I wouldn't have come just for the money." She squeezed his shoulder. "And neither would you."

Maybe he answered her. Maybe he told her she was dead wrong and didn't understand him one bit. But if he did, she didn't hear it. She had suddenly realized how good it would feel to let herself sink into sleep, just let it happen without a fight, and it did. It felt wonderful, the most peaceful feeling she could remember for a long, long time....

She must have slept for hours, because later, when she heard an anguished cry nearby, sounding exactly like a lost child, she woke from a very deep sleep with a start, terrified by the sound.

"It's okay." Gray's voice was soothing in the darkness. He sounded gentle, quiet, but as if he'd been wide awake the whole time. "It's just an elk."

An elk...yes, of course. How could she have forgotten that sound? She pushed her hair out of her eyes, trying to orient herself.

Sometime while she slept, she must have shifted, because she realized she was spooned against Gray, the solid wall of his torso behind her back, and his knees tucked in the hollow behind her own. His strong, warm arms were wrapped around her waist.

The elk cried out again, eerie in the deep, echoing night, which seemed to press blackly on the tent.

"It's all right," he said again. "I won't let anything hurt you."

She fuzzily considered that promise for a second or two... but not for long. On some very primitive level, she already knew it was true.

She wriggled back against him so that their bodies were a perfect fit, and not even a tiny black sliver of night could slip between them. Then she made a small, contented sound, hoping he knew it meant she believed him. It meant a lot of other things, too, but she was too blurry-minded to sort out what they were, or how to say them.

She purred one more time, tugging his arms tighter so that they encased her in warmth. And then, blanketed in bliss, she slid effortlessly back into sleep.

BY FRIDAY, SHE'D spent six nights with him in that big, wonderful bed. Not all of them had been as easily platonic as the first. Sometimes the comfort touches deepened, or strayed. Sometimes they kissed, because it seemed impossible not to.

Always, she felt the slow coiling of desire, low in her midsection, as her body readied itself for more. But his willpower was amazing. Though she knew he wanted her—he had no way to hide it—he never allowed either of them to reach the point of no return.

Only once did it seem that his iron control might weaken.

On Tuesday, the new guests had arrived, and she and Gray were busy in separate parts of the ranch. By the time they made it back to the tent, they were exhausted, which should have made restraint easier but didn't. Apparently it took a lot of unseen energy for him to hold the fire back.

Somehow, he held on then, too. He was just as charming, just as entertaining and intimate as ever, until it came time to actually sleep. Then he positioned himself with his back to her, a little farther over. And for the first time she didn't wake in the night to discover she'd spooned herself against him.

He hadn't been kidding when he'd said he thought they should wait. Wait for what, exactly, though? He'd said only that he had to be sure she was ready.

She had no idea how he would judge that, or whether she could make any promises. But she understood. She was, in her own quietly frigid way, still too mixed up—she could sense that he saw her as impaired. Or at least her emotions were. He wasn't the type to want to feel that he'd taken advantage. He clearly would rather not get tangled in her issues and end up feeling guilty for something that should have been purely fun.

So, though the awareness of desire was always present, he never let it get raw, or even disagreeable. It was more like a sense of always being plugged in, with the current flowing, potent, but for the moment harmless.

Sometimes a hum, a flutter, a pulsing, a warmth…but never an ache. Never pain.

The only really painful part was watching their days tick down.

On Friday, she found herself with a few free hours now that Rowena had hired more staffers. Three part-time children's counselors, half a dozen part-time wranglers and a full-time woman named Maura who would function as receptionist, reservationist and concierge had all come on board in the past few days. Maura, particularly, had been a coup. She had come out of retirement to take this job, and had decades of experience, making her easily the most useful employee in the place. Up to and including the Wright sisters themselves, who were still neophytes, and struggling to learn as they went.

Gray and Dallas were busy climbing around on scaffolding this afternoon, with hammers and nail guns and all kinds of tools they loved to play with. Rowena had accused them of being glad the contractor was running behind schedule for getting the arts and crafts building finished.

That way, he'd needed to call for help.

The upshot of all these changes was that Bree felt a little lost, as if she wasn't really needed anywhere. She wandered into Rowena and Dallas's wing and poked her head into the room they'd set up as a home office.

Rowena sat at her computer, staring at something on the screen.

"Need any help with anything?" Bree plopped herself on one of the chairs nearby. "Amazingly, I'm free until the bonfire tonight."

"No…" Rowena seemed distracted. "I'm just writing back to Bonnie. Though when, or even if, she'll check email again, there's no way to tell."

"Is she okay?"

"She says she is." Rowena chewed on her thumbnail. "I sure hope so."

Bree hadn't known Bonnie very well—she'd met her only a couple of times. Bonnie used to do some housekeeping work for Rowena, back before they decided to launch the dude ranch project. Though she'd apparently been a bit of a mystery woman, she and Rowena had become very close friends.

Some shadowy personal problem had forced Bonnie to disappear, though, right after Rowena and Dallas's wedding. Dallas's younger brother, Mitch, had gone with her, as protector and friend…and probably lover, too.

They'd been gone almost a year now, and Rowena clearly felt no closer to knowing what the problem was, or how to help her friend. Bree had seen how much it upset Ro, and she wished there was something she could do.

If only the private investigator would call with news. She tried to be patient. It had been only a few days, but maybe he'd get lucky.…

"Honestly, Bree, there's no emergency right now." Rowena closed the email and seemed to make an effort to be more cheerful. "Maybe we're getting the hang of it, or maybe this group is just easier." She sighed. "Lord knows *everything's* easier without Mabel Madison around."

Bree laughed. "I'm sure Gray feels safer now that she's gone. What a holy terror! You should see the bruises on his shins."

Leaning back in her desk chair, Rowena wriggled her eyebrows as if Bree had said something dirty. "No thanks. I'll leave that to you."

Bree rolled her eyes, and Rowena chuckled, clearly enjoying herself.

"Okay, seriously, if you're feeling that you must martyr yourself, Alec will be home from school in—" Rowena glanced at her watch "—two hours. If you could keep him out of my hair while I talk to the insurance guy at three, that would be fantastic."

"Sure. I want to add a couple of tables to the Horse Tales area. I'll make him help me paint them."

"Good." Rowena picked up a stack of unopened mail. "Between now and then, why don't you use the time to get some rest?"

"I'd rather be busy." Bree grabbed a superhero figure that Alec had left on the desk and made it wave its sword at Ro. "I'm Action Brianna. And I'm not tired."

Rowena grinned. "You're not? After spending all these nights at the tent? I'm sorry, sis, but sounds as if there's something you guys aren't doing right."

Caught by surprise, Bree felt herself flushing. Ro was joking, of course. She had no idea how close to home the joke had hit. And, while the sisters had made great strides during this long visit, Bree still wasn't ready to confide things this intimate to Rowena.

Or to anyone. She didn't know what was really happening with Gray. Their relationship, whatever it was, was fragile and utterly unique, at least in her life. She wouldn't even have known how to describe it.

Rowena didn't seem to notice Bree's hot cheeks, thank goodness. She had inserted the letter opener into the first piece of mail and slit it open. As she glanced at the letter inside, she moved on to another topic.

"Okay, well, maybe you can help me decide where to put the spa."

"Are we definitely getting a spa?"

"Yes." Rowena smiled. "We're definitely getting one *someday.* I'd love to build it as part of Phase Two, but it all depends on how much it costs. And that depends, to a large extent, on where we decide to put it. So what do you think? We've narrowed the location down to Cupcake Creek, where Gray's tent is now, and Little Bell Falls."

Bree shuddered. "Oh, not Little Bell Falls!"

"Why not?" Rowena lowered the mail to her lap. "What's wrong with Little Bell? It's beautiful out there."

"It's creepy." Bree thought about the heavily treed spot, with its horsetail waterfall appearing out of nowhere and its unnaturally round, disturbingly deep, plunge pool at the bottom. "It's too remote, anyhow. Do you think the guests will want to make a trek like that just to get a massage?"

Rowena's brow creased. "Are you sure you're remembering the spot correctly? It's really not *that* far. And it's not a bit creepy. How long has it been since you've seen it?"

Bree tried to remember. She couldn't.

"A very long time," she admitted. "I never liked it, so I didn't go there the way you did. I bet it's been twenty years."

"Well, then." Rowena looked smug. "You clearly haven't given it a fair chance. So there you go. That's what you're going to do with your spare time."

Bree gave her sister a sour look. It was strange, because she couldn't put her finger on exactly what the problem was. But she knew from the tightness in her gut that she definitely did *not* want to go out there.

Maybe she was just partial to Cupcake Creek, for obvious reasons, and resented any other location even being considered.

"Ro, it's clear as day that you've already decided you prefer Little Bell Falls, so what's the point in my going?"

Rowena had already found one of the maps they gave arriving guests, pulled it open and had begun sketching out a special, relatively convoluted back route to get to Little Bell. The longer she had to keep sketching, the more absurd it seemed.

"Ro, look how far you're having to draw that line. That's what I mean by 'too remote.' That's what anybody would call too remote."

Rowena held out the map, and Bree saw that she was wearing her dreaded stubborn look.

In spite of her reluctance, she had to laugh. "Oh, the horrors of being the younger sister," she lamented. "You're so sure you're the boss of me."

But exactly like in the old days, Rowena was not moved. "Just check it out. It's got charm. It's got moving water, a great view of the mountains, ancient trees and absolutely everything needed to make the guests feel they've been transported to another world."

"Well, they have. You have to get a passport, two airplanes and a Native American guide merely to find your way out there."

"What on earth is *wrong* with you?" Rowena scowled. "It's gorgeous. Don't you remember the columbine everywhere? The goldeneye? The bluebells?"

That did sound familiar. Something in Bree's chest tightened at the mention of the wildflowers, but she still couldn't

place any particular memory that caused such a negative reaction.

"Okay. Fine. I'll go look at it. Although you know it'll cost
more to put it way out there—"

"Go," Rowena commanded. This time she had picked up
the letter opener again and pointed it at Bree.

And so, out of a lifetime's habit—and a growing curiosity to find out why she had such an irrational dislike for the
spot—Bree went.

CHAPTER SEVENTEEN

IT TOOK HER twenty minutes to find the place. Though Ro's directions were great, she got lost twice—her subconscious still resisting the visit, perhaps?

Finally she spotted the gigantic, spreading live oak that Rowena had drawn on the map, aware, obviously, that the monstrous tree would be the most noticeable landmark for miles.

Even the tree gave Bree a chill. Something felt unnatural about a tree that had outlived several generations of Bell River owners and would undoubtedly outlive her, too. And every year it grew bigger, stretching its limbs out horizontally, and sometimes in fantastically twisted shapes, until it looked like a gigantic, deformed brown spider, crouching there by the plunge pool, waiting...for something Bree couldn't name.

The hiss of the falls bothered her, too. Partly because it sounded deliberately hostile, like the sound a snake makes to warn you to stay away. But also because the sound was so loud you just knew it might be covering other sounds.

Even more disturbing sounds.

It wasn't until she glimpsed the bluebells growing on the western edge that things began to fall into place. But the minute she saw them, she froze in her steps.

It was early for bluebells. She wasn't sure how she knew that, but she did. Bluebells weren't usually out, at least here by the falls, until mid-June, at least.

And then, as if the falls had suddenly roared to life and started racing toward her like a malevolent tidal wave, she was suddenly flooded with a memory so vivid, so powerful and so terrible…

For a minute she thought she could no longer breathe.

She felt herself going down onto her haunches, as if the pressure of it forced her toward the ground. She clutched some kind of small plant, as if it could keep her from being swallowed up by the earth, or falling off it. But the plant bent, too, crushed either by her or by the memory's dreadful weight.

She shut her eyes, spinning, dizzy. She didn't want to remember.

But she did…

She was about six. It was June. She was mad because she wanted to pick some bluebells for her dollhouse garden.

But there weren't any bluebells near the house. The only ones she'd ever seen were at Little Bell Falls.

She wasn't allowed to go that far alone, and usually that wasn't the kind of rule she ignored. She was always aware of what happened to Ro when she disobeyed an order, and it scared her. Ro didn't care, but Bree wasn't as brave as her big sister. She didn't like getting in trouble.

But today was about the tenth day in a row that her mother had hardly even come home to sleep. That wasn't fair.

So she'd saddled up Tommy, her paint, and hooked a wicker basket over the saddle horn. She needed something to carry the bluebells back in. Then she'd bumped Tommy's sides softly with her heels, and they'd cantered down to the falls.

She was only a little afraid. She didn't really think she was taking a very big chance. She didn't see how she could get caught.

She didn't have any idea where her mother was. She was too young to even consider the possibility that she *ought* to know things like that. Mom was just *Somewhere Else*. Somewhere Having Fun.

It never, ever occurred to her that *Somewhere Else* was Little Bell Falls.

Even now, more than twenty-four years later, she still had no memory, none at all, of what the man with her mother had looked like. He had been just a naked, white body without a face.

But why didn't he have a face? Had his face been obscured by a tree limb?

Even without a face, he had looked like a bad man because he was naked. Everyone, even her mother, had told her that if a man ever tried to make her look at his private parts, or touch them, he was a very bad man, and she should tell on him.

But she *couldn't* tell on him, because her mother was naked, too. Bree had no visual memory of that, just a memory of trying to hold in her reeling mind the confusing certainty that her mother was outside where people could see her, where this naked man could see her, and she had no clothes on.

Bree was so dumb she didn't even know she should run away, quick before they saw her seeing them. She just stood there, with the small twigs at the end of the oak tree branches scratching her bare legs, and heard herself make a whimpering sound.

Rowena called it Bree's spoiled-baby sound. Bree wished she could tell Ro that this time *she* wasn't really making it. It seemed to be making itself, using her throat and voice without her permission.

Her mother must have heard it because she turned her face toward the sound. She looked mad and embarrassed, and scared, too. Like when she took a bath at home and forgot to lock the door, then jumped when Bree came in, as if it was Bree's fault she hadn't guessed her mother needed privacy.

For a minute, her mother's eyes searched the big tree. And then, when she saw Bree and their gazes locked, she seemed to go crazy, as if she was having a fit, an epileptic fit, or a conniption fit, maybe, like Ro always said people did.

Her mother began pushing at the man's chest, using the hard, bony part at the bottom of her palms. And she started this awful, embarrassing scrabbling with her feet, as if she wanted to stand, but the man's big white legs were in her way. His legs were between her legs....

Bree couldn't look at it anymore. She might be watching her mother die right this very minute, or choke, or have a heart attack, or something. And she didn't want to see the man's face, but he was getting up, getting off her mother. He was going to turn around, and then she would see everything she wasn't supposed to see....

She ran back to where Tommy was standing, quietly eating grass, not even knowing what had happened with her mother. She had started to cry, and she almost fell down when she tried to get on Tommy's back.

But she made it, because she was too afraid to fail. And when she got the reins in her hand, she dug her heels into his sides. She must have dug hard, way too hard, because he started to run. He galloped faster than she'd ever gone, faster than she was *allowed* to go.

He knew the way home, so he just ran. When he tried to jump over Cupcake Creek, she fell off. She hit her head on the bank and it hurt, a lot. She got very wet, but she didn't pass out. She just lay there, crying, in the hot June sun, until her mother, who was now dressed normally and all alone, found her there.

Her mother picked her up, kissed her and hugged her and cried a little bit, too, though she didn't mention what had happened to make them both cry. Bree knew, right then, that her mother was never going to explain.

And she didn't want Bree to ask.

When they got home, Tommy was already waiting by his stall, looking as if he felt bad for knocking her off.

Bree forgave him. She was glad Tommy was okay because that meant there was nothing that would have to be explained to Daddy. She hadn't even torn her dress.

And so no one ever mentioned it again.

SHE HAD CHANGED, Gray thought. She looked…somehow… indefinably…

Different.

Okay, moron. That wasn't specific enough to mean a damn thing.

From his post by the back porch, where he handed sing-along booklets to each person who came out, Gray watched Bree. She moved around the bonfire, projecting almost as much warmth as the fire itself. She chatted with the guests, laughed at their jokes, squatted reassuringly to get on level with their shy children.

But she'd always been an accomplished hostess. That was her career. So what was actually different about tonight?

Well, for one, she appeared more confident. Less self-conscious, and yet at the same time more *un*consciously sensual. It was as though, for the first time in her life, she was wearing a skin that fit.

Blue moonlight in her hair, auburn-and-pink bonfire flames reflecting against her arms, golden sweater over her jeans…she looked like stained glass come to life.

Real, hot-blooded life. Yes, that was the difference—he'd guessed it from the start. The difference was the level of heat she sent out. She didn't move like an ice princess anymore. She moved like a woman who had fully and finally thawed.

Oh, really? How *convenient.*

Probably this was just his libido talking, doing a masterful sales job, hoping to weasel its way around his determination to keep from exploiting a damaged, vulnerable woman.

Naturally, the libido had been counting the days—just as the rest of him had. Every inch of him heard the clock ticking and knew he was running out of time. Five days from today, his bet with his grandfather came to an end, and he'd be on the next plane to Monterey.

So could he trust what his so-called "instincts" were telling him? Wasn't it just a little too opportune that somehow, in the twenty-four hours between the agony he'd endured all night last night and *now,* she had somehow cast years of emotional chains aside and been born again as sexual fair game?

The last guest came down the steps, and he handed out the booklet with a sense of relief. He felt the magnetic pull of her all the way across the backyard, and it had been practically splitting his body in two.

He made his way over to her with minimal detouring—if anyone was far enough away that it was plausible he couldn't hear them over the crackle of the bonfire, he just shrugged sadly, put his hand to his ear in the universally recognized sign for "too loud" and moved on.

Even so, three people snagged him. By the time he reached her, she was sitting next to Barton, who had his guitar out and had started to play.

She smiled at him....

Come on, boss, his libido taunted, *are you imagining* that? That sock in the solar plexus? She might as well have reached out her hand, struck a match and held it to his central nervous system. He was instantly on fire.

She glanced ruefully at the seats around her, which were filling up fast. Barton, still strumming, raised one eyebrow at Gray and grinned. "If you think I'm gentleman enough to give you my seat, son, you're mistaken. You snooze, you lose."

Gray laughed, even though he didn't much feel like it. He

glanced at her other side. Great. It was Alec, who had about as big a crush on Bree as Gray did, even if he had a much purer heart about it. His only dream was to buy her a horse of her own. He thought that might convince her to stay at Bell River.

Well, sure, Gray's libido observed nastily. *That's Alec's only Bree-dream because he's nine. It's easy to be pure of heart when you're nine.*

Alec scowled. "No way, Jose," he said without even waiting for Gray to say a word.

He glanced at Bree. She was laughing softly. But Gray smiled back, undaunted. He'd be darned if he was going to let an old man and a kid take his woman from him. He shrugged, as if to say "they made me do it," and then he sat in the grass right in front of her, with his back against her knees.

For a second, she seemed startled. No one else was sitting that close to the fire. He dropped his head back across her thighs and smiled at her upside down. Rowena and Dallas obviously already knew—and frankly, he didn't give a darn who else around here discovered they were a couple.

She laughed out loud, gazing down at his mischievous grin. But a second later she ran her fingers through his hair, slid them around to his ear and tugged on it gently. He had to take a deep breath. Who knew the earlobe was connected directly to the...other parts?

"Come on back here, you idiot, before you go up in smoke." She softened her legs just a little, so that he could wedge his torso between them. He was tall enough that he could rest his elbows on her kneecaps, and he did, mostly for the excuse to dangle his hands down the sides of her legs and stroke the underside of her knees with secret fingers.

He must have looked particularly comfortable and content, because, before long, husbands and wives, moms and kids, even brothers and little sisters had arranged themselves the same way. He gave Bree another upside-down smile.

"Yeah, you're a trendsetter," she said, her tone affection-ately mocking. For punishment, he stroked the sensitive flesh behind her knee until, with slightly unsteady fingers, she bat-ted his hand away.

A few minutes later, Barton launched into his signature version of "Red River Valley." The crowd stilled, listening to the elegant baritone sing the plaintive words about love and loss…about the man who was leaving the valley and the heartbroken girl who had loved him true.

Everyone knew the song, of course, so when Barton called for support, the guests responded. First just a few, the best singers who weren't afraid to stand out. Then, on the easy chorus, everyone sang along, even the children.

It should have been a mess. Gray could hear the boys whose unpredictable octave-changing squeaks announced that they'd officially hit puberty. He could hear the very old, whose sweet tones quavered. And of course the tone deaf added their own special harmonies. But in spite of all that, the effect of those gathered voices rising into the cool, crisp air was pure magic.

Three songs later, Gray eyed Barton suspiciously. Every single tune had been sad, every one about the pain of leave-taking, the heartbreak of saying goodbye.

Was Barton trying to tell him something?

On the other hand, maybe it was Gray's own hyperaware-ness of his impending departure that made the choices seem deliberate. "On Top of Old Smokey" was a pretty standard campfire song, and so was "Down in the Valley."

But then came "Shenandoah," which clearly belonged on the East Coast. And finally…

"Jamaica Farewell" at a dude ranch in southwestern Colo-rado? *Come on, Barton. Give a guy a break.*

When the old man caught Gray shooting him that ques-tioning glance, he grinned, admitting everything, and obediently switched gears. "The Bear Went Over the Mountain," "Puff the Magic Dragon" and "I've Been Working on the Railroad" brought the tempo up and finally got the tears out of everyone's eyes.

But right in the middle of the laughter and fun, in response to some signal only she could hear—or some vibration only she could feel—Bree tensed, and she began digging in her jeans pocket for her phone. When she found it, she looked at the screen, then almost fell over her own feet, and Gray's, trying to extricate herself from the bench.

She managed to stay erect, and hurried away, answering as she went. "This is Bree," he heard her say in a voice as tight as a guy wire.

He got up, too. In case she needed him.

It had better not be the fish corpse calling. Not now, and not ever again. The story of harem boy's birthday-party sex scandal had seemed funny that first night because she'd told it with charm and humor. But the more Gray thought about the humiliation she must have felt, the more he wanted to see how Charlie Newmark adjusted to life as a eunuch.

He made his way across the spotlighted lawn to where Bree had found a shadowed corner in which to take the call. He made sure she saw him, for support, but then he hung back out of earshot, in case she really needed privacy.

The call didn't last long. She paced as she talked, her golden hair and golden sweater moving in and out of a shaft of moonlight like a looping dream. He tried to read her face, but all he could be sure of was that she felt tense. Whether with excitement or with anger or fear, he couldn't make out from where he stood.

Behind him, Barton had begun "Loch Lomond." More goodbye music...

Before the short, sad song was over, Bree had returned.

Her eyes were shining, and his heart relaxed. Whatever it was, it was good news.

He waited, not wanting to ask. If she didn't volunteer, he'd just have to live with the question.

"That was the investigator," she said, her voice low and breathless. She glanced toward the campfire, as if she wanted to be certain Rowena was safely out of earshot.

He was surprised. That possibility hadn't occurred to him. It seemed too soon, either way. Bree had offered the man very little to work with, so definitive answers seemed unlikely after he'd worked on it less than a week. But surely no decent detective would have thrown in the towel so quickly, either.

"Oh, Gray." She clasped her elbows with her hands, as if to hold herself safely together. "He's found Rowena's father."

BREE SAT IN her suite until almost midnight, waiting for the guests to retire to their rooms and cottages. It took a while, because the campfire had been such fun, and because the spring weather was so lovely: no chilling wind, no rain, no frost, nothing to drive them indoors.

She'd sent Rowena a text message earlier.

Have you got a minute to spare later? I'd like to talk. Just us.

Rowena's answering text had been typically brief.

K. Front desk. Not till midnight. At least.

Trying to be patient, Bree watched from her window, holding the thick, sealed manila envelope the detective had delivered immediately after his call. She thought of Gray, waiting for her in his amber-lit tent by the creek, and hoped he understood why she had to do this first, no matter how long it took.

The parking lot, seen from her window, bustled with activity for a while, as robe-clad guests darted back out to grab the last paperback books and pill cases they'd forgotten earlier. But gradually the cottage doors stopped opening, and the area slipped into a trance, a misty film creeping across the windshields of the sleeping trucks and minivans.

One by one, the cottage lights went out. Even the scent of the bonfire finally disappeared, though it had lingered the longest, without its usual stiff breeze to fly away on.

Surely, she told herself, the coast was clear now. The ranch seemed to have curled up on its moonlit green hills and closed its eyes for the night. Its silence was broken only by the occasional hoot of an owl, a nicker now and then from the stables and the half-heard murmur of Bell River in the distance.

Even so, she waited another half hour because Rowena had asked her to.

Midnight. At least.

At twelve-fifteen, her patience ran out. Easing her door shut behind her, she moved noiselessly down the stairs. The silence was almost eerie, actually.

Then she heard a creak just below her. The skin at the back of her neck prickled, and for the first time ever she considered the possibility that she might see her mother on these stairs, just as the housekeeper still insisted she did, every day.

If Moira Wright were ever to materialize, wouldn't it probably be now? Now, when Bree was carrying her mother's deepest secret in this envelope, prepared to deliver the truth that might finally set Rowena free?

For a chilled second, her feet stilled, and she grasped the railing for balance. She realized, with a swooping sensation of suddenly being hollowed out, that she really didn't know how her mother would feel about what she'd done.

If the ghost could appear, would she be happy? Grateful, even? Would Moira be relieved to know that Johnny Wright couldn't hurt anyone anymore? That it was safe for Rowena and her biological father to find each other at last?

Or would her spirit manifest as a nightmare, blocking Bree's passage and declaring herself betrayed? Moira had kept the secret of Ro's real paternity her entire life. She'd carried it with her, as the cliché went, to the grave. Would she consider it a sacrilege for Bree to disturb the shadows now?

Oh, for heaven's sake. Bree gripped the envelope tighter and ordered her legs to continue down the stairs. She didn't believe in ghosts. Period. She had too much respect for the dead to believe any such thing. Why would unchained spirits, who had the universe at their command, feel the slightest desire to float around earth, ringing bells and tipping tables and dispensing cryptic advice that would be mostly misinterpreted or overlooked?

She reached the bottom of the steps without incident, of course. *No ghosts.* For better or worse, the people who got left behind were on their own.

Just as she rounded the corner to the registration desk, her cell phone beeped again.

GD sprinklers busted. Meet shed instead?

That was fine with her. More privacy out there, anyhow. Though…she did wish she'd brought along a sweater. Even on gorgeous spring nights like this, sometimes the bottom fell out of the thermostat and the temperature would plummet to near freezing in the blink of an eye.

But she didn't feel like traversing those stairs again, whether it made sense or not. So she just went on outside, around the western wing of the house, and headed for the utility shed.

When she got within a few yards, she heard Rowena cursing. Her feet froze one more time, which made her smile.

Truth be told, she was still far more intimidated by Ro in a mood than she ever could be by the prospect of encountering a ghost.

"What the Sam Hill is *wrong* with you?"

Oh, that's why the cussing was so loud. Bree had forgotten that the timer, and the valves, were all situated on the outside of the shed. Rowena stood just a few feet away, flashlight in one hand and a screwdriver in the other, staring at the still-locked green timer box.

"What's wrong?" Bree looked over Rowena's shoulder sympathetically.

"Everything. First the sprinklers didn't come on when they were supposed to, and now I can't even check the timer. The blasted screw is stripped."

Oddly, Ro's voice sounded almost on the edge of tears, and she smacked her screwdriver against the edge of the plastic box three times hard, not for any apparent purpose except to vent some intense frustration.

Bree wasn't sure what to make of the overreaction. This sprinkler thing wasn't likely to be a big problem—not the kind that cleaned out their cash reserves or shut down the ranch for days, anyhow. Ro handled tougher things than this without blinking, every single day.

But in the cold beam of the flashlight, which wandered around as Rowena yanked at the box and eventually ended up right in her face, Bree could see circles of exhaustion under Rowena's eyes.

Maybe, with one thing and another, Ro had just run into one problem too many.

When Bree saw her sister start to slide her nails in the groove of the timer-box door, ready to pry it open, she put her hand out. "Hey. Want me to try?"

As if Bree's question brought her to her senses, Rowena

stopped. She took a deep breath. Squaring her shoulders, she slid the screwdriver into her pocket and looked over at Bree.

"No, that's all right. I'll either bust it open with my bare teeth in a minute, or I'll calm down and call someone in the morning." She smiled wanly. "You said you wanted to talk. What's up?"

For no good reason, Bree felt suddenly nervous, as if she were in fifth grade again and it was her turn to perform in the oration contest. She had a little speech ready—she'd had plenty of time, up there in her room, to think about how to deliver her news. But, as little speeches so often did, it seemed too stilted and synthetic when it came face-to-face with the moment.

"I have some news," she said. She shifted the manila envelope to get a better grip. She felt, out of nowhere, as if she might drop it.

Rowena's gaze cut briefly to the envelope. "I hope it's good news."

"Yes, it is. I mean, *I* think it is. I hope you do, too."

"We won the lottery?"

Bree smiled. "Not exactly. But it is pretty exciting, anyhow. You see, I wanted to do something, something really special, to thank you for being so nice about…about my coming here. I didn't get off to a great start, but you gave me a second chance, and I wanted you to know how much I appreciated that."

Oh, dear. She had fallen back on the little speech, and it sounded just as bogus she'd feared it would. Ro had twisted her mouth sideways and started to frown, as if she thought Bree wasn't making much sense.

So Bree tried again. "Anyhow, I know you've been so busy…so caught up with the ranch, and with starting your life with Dallas and Alec, and…well, with everything, that you've hardly had time to think about yourself."

"Don't tell me—" Rowena raised her eyebrows quizzically "—you bought me a pedicure."

Bree laughed. As if she'd ever do that. Rowena had never needed to resort to such superficial trappings of beauty. She'd laughed at the girls who thought you could hook a guy like a fish just by dangling shiny hair extensions and acrylic nails in front of his face. And even if you could, she'd pointed out, why would you want a boy dumb enough to fall for all that?

"No," Bree said. She knew that the joke was Ro's way of telling her to get to the point, so she just inhaled hard, and did so. "What I did was…well, I hired a private detective. Remember you emailed me the picture you found of Mom—the one where she's on the ski slope with Rowan?"

She waited for Rowena to agree, or to nod, or make any sign at all to indicate that she was following. But, oddly, her sister didn't say a thing. She didn't even blink.

There was nothing to do but push forward. Get to the part that qualified as good news.

"Well, I gave it to the detective, and I asked him if he thought he might be able to identify the man in the picture. He wasn't very optimistic, at first. But I got a call from him tonight. And he did it, Ro. He actually did it." She held out the envelope. "He found out who your father is. This is his report."

In the silence that followed, Bree could hear her own heart thumping. What was wrong? Why was Rowena staring at her like that? Why did her face suddenly look, not just tired, but hard?

And why didn't she accept the packet?

"I—I didn't open it, Ro. It's still sealed. I thought you should be the first one to learn whatever it is he found."

Rowena laughed at that. The sound echoed into the still night harshly, like the sound of a wild bird. Still laughing, she reached out two fingers and plucked the envelope from her sister's hands.

But she didn't even look at it. She let it hang slackly at her side, never taking her flashing green gaze from Bree.

Bree's skin went clammy with fear.

"Well, that's very generous of you," Rowena said, the wild laughter still coloring the edges of her voice, making her sound like a stranger. "It actually occurred to you that I might want to be the first to know?"

"Yes. Of course." Though she wasn't sure how it happened, Bree was suddenly teetering on conversational ice skates, sliding all over the place, unable to find traction. "I assumed that...well, of course you would."

"I see. But it *didn't* occur to you that I might like to be the one who decided *when* I should know? Or even *if* I should know?"

"*If* you should know?" Bree shook her head, bewildered. "But of course you would want to know."

"Why 'of course'?" As she moved forward into the moonlight, Rowena's green eyes gleamed like animal eyes. "Because *you* think I should? Because, as always, Bree knows best?"

Bree flinched. And then, as comprehension finally dawned, she felt a terrible sinking in her chest. Like a comic-book character with the proverbial lightbulb going on over its stupid, stupid head, she finally, belatedly understood what she had done.

Of course Rowena would see this as interference. She would see it as bossy, prissy Brianna Wright at her most controlling.

Because...*dear God*...that's exactly what it was.

"Ro, please, really. I...I guess it was dumb, but that's honestly not what I was—"

Her sister held up her hand, the one that had accepted the

envelope. She glanced at it, as if surprised to discover she still had it.

"Don't bother, Bree."

She let the envelope fall. At the same instant, the angry fire in her face abruptly blinked out. It was as if the flame had been lit temporarily by a powerful spark of emotion, then guttered quickly, unable to maintain the intensity required to sustain itself.

In place of the anger, the old, exhausted look returned. Moonlight was not kind to the blue-black circles under her eyes, the white, tense skin around her nose, the jagged, too-thin cheekbones and the haggard lines around her wounded mouth.

Bree's heart ached as if someone had stepped on it with boots, twisting, to make sure it had been fully extinguished. She'd seen that beautiful, tragic face so often in her life. Even, during their lost years, in her dreams. Like a body with no protective skin, Rowena wore her pain on the surface, for everyone to see.

But this time Bree had put it there.

Like a bad joke, somewhere a mechanical click sounded, followed by a sibilant *whoosh, swish*...and then the sudden appearance of rising sprinkler heads, spraying tiny fountains of moonlit mist everywhere.

But neither of them reacted. What were a few drops of water right now? Bree couldn't tell whether Rowena even knew. She gave no sign that she felt the light spray that sparkled on her face like tears.

"You know, I really thought you'd changed," Rowena said flatly, no rise or fall in the monotone of her voice. "But you haven't. Maybe you can't. You still think you know better than everyone else, don't you? Especially me. I haven't made a decision in my entire life that you approve of."

Bree put out her hand, which had acquired a faint sheen

of moisture. Her shirt had begun to grow subtly heavier on her shoulders,

"Oh, Ro, that's not true. Sometimes I've said things that I—"

But Rowena cut her off again, wearily. "You know, it doesn't really matter anymore. I've learned to get along pretty well without your approval, through the years. But you should know that this time…this time you've gone too far. This was…" Without finishing the sentence, Rowena held up the detective's report. Bree could see that Ro had squeezed the thick envelope so hard she'd torn the paper.

But that was only possible because she'd been dangling the envelope all this time right where it took a direct hit from the misting spray.

The paper was growing darker, softening, taking on a sodden, ruined look.

"Ro." Even now, Bree couldn't bear to see the treasure lost, the ink letters running together to obliterate the name. It was all she could do to refrain from reaching out and grabbing it from her sister's hand.

Rowena shook her head, slowly, as if she was too tired to do anything very fast.

"You really should have stayed out of this, Bree," she said. "It wasn't your decision to make. It was *mine*."

CHAPTER EIGHTEEN

GRAY HAD BEEN waiting so long, sitting on the deck with his computer propped on the arm of the chair, that he'd read all today's reports, and then caught up on all the other reports he'd been inadequately skimming for the past three weeks.

The three-ring circus that was horse breeding—foals that had been born this past January, mares that were already carrying the foals that would be born next year and the purchase of new breeding stock for future foals—generated more paperwork than anything else he'd ever done. If he wasn't a little bit crazy, and in love with every trivial detail about horses, he would have pitched the computer in the creek hours ago.

At least the work had made the time pass a little more quickly. He closed the laptop, stretched to loosen the kinks in his shoulders and then glanced at his watch. One-thirty in the morning. He stood, stretched again and decided to walk down to the water's edge to get his blood moving.

He had no intention of going to sleep. He refused to believe she wasn't coming, sooner or later.

It was one of those preternaturally quiet nights, when the wind seemed to have blown into some other corner of the world. The creek was as still as a painting of water. Even the gauzy moonlight didn't bend or refract or twinkle, as it usually did where it touched the creek's surface. It might have been a lifeless strip of silver foil bisecting a hard pane of black glass.

Lifeless. That was how he felt. Not dead, but too still. A picture of a man, a video indefinitely on pause. Waiting for Bree to arrive so that real life could begin again.

He put his hands in his pockets, trying to banish a nagging feeling that something had gone wrong. When Bree had first told him about hiring the P.I., he'd felt a twinge of foreboding.

Would Rowena really be as excited about this as Bree obviously believed she would? Would she really welcome anyone poking around in her personal business—even her own sister?

He hadn't ever known Rowena intimately, but he had one intensely vivid memory of her that made him wonder…

After Moira Wright's murder, Gray's grandfather had insisted that the two of them go to her funeral. Gray had protested vehemently. He thought the idea sucked.

He knew firsthand how much drowning people hated being patronized by people who weren't. Hated even being *looked at* by them, as if they were the two-headed boy in the circus, and the normal people could pay their fifty cents and ogle them all day.

The not-drowning people had two reactions to the drowning ones. Only two—each as loathsome as the other.

One was a lascivious curiosity. *Ooh, I wonder what that's like?* The other was a smug certainty that they'd earned their own good fortune. *Oh, thank goodness that's not me…but then, I know better than to*—insert appropriate tragedy-attracting behavior here—*at least I know better than to drive drunk. At least I know better than to marry a madman.*

He didn't fit in either category, and he didn't want the Wrights to think he did. But his grandfather had insisted, and Gray was only in ninth grade, old enough to make the battle ugly, but too young to win it. And so they went.

Sometime during the service, a woman had commented on the little sister's bloodstained dress, apparently shocked, as if Emily Post simply wouldn't approve.

Gray had felt like snorting. *Idiot.* As if Emily Post would be fine with the rest of it, with the adultery, and the murder, and the orphaned little girls…as long as the funeral clothes were clean.

Rowena must have heard the comment because, though she'd been staring down at the ground almost the entire time, she suddenly lifted her head and stared straight at the stupid woman.

Gray would truly never forget the set of that bony, Greek-tragedy face. Haughty, pointed chin and blazing eyes, lips curled with contempt, nostrils white and flaring. If looks could kill, he'd thought, and he'd liked her then. She had guts. She had pride. Too much pride, but as far as he was concerned, that was better than not enough.

Rowena seemed much happier now, mellowed by marriage and by a fulfilled life at the dude ranch. But he knew, unfortunately, that pride never really went away—it was like a river that sometimes dived underground and sometimes branched off into new directions, but rarely really disappeared for good.

He felt guilty now, wondering if he should have said something. Shared his worry that Rowena was too complicated for Bree to take any of her reactions for granted.

But Bree had been so excited, so happy to have this great surprise in the works…. He hadn't wanted to burst a single bubble that night because they had needed every one.

He turned around, scanning the trees. What was happening back at the main house?

It was almost two before he heard her footsteps on the deck. He climbed back up the creek bank and reached the tent just as she finished scanning the room, and turned around again, looking bedraggled and oddly lost.

"Oh, there you are," she said softly. Her eyes were shadowed and dark, and every inch of her body language was written in the code for pure distress. "I'm sorry…I'm sorry I'm so late."

Without a word, he crossed to her and took her in his arms. "You're here now," he said. Her shirt was wet, and so, he realized, was her hair. He pulled wet strands of the golden silk from her pale cheeks. "What happened?"

"Ro thought the sprinklers were broken," she said, apparently taking his question literally. "They came on all of a sudden, while we were standing there."

But he didn't care about the wet clothes. "I mean, what happened with Rowena?"

She looked at him, her face momentarily blank. She shook her head, but he couldn't be certain she was conscious that she did it.

"I've made such a terrible mess of it all." The expression on her face broke his heart. "I thought I had learned my lesson, but I was so wrong. She thinks I haven't changed a bit. She believes I disapprove of everything she's ever done."

"But you don't," he said.

"I know. But I keep doing things that make her feel…unloved. And now I've done it again. Why on earth did I think it was all right to meddle in anything as personal as that? Why couldn't I see that it was her life, not mine? Her father, not mine? Why didn't I respect her decision to do nothing?"

He tightened his arms around her. "Because you love her. You can't be happy unless she is."

Strange. He'd never been able to come up with a working definition of love before—probably because he hadn't ever been sure it existed anywhere on this earth, now that his parents were gone. But suddenly it seemed like the most obvious thing in the world.

"You love Rowena, and you always will. That makes her happiness your business. And you thought connecting with her real father would make her happy."

"Well, I was wrong." She tried to smile. "And I've paid such a high price for my selfishness, Gray. I was on my last chance with her. I'd been so unforgiving for so long, so judgmental. This was my last chance to make it up to her."

"No," he said, on instinct rather than experience. He knew all too well how intractable stubborn pride could be. But not Rowena's, surely. Not to the point that she'd permanently reject her sister.

"Yes, it was," she repeated with certainty. "And I threw my last chance away because I wanted to be the hero. I wanted to be the one who showed her the right path to take."

"I don't believe that. Whatever she said tonight, Rowena loves you, too. And when you love someone, there's no such thing as a last chance. There's always one more. *Always.*"

He wondered, actually, whether he really believed the corny, mawkish phrases he'd just uttered. These weren't sentiments that had ever passed his lips before.

But so what? Even if they weren't true for him, it was different for the Wright sisters. For them, it was true. They loved each other, and they *needed* each other. They'd survived the same unspeakable shipwreck, and they bore the same scars. Their psyches were littered, no…they were *mined*…with the same dangerous detritus.

No one else on this earth, except those three, could ever say, "I understand how you feel" and be telling the absolute truth.

Not even Gray.

Bree looked at him, and though he still saw worry and regret in her eyes, he didn't see…

He didn't see fear. The change he thought he noticed earlier tonight…a lifetime ago, at the campfire…was still there.

"You're a very kind man," she said thoughtfully.

He shook his head vehemently. He would walk out of this tent, this ranch, this city, this state, in only four days. He'd be leaving her behind, collateral damage in the mindless determination to escape his grandfather—and his memories.

And he wasn't even going to try to stop himself.

"I'll be gone in four days, Bree. You know damn well I'm anything but kind."

"You've been very kind to me. These past few weeks… your patience, and your friendship, and your faith in me…" She blinked, and swallowed hard. "It gave me the courage I badly needed, courage to face some old demons. And I did. Thanks to you, I did."

He frowned. "Don't be ridiculous. Your courage has been with you all your life. What you've been through would have broken most people. But it didn't break you. It didn't even make you hard, or selfish, or cruel. I wish I could say as much for myself."

She smiled up at him. "Maybe I should say it for you. You're a very kind man, Gray Harper."

"And you're amazing, Brianna Wright." He meant to be sincere but lighthearted as they exchanged compliments. Instead, his voice sounded oddly thick. Why did this feel as if they were already saying goodbye? He had four more days…. "You're amazing, and beautiful, and good. Don't you ever lose track of that."

For a minute, she just let her head come to rest against his chest. Her ear was pressed against his heart, and he wondered if she could hear what the erratic beat was saying.

Then she lifted her head. Her clear blue eyes searched his.

"Will you please make love to me, Gray? I think it's time. I think we've waited long enough."

For a minute he could hardly speak. He burned, instantly, but he had trained himself not to feel it. He was terrified to let go of that control. It had been so difficult to achieve and, once peeled away, he knew he'd never be able to get it back.

"Bree." He met her searching gaze. "Is that really what you want?"

"What I want, and what I need." She took a deep breath.

"I'm ready, Gray. I've learned a lot about myself today. Some of it was very hard, and some of it breaks my heart. But none of it changes the fact that I want you. I want to be in your arms when I finally…stop being afraid."

He tried to find his moral compass…he tried to find true north, where honesty stood out clearly from lies and wrong never could pass for right.…

Where was it? Where was the line he mustn't cross? He had seen it so clearly just yesterday. He'd seen it in her sad eyes, her anxious smiles. But tonight the line seemed to be moving, shifting, evaporating beneath this new confidence he felt in her.

She was even more erotic now, with this new light in her eyes, this new certainty in her voice, than she had ever been, even that first night, when he had turned to putty in her hands.

Even more beautiful, even more impossible to resist. He had to breathe shallowly because even deep movements of his diaphragm put pressure in places that were already about to explode.

"If you're just upset about Rowena…if you're just dreading being alone…"

"I'm not. I am upset about her. And I do dread being alone. But that's not why I want to make love to you."

"You don't have to do this. You don't have to do anything. You know that, don't you?" He touched her face. "I'm here, if you want me here. There's no price to be paid for that."

She groaned, tilting her cheek into his hand to deepen the touch.

"Gray," she said, her voice tight, thready with her rapid breaths that exhaled warmly against his palm. "Gray, please. Stop talking and make love to me."

After that, it was too late. He couldn't have stopped himself from touching her unless he'd been ready to stop his own heart from beating. He kissed her first, but she had no patience, and her hands went everywhere. Their mouths clung, but the mad rush to discard clothes, to reveal and discover and explore every inch of naked skin, made the kiss loud with panting and laughter, all probing, primitive wetness and heat.

They fell onto the bed, giddy, needing air but unwilling to part long enough to breathe. She tried to touch him, but he couldn't have survived it, so he laid her back against the pillows and used everything he possessed to make sure she was far too distracted to try again.

He used his lips, his tongue, his fingers, his voice. He even trailed his hair across her breasts until she cried out, begging for something firmer, something hotter. He suckled her till she was pebbled and panting, and then he let the wetness grow cold before closing over her again with a heat that shocked and made her arc upward in small jerks of uncontrollable fire.

He kept her loud, rewarding every cry, every whimper, every groan that proved she wasn't holding back a thing. He made her laugh even while she screamed. He made her tell him what she wanted, and then he gave it to her, and more, too.

Finally, because he couldn't wait any longer, he slipped his hand between her legs, and then the shock was his. She was open and ready, desperate with pulsing moisture, moaning with swollen heat.

"It's going to be wonderful," he whispered. "It's going to be as beautiful as you are."

She twisted under his hand, and he smiled, feeling that tiny, half-bursting, delicately engorged pearl trying to throb itself into his hand, where it might find release. He carefully folded back the skin in which it was nestled, like pink petals opening around a treasured seed.

He placed his hands under her hips so that she was cantilevered against them, her pelvis tilting up just enough for him to see clearly the damply throbbing spot he'd laid bare to the moonlight.

Later, he thought as he lowered his hungry mouth to the spot. Later, they would start again, and he would fill her body with his body, her heart with his heart.

But right now, he was going to give her the crazed, spinning bliss she'd been waiting for for so long. He lowered his head, took the pearl gently, so gently, between his lips and pressed his tongue against her.

Just the warm tip of his tongue, burrowing into the secret, pink and painfully erect nub. She whimpered once, a shocked and helpless sound.

And then, nothing, nothing could have stopped what followed.

She was half-mad with it, writhing, her limbs jerking and breaking out in cascades of rippling shivers. Between his lips, a series of endlessly contracting spasms pulsated against his tongue.

When she started to calm, he started again, catching her unguarded, and the pulsing never fully stopped between one orgasm and the next. She cried out, over and over, sometimes his name, and sometimes just animal vocalizations of release. Her buttocks bucked against his hands, her legs wrapped themselves around his shoulders and her hands tugged frantically at his hair, until finally her muscles gave out, the shivering ebbed and her head fell back limply against the pillow.

Later, he thought, laying his cheek against her satin thigh. Later, they would start again.

WHEN SHE WOKE, she woke him, too, and this time she made love to him, just as she'd wanted to do that first night.

And with all the times after that, they eventually lost track of whose turn it was, until it was just bodies, and sensations, and joy.

Around the time she felt dawn stirring the shadows with its golden fingers, she knew she couldn't stay awake a minute more, not even to feel his magic hands on her skin.

At the moment, he lay across the bed, glorious in his nakedness, his head against her belly. She touched his hair and wished that she could tell him how beautiful this night had been. If she never made love again in her life, she would live a fully satisfied woman.

But she was too tired for words. She tugged tenderly on his hair, trying to urge him up to his own pillow. He must be tired, too.

He came, understanding her unspoken signals so well— as he had done all this marvelous night. He kissed her once, softly on the lips, and then he lay on his side, watching her as she drifted into sleep.

She smiled. She wanted to tell him he could sleep, too. He needed rest, and there were no more monsters to guard her from. But she couldn't think of those words, either.

Finally, she just whispered, "I love you, Gray," through her half-sleeping lips.

She felt his hand go very still against her breast. Forcing her eyes open just enough to see his profile in the gloamy dawn, she smiled.

His eyes were wide and very dark.

Oh, dear, she thought, although she couldn't really find any true sense of alarm. She knew what he must be thinking. He was afraid she was trying to hold on to him. He thought she was clinging…trying to make him feel so guilty, perhaps, that he would stay?

She could fix it. In the morning, she told herself, she would explain. She knew he would leave in four days, and she had always known it. She regretted nothing. She would change nothing.

She loved him, that was all. In the morning, she'd explain

that the declaration didn't come attached to strings. She could make him understand.

Several hours later, when her cell-phone alarm finally did rouse her from the half-drugged, blissful slumber, she raised up on one elbow.

Something was different. Blinking to clear her tired eyes, she slowly scanned the strangely empty, brightly sunlit tent.

Birds were singing outside, and the creek was luffing in a fresh morning breeze. Between them, they filled the tent with music. But other than that, and the luxury furnishings provided by Barton James—and of course Bree herself—the tent was empty.

Gray's things were gone. All of them.

His computer and papers and phone were gone. All of them.

His clothes, his coat, his watch and shoes were gone, too. All of them.

One last hope crossed her mind. Perhaps he'd left a note. He might have been called to his grandfather's hospital room, or…

She raised up again, checking the chair, the desk, the little wooden platform on which his suitcase had once been stored. The surfaces were bare. All of them.

Then she saw the note lying across his pillow. She picked it up, registering that her fingers felt cold and a little numb. His handwriting was bold and black against the pure white.

It was perfect. And so are you. Never forget that.

Never? She stared at the black masculine slashes. It wasn't a cruel note. It obviously had been meant as a kindness, a touch of soothing ointment to put over whatever wound his departure might leave behind.

Never was the word she hated, the word that told her exactly how long he would be gone. Never was such a vast, echoing word. Such a final word.

Never meant forever.

She dropped back against the pillow, holding the sheet to her naked breast and trying to understand.

Last night she told him that she loved him. And now, this morning…

Gray Harper, who would have been a millionaire in four short days, was gone. All of him.

CHAPTER NINETEEN

SHE WAS SCHEDULED to lead the Saturday-Morning Horse Tales, so thankfully she didn't have time to brood. She'd slept till the last minute—she hated to think what would have happened if she didn't have a strict habit of always setting her own alarm, never relying on anyone else to wake her. She barely had time to grab a shower and still make it to the old barn by ten.

The hour didn't go quite as well as last week's, but what else could she have expected? Last week, she'd felt so at home here, growing more relaxed around Rowena every day, and excited at the possibility of seeing Gray again that night. She'd been brimming with enthusiasm, delighted by the children and turning over a hundred ideas to make everything better.

Yeah. Great ideas, like hiring a private investigator to poke around in Rowena's personal affairs—then taking the information and offering it to her sister, gift-wrapped, and expecting a pat on the head.

What a difference a week made!

Today, Gray was gone with no goodbye. She had taken two giant steps backward with Rowena, if she hadn't destroyed their chances altogether.

And she felt like a hopeless interloper at Bell River. Or, even worse, she felt like the disagreeable relative who had invited herself over, and who was barely endured out of duty until she finally got the hint and took herself home in a huff.

Small wonder she was a little short on the enthusiasm and delight.

Still, she tried not to let the children notice, and she was relieved when, the hour over, Rose showed up to escort the kids to their next adventure. Today, they'd go bird-watching.

She was moving systematically through her cleanup routine, had just shelved the books and dragged out the cushion cleansers, when a long, lean shadow moved into the rectangle of sunlight formed by the open barn doors.

Her heart skipped a beat. That was Gray's outline, right down to the wave of hair that lifted up with the hint of a cowlick at the hairline, then tumbled sweetly back down onto his forehead.

"Well? Is it true?" The shadow entered the barn, and the movement alone told her it wasn't Gray. Her heart slumped back into its previous sluggish pace. It was Gray's autocratic grandfather, leaning heavily on his cane and scowling down his aristocratic nose. "Is it true that he's run away?"

She spritzed cleanser on the first cushion and began wiping it down with rougher strokes than usual. The old man really got under her skin.

"Gray is a grown man, Mr. Harper, so he doesn't have to 'run away' from anything. He leaves however and whenever he chooses. But if you're asking whether he's gone, the answer is yes."

She finished the cushion, tossed it in the pile and began another, all without meeting the old man's gaze.

He made a small, disdainful sound. "So. He left you, too. I wonder why."

And he'd just have to go on wondering. Bree certainly wasn't going to indulge in a cozy little sit-down so that she could fill him in. Besides, surely he knew better than anyone why his grandson didn't want to spend an extra minute in Silverdell.

"It's usually a matter of his having been asked to do something boring," he said sarcastically. "Like real work. I gather he's commitment-phobic, as well, though. I hear that no one woman has ever lasted a full month with him, so don't take it personally, Ms. Wright."

She set her bottle, rag and gloves on the table. Then she walked right up to the old guy and stood toe to toe with him. He had really, really picked the wrong day.

"I'll tell you what I take personally, Mr. Harper. I take it personally when I tell you not to set foot on Bell River land, but you decide to ignore me."

He smiled, and she had to steel herself not to see echoes of Gray. "I didn't ignore you," he explained reasonably. "I overruled you in an emergency. There's a difference."

"Not much," she countered. "But if you'll excuse me, I'm expected in the kitchen."

"No, you're not." He smiled again. "I was just in the kitchen, talking to your lovely brother-in-law, Sheriff Garwood. We're old friends. He told me you were probably out here, and that you'd have an hour or two before your next scheduled session."

She started to flush, but forced herself not to. "My excuse about the kitchen was a conversational nicety, Mr. Harper. Like when the person you're talking on the phone to says, 'well, I won't keep you.' You're not supposed to believe it's true. You're supposed to understand you've been politely disposed of. I told you that last time you came around that I wouldn't listen to you denigrate Gray. I won't listen now, either."

Harper's face darkened, and she was reminded uncomfortably that he had been in the hospital only yesterday.

"No? Are you really still determined to defend him? Even after he *disposed of* you, too? Even though he clearly played you for a fool every bit as much as he played me?"

Bree clenched her jaw. She wasn't going to let this angry old man draw her into a fight. He clearly needed someone to agree that Gray was an evil, selfish bastard, and thought that maybe the woman who had been left behind might be in the mood for a little fickle-lover bashing.

But he was dead wrong.

"I regret nothing about my friendship with your grandson, Mr. Harper." She held her chin high. "*Nothing*. Gray is a remarkable man. In fact, I would go so far as to say he's amazing. I'm even more impressed now, because I can see that he had to develop his integrity on his own, without any role model to follow."

"*Amazing?*" The furrowed face drew back slightly, incredulous. "*Integrity?* I would laugh if it weren't so pitiful. I know you've been sleeping in that ridiculous tent with him, but still…sex is one thing. This misguided loyalty is another." He shook his head, as if she'd disappointed him. "I wouldn't have thought you'd be so easy to dupe, Ms. Wright."

She returned his gaze icily. Obviously, he was trying to sting her, and was waiting for her to squeal. She wouldn't give him the satisfaction.

He tried again. "I don't know how you feel about my grandson, Ms. Wright, but you need to understand this. He doesn't know how to care about anyone. Maybe it isn't his fault. Things happened to him when he was very young, and those things may have damaged him beyond repair. But please. Don't romanticize him. He is far from amazing, I assure you."

She gave the old man a hard, level look. "So *that's* where he gets those ideas about himself."

He frowned. "What are you talking about?"

"He says those same things about himself. Apparently, you've taught him well. But maybe you need to ask yourself how well you really know your grandson anymore, Mr.

Harper. Ask yourself why you think he's incapable of love. Is it simply because he doesn't love *you?*"

He banged his cane on the ground, an imperial gesture, as if to command that she watch her tone. But the barn floor muffled the sound, and his action had no power here.

"Here's one important difference between you and me," she went on. "When my relationships don't work out, I'm learning to take responsibility for my part in the failure. If I love someone, but they don't love me back, I won't any longer automatically assume it's because they're bad people, or because they don't know how to love."

"If you love someone?" Harper slumped suddenly, bending over his cane as if the effort to hold himself upright was too great. "*Love?* Damn that selfish boy. It went that far? He made you fall in *love* with him?"

The truth was, when she spoke she hadn't been thinking only about Gray. She'd also been thinking of Rowena, and her mother, and maybe even her father, too. She'd been thinking about all kinds of love, and all kinds of heartache.

And what it took to make a relationship last over the long haul. For the first time in her life, she felt she was beginning to understand how much work went into that.

It took the courage to face life squarely, not to run away when it got scary, not to dodge hurtful truths or deny even the memory of old traumas. It took honesty and self-awareness and the ability to live with uncertainty and risk.

But most of all, it took mercy and compassion. You had to be willing to forgive the people who hurt you, and, even more challenging, you had to be willing to forgive yourself.

Even in his eighties, old Mr. Harper clearly hadn't yet been able to do any of that. She wished she could make him see how impossible it would be for him to bring about any real changes when he wouldn't admit that he might be part of the problem. She'd been stuck in that rut for far too long.

"*Made* me fall in love?" She shook her head sadly. "I think you're still missing the point."

"Is that so? And what would the point be?"

"Love can't be mandated. It has to be earned. In a hundred ways, Gray earned mine. If I didn't earn his, then I just have to live with that. Maybe I can even learn from it. But if I lash out, if I try to ease my pain by blaming him and trying to devalue him…"

She stared at Harper intently, wondering if any of this was getting through. She hoped so. She had suddenly glimpsed, with a raw clarity, exactly how much agony, loneliness and guilt lay beneath his surface fury.

Just as fear and insecurity had always lurked below her own judgmental, icy crust.

"Then can't you see, Mr. Harper? Lashing out doesn't make him change his mind and decide he ought to love me after all. All it does is prove how right he was to walk away."

Apparently, Gray had somehow notified Rowena that he was quitting, because when Bree hustled out to referee the after-lunch horseshoe contest that should have been his task, it was already covered.

Arkansas Muldoon, one of the older men who had signed on as part-time waitstaff, had already been drafted to fill in for Gray.

Actually, she was relieved. Most important, if Rowena already knew, at least Bree didn't have to break the news.

But she was also relieved because, while horseshoes ought to be a sleepy time-waster, around here it got surprisingly competitive. The last set of guests had nearly come to blows once over a fine point in the rules—a problem that Arkansas, a six-foot-three former NFL quarterback, would be far better qualified to squelch.

She thanked Arkansas for helping, then glanced up toward

the house. The back-porch swing and wooden rocking chairs were all swaying under the weight of a dozen or more guests who'd gathered to watch and cheer.

"You don't happen to know where Rowena is, do you?"

Arkansas stared at his stopwatch, obviously having been warned about how seriously the thirty-second tossing rule was enforced by the players. "No, sorry. She's gone, I know that. I saw her drive off in the car."

"Foot foul!" Ethan Shipley stood beside his opponent, sweet, freckle-faced Chad Bartlett, who was Dallas's deputy and an overall good guy. Shipley thrust out his arm, finger pointing at the ground as dramatically as if he needed to make the gesture visible for a worldwide television audience, like a football referee. "Dead shoe!"

Chad backed up, eyeing Shipley as if he were a volcano about to erupt, and extended a conciliatory hand.

"No problem," he said, stepping off his pitching platform. "It's all yours."

A few catcalls from the audience on the porch seemed to indicate the foul wasn't quite that cut-and-dried. Though Bree had been going to ask Arkansas about Dallas's whereabouts next, she saw that this wasn't the right time to distract him. She smiled to let him know she understood.

He winked back before jogging over to the contestants. "Now, boys, let's take this slow…"

With a little help from Barton, she finally found Dallas out in the east field, a chain saw on the ground beside him and a sawhorse beside that. Sometime over the past few days, a large oak limb had fallen, crushing several feet of paddock fencing. He'd clearly been working on the repair a long time, judging from the sweat around his T-shirt and the wood chips in his hair.

She'd brought out a bottled water, which he took gratefully. "Sorry to interrupt," she said.

He laughed. "Interrupt away." He drank half the bottle in one swig. "In fact, if you could manufacture a bank robbery or something requiring the sheriff's immediate presence in town, I'd be seriously in your debt."

"I'll work on that." She smiled. "I was just wondering if you knew when Ro would be back."

"No. Sorry. I've been out here all day. I know yesterday she talked about picking up some light fixtures for the arts building." He took another drink, then bent to set the bottle on the grass. As he did, he glanced up at her thoughtfully. "But today the errand didn't seem high on her list. She acted a little down. I take it you guys haven't patched things up yet?"

Bree shook her head. "No. That's why I wanted to find her. But to tell you the truth, I don't think she's all that interested in patching things up."

"Sure she is."

Bree raised an eyebrow. "You didn't hear her last night. She was furious."

"Still. I know Rowena. She wants to make up, all right. She's just not very good at *admitting* she wants it."

Bree hoped he was right. "I'm not sure what she's told you about it, but I want you to know I meant well when I asked for the search. I see now how dumb it was, but I got caught up in the excitement of surprising her. I hadn't even considered the possibility she might not want to know. I thought that, especially if there was a baby on the way..."

Dallas put one hand on the sawhorse and wiped his brow with the other.

"About that," he said quietly. "Since you asked me before, you should know. There's not."

She blinked. She heard him, but the news didn't really sink in, not in the first instant. "There's no baby?"

"No." He shook his head, as if the fact needed corroborating. "She just found out for sure—which is probably why her emotions are so intense right now. I think she was hoping. Entertaining the possibility. Just as you and I were."

"Does she know that I—?"

"Of course not." He smiled, but it was a poignant smile… a rarity for this sunny man. "You know how proud she is. She wouldn't want anyone to think she wanted something she can't have."

"Can't have?" Bree's heart thumped. "Is there any reason to believe she can't….?"

"Of course not. Not in real-world facts. But in Rowena-world fears…" He let that dwindle off.

Bree understood. "She hasn't ever really believed she deserves to be happy. And she's so ridiculously contented now, with you and Alec, and the ranch. So I guess she's always waiting for the other shoe to drop."

"Exactly." He hesitated a second, absently brushing sawdust from his forearms. Then he seemed to decide to simply say what was on his mind. "I hope you understand that her anger about what you did…well, it has very little to do with you, or anything you supposedly did wrong."

"Of course it does." Bree appreciated the effort to console her, but she wanted to be honest with herself. "I shouldn't have interfered. It's a lesson I'm having a hard time learning. I'm not very good at accepting people as they are and not trying to change them."

"Well, that's for you to say, I guess." He smiled again. "But you should remember that Rowena's fear of rejection runs deep. She's spent a lifetime trying to beat other people to it—rejecting them before they can reject her."

Bree nodded. "Our father…I mean, Johnny…"

"Yeah." Dallas's face darkened. "I sure would have liked just five minutes alone in a room with that bastard." Then one side of his mouth ticked up wryly. "But she doesn't need me to do her dirty work. Now that she knows the truth, she could handle it with her own five minutes."

"True." Bree had to chuckle. Ro wouldn't have laid a finger on Johnny, but she'd have flayed his skin right off his body anyhow, using only her whips of words. "That's why I felt so sure that, if she could connect with her *real* father, she'd jump at the chance. To have him accept her, show that he wants her, after all those years of—"

"But what if he didn't?"

Bree frowned at Dallas's quiet interjection. "Didn't what?"

"Didn't want her. Didn't accept her."

"Oh."

The simple sentences opened up a void at Bree's feet, as if the ground she'd thought she was standing on had been merely a clever illusion. She wondered, suddenly, if this was how Rowena had felt when she learned her whole childhood had been a lie.

"But he would want her. Of course he would." Her mind backed away from the emptiness instinctively, as if she were scrabbling back from a near fall off a high cliff. "It's obvious our mother never told him. He never even knew he had a child—"

"I agree," Dallas said mildly. "But it's not enough for *us* to be sure. She isn't. And, after a lifetime of rejection, can't you see how terrifying it is to risk facing another one? And this time it wouldn't be from an angry bully who resented having been tricked into accepting another man's child as his. It wouldn't be from a madman with a brain tumor scrambling his judgment. It would be from her own flesh and blood."

Of course Bree could see. Terrifying, indeed. She shivered, in spite of how balmy the spring afternoon was and how brightly the sun was shining on the green pasture, picking out the pink-and-yellow wildflowers that had sprouted up as May wore on.

"In spite of that, I still believe she'll come around eventually." His voice was low and thoughtful. He, too, gazed into the middle distance, as if the peaceful day bolstered his optimism. "She's not the type to run scared forever."

Bree smiled. Once more, she felt a twinge of envy that her sister had found such a wonderful life partner who saw her clearly and cherished everything he saw. She wondered whether any miracle like that could possibly be waiting around some corner in her own life.

Or whether she'd just met her miracle. And lost him.

"How about you?" Dallas tilted his head, suddenly, surprising Bree by looking at her with a quiet intensity, almost as if he knew the direction her thoughts had taken. "It's been a rough couple days, hasn't it? First Ro losing her cool, and then…"

She flushed.

"I heard about Gray." Dallas shrugged, as if that was enough to say. "Are you doing okay?"

She thought of the anchor that seemed to have been hooked to her heart, making it ride low and heavy in her chest.

"I'm fine," she lied. Then she scrunched up one corner of her mouth and decided to be honest. "Or I will be, soon enough. He never pretended he was going to stay when his four weeks were up, so I don't have any complaints. I may not be as tough as Rowena, but I'm not likely to curl up and die just because he left a few days early."

He nodded. "Yeah. That's what I thought. You Wright sisters are a mighty formidable posse." He picked up the chain saw, smiling at her over its big chain of metal teeth. "If you ask me, Gray Harper is a damn fool. And if I ever see him again, I'll be happy to tell him so."

CHAPTER TWENTY

BREE DIDN'T THINK of herself as a woman who operated on instinct much of the time. She'd always been too walled off, too frozen inside, maybe, for instincts to stand a chance.

But today, her gut was making itself heard in no uncertain terms. She wanted to find Rowena, and her gut said that Silverdell Memorial Cemetery was the place. Bree hadn't visited in years, but she had heard Ro make a few comments—about reminding the city to keep the grass mowed or the litter collected—that indicated she no longer avoided the site.

Set out of town by a few miles, and a long hike up into the ponderosa pines of Sterling Peak, the cemetery had been around at least a hundred years. Up high, angels and lambs and clasped hands made of marble joined with heartbreaking verses to memorialize the dead. But as the plots moved down the hill, the dates grew more recent and the tombstones simpler.

"Moira Wright, beloved mother" was among the newer graves. But no longer the newest, Bree noticed as she parked her car—right next to Rowena's.

This once, her gut had been telling the truth.

She opened her door and got out, glad she'd tied her hair back in a ponytail. Up here, the wind blew stronger, bending the heads of purple asters and yellow potentilla bushes—and even ruffling the bouquets of plastic flowers that were slowly fading under the hot spring sun.

She could see Rowena sitting on the small marble bench

that overlooked Moira's grave. The detective's manila envelope lay in her lap. It had dried since the sprinkler's soaking last night and once again shone gold in the sunlight.

For a minute, Bree couldn't force herself to go any farther. Her feet simply wouldn't start walking. The last time she and Rowena had been here together had been the day of the funeral. Penny had swayed groggily between them, her brown eyes wide and uncomprehending. Drugged by the doctor almost into catatonia, she still had refused to remove her party dress, with its terrible red trimming of blood.

That was the last time they had been safe inside their sisterhood. Bree's eyes stung, remembering.

Why had the grown-ups, with their unassailable "logic," decided to split them up? They had needed each other—desperately. They had needed the security of knowing that this one bond, at least, had not and could not be broken.

They would have been better off begging crumbs from neighbors until Rowena or Bree, or both, had been old enough to get jobs and take care of Penny.

Together, they might have been able to survive intact. But once they'd been so clumsily separated, like conjoined souls subjected to a botched amputation, they'd been forever deformed.

Somehow, Bree had to find the words to make Rowena forgive her so that they could work toward becoming whole again.

But what if it really was too late?

Rowena had obviously come here to commune with her mother, to ask her what she should do about the man whose name lay in the envelope. And maybe Moira would give her an answer. She and her firstborn had always been so close.

For the first time, no pang of envy pinched Bree's chest when she remembered how forgotten she'd always felt. Everyone had paired up so neatly. Moira and Rowena. Penny and their father. But Brianna stood alone.

She'd always understood that their father preferred Penny because she was no threat, always gentle, always the peacemaker. But now, finally, Bree also understood why her mother's obsession with Rowena had been so absolute.

Moira had wrapped her heart around Rowena like a bandage, trying to protect her from Johnny, trying to make up for the father, the real father, she'd never allowed her daughter to know. That didn't mean she didn't love her other daughters, too. It meant only that she felt she had injured her eldest daughter and wanted to set things right.

Oh, Mom, she thought with a piercing pity. *You must have been so lost. I'm lost now, too. Please help me find the words. Please help me get this right.*

The wind picked up suddenly, and it seemed to carry a whisper on its back. A woman's voice, as gentle as a cool palm on Bree's hot forehead.

Don't be afraid, Brianna. I love you very much.

Startled, Bree glanced around, her heart racing even as she felt incredibly foolish. She knew full well the words weren't real, couldn't be real. It had sounded like her mother's voice. But of course she was alone, except for Rowena, who, fifty yards away, had not moved a muscle since Bree arrived.

It must have been the wind breathing in the pines, or sighing across the old mining scars that mottled the sloping hillside.

Or the overwrought nerves in her own psyche, thrumming in response to her thoughts, summoning up the words she wanted to hear. An auditory hallucination.

Or, more simply put, a plain, vanilla case of wishful thinking.

But whatever the source, the sound had relaxed the anxious place inside her and thawed her fear-frozen feet. The tall iron gates were never locked, so Bree simply walked in.

Though tall, still-unmowed grasses muffled her steps, Rowena must have heard something. When she was within a few gravestones of her sister, Rowena turned.

Her green eyes sparkled with tears. But when she recognized her sister, she smiled, like sunshine breaking through clouds. She smiled as though she'd just received the answer to a prayer.

"Oh, Bree," she said, her voice trembling with intensity. "Can you ever forgive me? I've been such a terrible fool."

BY THURSDAY, EVERYTHING was falling into place so well that Bree sometimes caught herself playfully indulging the fantasy that some supernatural hand really might be directing the sails of her life after all.

Isamar, the housekeeper who had continued to see ghosts for the past month, assured her that Moira's spirit was still smiling. But then Rowena reported that Isamar also occasionally "saw" the ghost of Pippi Longstocking, and no one could convince her that the little girl was a fictional character and thus really didn't qualify to haunt anyone.

Okay, so Isamar was a little teched, as the other maids said, on the subject of the paranormal. It didn't matter. Bree knew that her "supernatural hand" idea was just a lovely piece of make-believe, but it made her smile all the same.

That day in the cemetery, Rowena had asked her to stay at Bell River permanently, either as the social director or just as family. She didn't want them ever to be separated by so many miles again.

Though the offer was a dream come true, Bree had briefly asked herself whether the memories—both of the family tragedy and of the joyous days with Gray—would be too difficult to live with.

Very briefly.

Ten seconds later, she'd accepted Rowena's offer, hugging her sister and laughing, with waves of joy washing through her. She wanted the social director job. She loved the work, as she hadn't loved her event planning business in a long, long time.

She and Rowena, Dallas and an ecstatic Alec—with Trouble, of course, putting his two cents in occasionally—had held a family meeting and worked it all out. River Moon would be her personal cottage—Rowena had to admit that, subconsciously at least, she'd designed that cottage as a home for Bree all along.

Now they were all hip deep in plans for the summer season, which would open in just a week. June first to September first, seven-night minimum...and they already had enough bookings to make payroll, which amazed and thrilled them. Not to mention how much it thrilled the bank that had said yes to the business loan in the first place.

The soft opening had generated so much goodwill—all that word-of-mouth publicity had more than paid for itself. Bree thought about calling Georgia Brooke and apologizing for being such a judgmental grouch that first day. Two-hundred-dollar banner? She would gladly have doubled that, now that she knew how all-important the good first impression had been.

Rowena was still not ready to open that envelope from the detective, but as she had sat on the marble bench in the cemetery that day, explaining why she needed more time to think, Bree had not uttered a single syllable of protest. She still hadn't. It was Rowena's life, and Rowena alone would decide when, or if, she was ready to reach out to her father.

Amid all these gifts, there was only one dark spot left in her heart. Bree actually felt a little spoiled, a bit childish and ungrateful, to realize that she still wasn't completely happy.

Though she knew it was pointless, she still carried the anchor of Gray's memory hooked to her heart. She still dreamed of him at night—and saw his shadow fall in every sunlit doorway, always throwing itself between her and the perfect joy she knew she should be feeling.

Once she would have said it was impossible to fall in love in four weeks. Now she knew she'd fallen in love with him the first day. The moment he touched her shoulders and turned her toward the creek so that she could watch the otters playing in the water, her body and her heart had belonged to him.

The fact that he clearly didn't want them was apparently irrelevant.

She tried to be mature. *Patience,* she told herself. Time really did heal things that seemed irreparable. A year ago, she wouldn't have believed she and Rowena could be so close... and yet they had found their way back to each other.

Once she would have said she could never live in Bell River again. She would have said that no one could live in this doomed structure and be happy.

And yet here she was, feeling *home* again for the first time in sixteen years.

Someday, she'd think of Gray without heartache. Someday, she would stop feeling a burst of painful electricity through her nerves whenever she saw a long, lean cowboy walk down Elk Avenue, or watched a brunet wrangler saunter into the barn.

Someday. But not today.

Today, she was interviewing for the position of assistant social director, and every single candidate fell short, simply because they weren't Gray. They didn't have his laughing eyes, or his teasing voice, his soft brown hair, strong hands, easy grace and smoldering...

Oh. Groaning at the flame of longing that burned rapidly

through her, from chest to pelvis, she put her head in her hands. She had to stop this. She was going to make herself ill.

She sat like that for several minutes, trying to collect herself. Her new office had been carved out of a back room in the recently completed arts-and-crafts building, and it smelled of new paint and unpacked boxes.

She didn't have a lot of furniture yet. Just a desk, a chair, a computer and a lot of empty filing cabinets waiting to be stuffed with the mounds of documents, contracts, bills of lading, applications and correspondence that now stood in two-foot piles all over the room.

Just thinking about the mess made her head feel heavier, and she kept it in her hands. It was ironic, really. She dared to be picky about her job candidates? What a joke! The applicants probably got one look at this mess and decided she'd be a hellish, disorganized boss, impossible to work for and chronically unprepared.

Not to mention a little scatty. Sometimes, when one of Bell River's taller cowboys passed the window, she'd get a far-off look in her eye, and it would take three tries to make her focus on the interview again.

So, who was next…? She couldn't face shuffling through the papers to figure it out. She rubbed her eyes with the heels of her hands and tried to remember. She'd seen three…no, four…

"Ms. Wright? I'm here about the position?"

Great. Now she'd been caught half napping, or whatever you called it when you daydreamed about having the best sex you'd ever dreamed of having…but never would again.

She sat up with a smile, trying to look bright-faced and professional.

And found herself looking into the laughing hazel eyes of Grayson Harper the Third.

He stood in front of her desk, dressed in denim jeans and

a white dress shirt, with his cowboy hat held in front of him, two-handed and humble.

But his grin wasn't humble. His grin was all Gray.

"I've come about the position?"

Without the anchor to hold it down, her heart felt as if it was trying to lift its way out of her chest. She held it in with deep, careful breaths.

"I'm afraid I don't have you on my calendar." She moved papers around blindly, just for show. "Perhaps we should start with…um…what position, exactly, are you applying for?"

He tilted his head. "Well, that depends, I guess, on what you're looking for. Because whatever that is, that's the one I want."

So he had come intending to be charming. She bought time by looking at the papers again, though she barely registered a single word. Her conscious mind was trying to put the pieces in the right places and figure out what this could possibly mean.

But all the primitive, subconscious, instinctive parts of her were smiling, and trilling, and bouncing for joy.

Who cares what it means? He's here.

But she had to care. Didn't she? She had to protect her heart from being broken all over again.

Didn't she?

"Mind if I sit?"

She shook her head.

"Thanks." With an exaggerated display of diffidence, he pulled out the chair and sat, resting his hat on the edge of the desk. She picked up her pen, as she'd done with all the other applicants, and tried to think what her first question should be.

Continuing the charade seemed silly, but even if she abandoned it, she couldn't be truly authentic, could she? She couldn't just burst into tears, or start beating his chest, weeping, "Where *were* you, damn it? Where did you *go?* Why didn't you say goodbye?"

And she certainly couldn't jump into his arms and say, "I don't care where you've been. Just make love to me, right now, before I lose my mind."

All of that…out of the question. Humiliating, to have such a storm raging inside her…especially considering he'd been gone only five days.

Five days that had felt like five years.

So she'd have to say something civilized, something poised and unruffled. Something like, "It's good to see you, Gray. How have you been?"

Which was every bit as artificial as the applicant act.

And less likely to allow her to ask the questions that mattered. So she held the pen over her notebook and glanced up at him.

"Perhaps you should tell me about your work experience. Have you ever worked on a ranch before?"

"I have." He held up his hand to tick off the dates. "My first job was a cattle ranch in Texas. I was there two years. Then three years at a ranch in Wyoming, where they also bred horses. The past eight years, I've been in California, on a ranch that breeds quarter horses."

She raised her eyebrows. "No experience on a dude ranch?"

"Well, very little. About three weeks."

"I see." She had to fight the urge to correct him. *Not three weeks, Gray.* Twenty-four days. Just four days short of his allotted time.

She rotated the pen through her fingers, picking her words carefully. "Why such a short time? Did you not find the work…compatible?"

"Oh, *very.*"

"So…" She made a meaningless note on the paper. Her

fingers on the pen weren't as steady as they should be. "It's customary to ask…why *did* you leave your last job?"

He touched his hat, pinching the dent in the brim. Then he gave her a look so direct she felt her cheeks burn. "It's a long story. Before I bore you with it, I'd like to be sure you're really…interested."

She raised her chin. "I'm listening. I have half an hour before my next interview, so take your time."

"Okay." He settled back in the chair, crossing his ankle over one knee. The gesture outlined his strong legs, from the long, graceful thigh to the soft boot that cupped his lean, elegantly muscled calf.

An invisible coil inside her midsection tightened, and she looked back down at her paper.

"Actually," he said, "the answer is long because it's not just one simple answer. There are many parts to it. I'll start with the easiest—and that was that I couldn't keep the job because I'd taken it under false pretenses."

She shot a glance up at him. "False pretenses?"

"In a way. You see, I didn't tell the truth about who I was, or where I come from, or what I really wanted."

"Go on."

"I let it be assumed that I was just a ranch hand somewhere and fairly hard up for money. I implied that I'd taken the job because I wanted to be reinstated in my rich grandfather's will."

"And that wasn't true?"

"Technically, it was. I do work on a ranch. And I did make a bet with him that I could keep the Bell River job for four weeks. If I could, he had to put me back in the will. If I couldn't, he had the right to disinherit me, and I would never mention it again. So the part about the job being my way back into the will was all true."

"What part was a lie?"

"I did want him to give me the money, but not because I was particularly hard up for it, as I let everyone assume. I wanted him to acknowledge that he owed it to me. I wanted him to admit that he'd taken money from my father, supposedly to invest for him, but then refused to give it back because he didn't approve of my father's lifestyle and wanted to be able to control him."

She thought of old man Harper and decided it wasn't impossible to believe this.

"All right," she said. "So now are you back in your grandfather's will? Did your plan work?"

"Not really." He shrugged. "Unfortunately, when I spent time in Silverdell, and with my grandfather, I began to doubt the black-and-white version of events I'd clung to ever since my parents died. I didn't want to let go of that comfortable old story, that my father was a martyr and my grandfather was a beast. But being home again brought back memories that just didn't line up with such a simplistic version. I had to recognize that my father had problems, serious problems. My grandfather didn't handle them well, and that's an understatement. But even so…"

She could hear tension in his voice. She didn't speak. Empty platitudes wouldn't help, and because she didn't know the characters involved, she had nothing else to offer.

"In the end, I saw that they were probably both made up of a little bit of the martyr and a little bit of the beast." His smile was slightly twisted. "As most people are, I suppose. As I am myself."

She nodded. Her own homecoming had been a relearning of the past, too. Abandoning the old thinking was surprisingly difficult.

"I'll probably never untangle the whole truth of what happened to my father's money, but I knew I no longer wanted it. Somewhere along the way, I saw how empty that victory would be. Getting the money back wouldn't vindicate my father. My father is dead, and beyond caring. And so I had to leave."

"You didn't tell your grandfather, though." She thought of old Harper's fury the other day. "You didn't explain to him why you were leaving."

He shook his head. "He wouldn't have believed me. He's a stubborn old coot, and he sets a lot of store by his money. So of course he assumes everyone else does, too. He would have accused me of merely choosing another route to weasel myself back into his good graces. He'd have thought I was switching to the flattering-toady route, feeding him empty hypocritical words because it was easier than working hard."

He chuckled. "And that would have got my dander up, and we would have been right back where we started. So I just left, before the four weeks had elapsed, so that he could see I had voluntarily forfeited the bet. When I left, I didn't think I wanted to have a relationship with him. All I knew, or all I was willing to admit to myself that morning, was that I didn't want him to be able to accuse me of being what he calls a 'deathbed vulture.'"

She heard the small added clause... *All I was willing to admit to myself that morning...*

"Have you changed your mind since?"

He smiled. "Well, you see, that brings me to the more complicated part of the whole mess. There was a woman."

"Ah." She tapped her pen on the paper, hoping it looked like detached amusement, but aware that, at least to her, it sounded jittery and uncomfortable. "There always is."

"You see, I met someone who insisted that what I really wanted, though I wasn't admitting it, even to myself, was another chance to work things out with my grandfather. I wanted to understand him and make him understand me. I wanted to forgive and be forgiven. The money, she said, had always been merely my excuse to put myself back in his life long enough to do that."

She was the "someone," of course. She remembered the night she'd told him that. He had seemed to laugh it off. It had never occurred to her that the thought had taken root... and might somehow have changed his course.

"And...?"

"And sometime over the past few days, I began to see that she might have been right. When I leave here, I'll go to Harper House, and see whether any of that is possible."

"I see. I guess the only part I still don't understand is—" she bit her lower lip "—why you had to leave in such a hurry. Without...time to really say goodbye."

"Well, that's where the explanation gets really complicated. Or maybe...maybe it's almost ridiculously simple. I left because I was a coward, and a fool."

"A coward?"

"Yes. The thing is...I don't have long-term relationships. When I was just a kid, I decided that caring about other people was simply too damn dangerous. I almost didn't survive the loss of my parents, quite literally, and I didn't intend to risk ever feeling like that again. Caring about anyone at all seemed risky. Love—" He shook his head. "Love seemed like something only an idiot would consider, like standing too close to a bomb that's already ticking. So I keep my relationships light, and I am always honest about what I am willing to give. Every affair I ever entered into had an end date, stamped and officially announced, even before it started."

She nodded slowly. He had been honest. She'd never had any reason to fault him there.

"So this woman...she was supposed to be another short-term affair. Good times, fun, no hard feelings when it was over. But then...then, one night, she told me she'd fallen in love with me."

She lowered her gaze to the pen. "Obviously that was a big mistake."

"Yes, it was. But only because I was, as I say, a coward and a fool. Predictably, I panicked. I could see that, for the first time, my carefully constructed walls were in danger of being breached. She had a way…a way of suddenly getting close, and making me feel things I wasn't comfortable feeling."

"So you ran."

"I ran. It's what I do. But this time, something went wrong. I hadn't been gone forty-eight hours before I realized it was too late. I couldn't run away this time. Because she was already inside me. She was already in my head, and in my heart, and in my dreams. I hadn't left her behind in Silverdell at all. I'd brought her with me. And the pain I was so afraid of feeling? It was already inside me, too."

She realized she was holding her breath. She tried to loosen it, but her chest felt too tight.

"Do you understand, Bree? There was no point in running anymore, no point trying to protect myself, trying to prevent getting hurt. I wasn't *in danger of* caring. I wasn't *in danger of* falling in love. I had already done it."

Little fireworks had begun to detonate inside her. But it seemed impossible. She wondered whether she might be dreaming, or whether, in some terrible way, he was teasing her, or just being nice. Or trying to get his job back for reasons of his own…

On some deeper level—the detonating-fireworks level—she knew those doubts were absurd. But…the old cliché "too good to be true" seemed to make sense in a new and concrete way.

She took a shaky breath. "And how does she feel about you?"

He let his gaze slide over her face. "She loves me, too. She doesn't trust me, and she doesn't really trust herself. But she said she loves me, and I believe her." A slow smile tugged at the corners of his mouth. "That is…unless she said it as the result of a sexually induced endorphin high. You see, the sex was pretty phenomenal, so I suppose it might have been that."

She raised her eyebrows, flushing all the way down to her collarbone. "Oh, really? That's smug, don't you think?"

"No. It's actually an understatement. The sex was amazing."

Amazing…the drumbeat in her belly sounded those three syllables slowly, over and over, as heat gathered. But she couldn't give in to that yet. There was still one piece that didn't seem to fit….

"Something you said, right at the beginning…about taking the job under false pretenses. You said you let people assume you were 'just' a ranch hand. You let them assume you needed the money. Are you saying you *don't* need the money?"

"I'm not saying I have sixteen million dollars in my hip pocket, if that's what you mean." He smiled easily. "But I am saying that I won't go hungry, even now that I'll never inherit the Harper millions. The ranch I work on is my ranch. The horses we breed are my horses. I have five hundred acres and fifty employees. I'm doing just fine."

She tried to take it in. She was happy for him, of course. But five hundred acres of horse ranch in California, a thriving breeding business…

Even if he had been serious when he said that he loved her…how could they ever have a real relationship? There was no way he could do that kind of work from Colorado.

And how could she leave Bell River and Rowena, now that she'd finally found them again?

He frowned. "Actually, I thought you might take that new

a little better. Surely, when a man declares his love for you, it's preferable to learn that he's solvent?"

"I—" She shook her head, abandoning the job-interview pretense. "I'm not sure I can absorb all this. I'm not even sure how much of what we're saying is serious, and how much of it is just a game and…"

"The part about my loving you is serious." His gaze was dark on hers, and yet its depths seemed to reflect a banked fire that made her breath come faster. "Deadly, forever serious."

"I—" Her tongue tangled on whatever had been supposed to come next.

"But you're right. The rest of it is a game—and I hope the rest of our lives will be, too. I want to make you laugh, Bree. I want to fill your life with so much sunshine that you forget what darkness looks like."

She felt a strange stinging behind her eyelids. Surely she wasn't going to cry, was she? Not when he was talking about sunshine and laughter.

"We've both been through enough," he said, his voice intense and determined. "Too much sadness, too much fear. I want us to put all that behind us. I want our future to be filled with fun, and work we're passionate about, with sex and joy. And love."

She shook her head, afraid, so afraid, that in a minute she'd wake up. Or he would. "But what future? A future…*where?*"

He looked at her as if confused. Then he laughed.

"Here, of course. Do you think I could have failed to see how important Bell River is to you? I've just spent the past twenty-four hours negotiating with Rowena and Dallas. As long as you and Penny agree, it looks as though Gray Stables will be setting up its breeding operations here on Bell River land. I'll rent about a hundred acres on the western slope."

She widened her eyes. Rowena had known for twenty-four hours that Gray was coming back? When she saw her sister next, she was going to...

Kiss her.

Suddenly, her heart was pumping a gold-shining liquid through her veins, and she wondered whether, if they turned off the office lights, she might glow in the dark.

And then the thought of being alone in the dark with Gray just made her heart pump the magic liquid faster, and she heard her breath coming fast and shallow.

She picked up her pen, trying to create space for air. "It sounds as if you're significantly overqualified for the assistant social director position, Mr. Harper. Why would you be interested in such a menial job?"

With a slow smile, he stood, then made his way around the desk until he reached her chair.

"Because," he said softly, "I'm hoping that, once I'm back in the Bell River family, I can, slowly but surely, work my way up the ladder."

He put out his hands. She took them, and he tugged her slowly to her feet. She wondered if her gold-shining limbs could hold her erect, or whether they would simply melt under her.

"And what job do you have your eye on?" She kept her interview expression in place. "Where do you see yourself in, say, five years?"

"I see myself right here," he said, pulling her closer, and then closer, until their bodies melded from chest to knee. "Beside you. Inside you."

She made a soft sound without meaning to. He kissed the edge of her mouth, as if to catch the whimper, and then slid his lips around to her ear.

"Of course, by then we'll have to fight for our privacy," h

said, "because we'll have two children and a dog. And maybe another on the way."

She shut her eyes, shivering as he tugged on her earlobe. "Another dog?"

He laughed, and the vibration passed through her like a tiny, hot earthquake. "How about two children, two dogs, three cats...do you like cats?...four horses *and* a baby on the way?"

She smiled. "So this ultimate title, the one you're climbing the ladder to reach...it's zookeeper?"

He lowered his lips, letting them hover tantalizingly over hers. "The title I want is *husband,* Bree. It's *lover.* Your lover, your partner, your friend. If you'll allow me to be all those things to you, it will be the title of the luckiest man in the world."

If she'd allow it? Torn between laughing and crying, she nodded, unable to trust her voice. With a low growl of triumph, he finally lowered his mouth to hers and kissed her with all the fire she'd thought she'd lost forever.

She had just surrendered to the shivering joy, and had let her hips move, finding the rising heat between his legs, when she heard someone knock on her office door.

She groaned, but he ignored both knock and groan, instead teasing her lips open wider with his tongue. And then she, too, ignored everything but that dark, wet place where they were joined.

"Bree?" The door creaked open. "Bree, your three o'clock interview is—"

A beat of silence, during which Gray continued to assault every sense Bree possessed. Whoever knocked had better leave, because Bree might just fracture into a thousand pieces right here, right now, standing up....

And then she heard a small chuckle from the threshold. *"Oh."*

Finally, the sound of the door closing. And Rowena's laughing voice speaking to someone unseen.

"I'm very sorry, Mrs. Brimley. It appears as if that position has just been perfectly—and *permanently*—filled."

* * * * *

Look for the next THE SISTERS OF BELL RANCH story
by Kathleen O'Brien!
Coming in December 2013
from Harlequin Superromance.

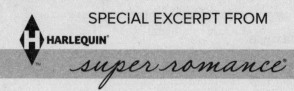
Allison tapped her fingers against her upper arm as she turned
over his conditions in her mind. No matter how she looked
at it, she had zero negotiating room. "So. We're stuck with
each other."

"Looks that way." Joe's expression was stony.

"I didn't come prepared to stay, let alone work," she said.

"I can see that." He looked askance at her outfit. "You'll
need work boots. I suggest you make a run to the hardware
store. Get something sturdy. No hot-pink rubber rain gear."

"I'm assuming you have a separate room for me. One with
clean sheets and a working toilet."

"You'll get your own room." In four steps he was across the lobby and at the door. He pushed it open. "Hardware store's on State Street. You can't miss it."

When she made to walk past him, he stopped her with a hand on her arm. His nearness, his scent, the warmth of his fingers and their movement over the silk of her blouse made her shiver. *Damn it.*

Don't look at his mouth, don't look at his mouth, don't look—

Her gaze lowered. His lips formed a smug curve, and for one desperate, self-hating moment she considered running. But she'd be running from the only solution to her problems. "If I'm going back to the agency and delaying renovations for a month," he said, "then I get two full weeks of labor from you. No complaints, no backtracking, no games. Agreed?"

She shrugged free of his touch. "Don't worry, I'll do my part. Your part is to keep your hands to yourself."

"You might change your mind about that."

Will they keep their hands to themselves?
Or will two weeks together resurrect the past?
Find out in STAYING AT JOE'S
by Kathy Altman, available August 2013 from
Harlequin® Superromance®.

REQUEST YOUR FREE BOOKS!
2 FREE NOVELS PLUS 2 FREE GIFTS!

HARLEQUIN

super romance

More Story...More Romance

HSR13R

The clock is ticking for Angela Taylor

Angela Taylor came to Templeton Cove to start over. But when the press photographs her in Chris Forrester's arms during a flood rescue, it's only a matter of time before her peaceful new life takes a frightening turn....

Suspense and romance collide in this sensational story!

A Man Like Him
by Rachel Brimble

AVAILABLE IN AUGUST